DEAR MOTHER

Also by Angela Marsons

Detective Kim Stone series:

1. SILENT SCREAM
2. EVIL GAMES
3. LOST GIRLS
4. PLAY DEAD

Other books:

THE FORGOTTEN WOMAN
(originally self published as MY NAME IS)

Angela MARSONS

DEAR MOTHER

bookouture

Published by Bookouture

An imprint of StoryFire Ltd.
23 Sussex Road, Ickenham, UB10 8PN
United Kingdom

www.bookouture.com

ISBN: 978-1-78681-042-7
eBook ISBN: 978-1-78681-041-0

Previously published by Angela Marsons as
The Middle Child in 2014.

This book is dedicated to any person who has suffered any type of childhood abuse and made it out the other side.

You are true survivors.

CHAPTER 1

Catherine

Catherine adjusted the Hermès wrap around her shoulders. Despite the chill of the September breeze she loved the promise of a new day ushered in by the morning chorus. It was a sound that she'd trusted many years ago to herald a new beginning, an awakening from a horrible nightmare.

These days she didn't need to force herself upright to fight off sleep in order to be ready for the evil across the hall. Or to squint at the bunk beds opposite to watch over her younger sisters. She didn't need to make sure Alex's limbs jerked occasionally expelling her boundless energy or that Beth's intermittent sighs spoke of ice cream and candyfloss. She no longer had to fight off the growing warmth of the bed covers to keep her sisters safe.

Those long, anxious nights were long gone but she still enjoyed the unspoilt canvas of a fresh day. As the day dawned anything was possible, everything could be reversed, changed, started, finished. The day could be anything that you wanted it to be. Right up until the moment it became infected with people, thoughts and memories.

Her daily ritual always began on the patio of the three-bedroom cottage on the outskirts of Bridgnorth, a small market town south-east of Shrewsbury. The property was picture perfect from the front, complete with white picket fence and mature cottage garden plants. The rear of the house faced west to the Shropshire hills.

This was Catherine's piece of paradise and she had fallen in love with it at first sight. That had been almost eight years ago, before the girls had been born, and if she was honest with herself, the last time she'd experienced true happiness.

She glanced at her watch. Could she fit in another cigarette and coffee before Tim rose? At six fifteen she was cutting it fine but decided to chance it anyway.

There was a strangeness about the day that she couldn't fathom. She had woken with a sharp intake of anxiety. There weren't butterflies in her stomach but elephants wearing hobnail boots. Even the peace of the bright, fresh morning had done little to eradicate the trepidation and sense that today something was going to change. It was a feeling in her gut that was a middle ground between her head and her heart and she trusted it implicitly.

She poured the last cup of coffee from the percolator and immediately prepared a fresh pot. Tim had berated her many times for breaking percolators due to not waiting for the thermostat to cool down. Catherine shrugged. She needed coffee and they could easily afford it.

As she reached for the cigarettes peeping out from the top of her handbag she heard the sound of footsteps above. Her window of opportunity had firmly closed and all too soon she would be thrust against the first obstacle that obscured the promise of a new day full of hope.

Tim wrinkled his nose in distaste the second he entered the kitchen. 'For goodness' sake, Catherine.'

She didn't need to question the source of his disapproval. He expressed it most mornings. 'I was outside,' she snapped back. 'I can't control the bloody breeze.'

'Shut the door, then.'

'I am not shutting myself out of my own home to have a damn cigarette.'

'It's a filthy habit anyway. The smell gets on your clothes, in your hair… '

'Okay, Tim. Enough.'

He shrugged and relaxed his features. 'I'm only thinking of the girls.'

Of course he was, Catherine mused. Wasn't he always?

'It's not healthy for them to inhale—'

'For Christ's sake, Tim, leave it alone. I had a couple of cigarettes in the back garden in the early hours of the morning. I hardly think that'll have any lasting effects on their long-term health.'

Tim's face tensed up again. 'It's a proven fact that children from parents that smoke have a higher percentage—'

'Don't quote figures at me and don't speak to me as though I'm in your classroom. You don't smoke and I smoke a couple of cigarettes a day away from the girls so I'd say the odds are reduced to roughly six and a half per cent. You should be more concerned about drugs, alcohol and teenage pregnancy.'

His studious expression told Catherine that he was trying to dig more quotable facts from his mind with which to continue the argument. She turned away and began preparing breakfast. He sighed heavily behind her.

'Not the best way to start the day, is it?' he asked, gently.

Although in physical terms they were less than ten feet apart, the words travelled the real distance between them.

'Seems to be the only way these days,' she replied, dropping the knife and heading for the bathroom.

She jumped under the shower, the lukewarm needles waking every inch of her skin to alertness. She'd already showered after her first coffee, but it was an extra few minutes of peace. Tim wouldn't disturb her in the shower. Maybe once he would have done but not any more. The girls might come in.

She stepped out feeling calmer and more relaxed. She focused on the tasks that needed completing before she could get off to work, and padded back into the kitchen to prepare scrambled eggs for herself and Tim and cereal bowls for the girls.

She worked quietly while Tim read through the national dailies. She stole the occasional glance at his fair head bowed in concentration on a page he hadn't turned in minutes. She served up eggs with a scorched brown underbelly. Oh yeah, life was perfect.

'Breakfast is ready,' Catherine offered. Her daily signal to Tim to wake the twins.

'You wake them,' he said, folding the newspaper.

She threw the spatula into the sink, clattering against the stainless steel edge. 'Is everything going to be a battle today?'

'You never wake them,' he observed with a glint of challenge in his eyes.

She turned away and began wiping the surface. 'They respond better to seeing you first thing in the morning.'

He opened his mouth to speak but just stared at her for a long minute. Was he going to push it?

He shook his head and went for the stairs. Catherine breathed a sigh of relief.

Within seconds Lucy was at the table, clad in teddy-bear pyjamas, her feet dangling in mid-air. Lucy was always the first, Catherine realised. First out of the womb, first to crawl, first to walk, first down to breakfast every morning.

The sound of rice popping in milk filled the kitchen. Catherine smiled fleetingly at her eldest daughter, older by about ten minutes. The silences between her and Lucy were easy, companionable. This child demanded nothing.

Within a few moments Jess flew into the kitchen, as always trying to catch up.

Catherine viewed her daughters from the corner of her eye as she buttered toast for Tim. As twins the girls had similarities but weren't identical. Lucy's hair was slightly fairer than Jess's, her face more angular. Lucy's serene demeanour reminded Catherine of her sister, Beth, who had cried little as a child. Jess reminded her of Alex, full of rebellion and fire. She saw nothing of herself in her children.

'I want Coco Pops,' Jess moaned, eyeing the Rice Crispies with distaste.

'You ate the last ones yesterday,' Catherine explained without turning. She'd meant to get some on the way home from work but it had slipped her mind.

'Want Coco Pops.'

Catherine turned to face her. 'Eat your breakfast, Jessica.'

Jess picked up a handful of Rice Crispies and threw them on to the floor.

Catherine's temper flared but she held it in check. 'Jess, clean that mess up right now.'

Jess eyed her coldly and with one swift movement used her forearm to send the bowl crashing to the floor.

'Jess, I'm warning you. Pick that mess up or I'll… ' Her words trailed off as Jess pushed the milk carton over the edge of the table.

Catherine advanced on her youngest daughter, blinding red rage clouding her vision. Jess, it was always Jess who had to test her, challenge her, demand something from her.

Within seconds she was beside her youngest child. She felt her right arm begin to rise.

'Catherine, what the hell are you doing?' Tim cried, his hand grabbing at her wrist that was suspended in the air. 'Jesus, you were going to hit her?' he asked, stunned disbelief in his voice.

Catherine pulled her hand out of his grasp and turned. She saw the expression of fear on Jess's face and she felt sick. Lucy stared down into her breakfast and hummed softly.

'Go and get ready for school, girls,' Tim instructed. Forced cheerfulness dripped from his words.

Once she heard the sound of their small feet pattering out of the kitchen, Catherine began to clean up the mess.

'What the hell is wrong with you?' Tim asked as soon as the girls were out of earshot.

'She just won't listen.'

'She's six years old. She's not supposed to listen.'

'Lucy does.'

'Lucy's the exception and you know it. She's too damn scared of you to do anything else. Jess is a little braver, that's all.'

'Defend her as always,' Catherine accused, wiping the last of the milk away. 'You take her side against me every time.'

'This is not a damn competition. They're our daughters. Jess spilt some milk, that's all.'

'She didn't spill the milk. She deliberately threw it on the floor because she couldn't get her own way.'

'And that's a reason to hit her?'

'Don't be ridiculous,' she spat. 'I wasn't going to hit her.'

'Your hand was in the air about to strike her. I caught your wrist just in time.'

'Don't be so dramatic,' Catherine snapped, unable to meet his gaze.

Tim sat back on the chair, deflated. When he spoke his voice was low and weary. 'You know, Catherine, there are many things I can put up with in the hope that they'll change. I put up with your disinterest in what your children do at school. I accept your lack of physical contact with them. I ignore the fact that you've barely entered their bedroom since they were born except to clean. I ignore the fact that, despite me telling you a dozen times, you still don't know the name of their teacher. I even accept that your work is probably your highest priority, above myself and also above the girls.' He paused and looked at her sadly. 'I accept all of this and try to compensate for your distance, but not physical violence, Catherine. I can't accept that.'

The words brought tears to her eyes. She moved towards Tim, anxious to feel his arms around her, eager for his soothing words of comfort that would erase the deadened feeling in her stomach.

As she reached him, Tim stood and turned away. 'I'll drop them off at school.'

Catherine nodded at his back as he turned away, not waiting for a response, and then fell down into a chair, deflated and scared. She heard the front door open and close behind muted goodbyes.

A collared dove landed on the bird box to the side of the house.

'You lied to me again,' she murmured, as the tears rolled over her cheeks. The day was not filled with promise, after all.

The phone began to ring.

CHAPTER 2

Alex

'Get the fuck out of my bed, now,' Alex growled. The water in the kettle was beginning to jump with heat and would be boiled in less than a minute. And one thing she couldn't stand was peering at the face of a one-night stand over her first shot of caffeine.

'You weren't saying that last night,' said the coy female voice from the bed.

The words and tone irritated Alex as she wondered if Yolanda, Ulanda or whoever the hell she was had the hide of a rhinoceros.

'Do I look like I'm fucking joking?' Alex snarled, turning a cold gaze on the smiling figure in the bed. The girl's expression became puzzled.

'You were nothing like this last night.' The girl was unsure whether Alex was serious. Alex decided to clarify.

'Last night I wanted someone to fuck and you were available. End of story.'

Alex turned her attention back to the boiling kettle. She listened keenly and smiled at the sound of the covers moving. Finally, the stupid tart was getting the message.

She held her breath, hoping the girl wouldn't ask to take a shower. Alex just wanted her gone.

She decided she would need to hone her selection process in future. She had known that the girl was inexperienced the moment she offered to buy her a drink. With seasoned 'hunters' one drink was enough to convey the message before leaving for the nearest bed. This girl had cost her three brandy and Cokes and an hour of pointless conversation.

She smiled ruefully. It had been worth it, though. The girl's fair hair and milky complexion had belied her voracious sexual appetite and Alex had been lulled to sleep by the sound of the refuse collection, truly exhausted.

But once she'd woken the bed had closed in. It was a space she struggled to share. Like mother, like daughter, said a small betraying voice in her head. Fuck off, she replied, but the memory had already formed…

* * *

She'd been five, maybe six, when a nightmare had propelled her from her bed. She had instinctively aimed for the door across the hall. Catherine had blocked her path.

'Where are you going?'

'To tell Mummy about my dream,' she said, trying to hold back the tears.

'No… ' Catherine protested but Alex didn't hear any more as she marched across the hallway.

She pushed the door open and touched the bare arm protruding from the yellow sheet.

'Mummy, I had a nightmare,' she murmured, her voice still weak with fear. There was no response. She tapped harder. 'Mummy… Mummy… wake up… '

The form stirred and peered at her in the dark.

'I had a nightmare,' she repeated.

'So fucking what?' her mother said, gruffly.

'There was a monster with claw hands and big teeth and he was chasing me down the street. He was running after me and he wanted to eat me and his claws were sharp and they were going to rip into—'

'Get out, Alex.'

Alex knew that she had made her mum angry, but she tried to climb into bed beside her to feel safe from the monster.

'I said, fuck off,' her mum growled, pushing her harshly to the floor.

Alex began to cry, the residual fear of the nightmare finally spilling over her cheeks.

'But I—'

'This is my bed, not yours, now get out before I call the monster back. I control his claws and teeth and they'll rip you apart if you don't piss off.'

Alex screamed once and darted back into the opposite bedroom. She threw herself beneath the covers and hoped they would protect her.

She tried bravely to stem the tears and the sobbing. The monster might hear her and come back. If she could just be quiet then she'd be safe.

'It's all right, I'm here,' Catherine said, kneeling beside her.

Alex popped her head out from beneath the covers. The monster wouldn't come if Catherine was with her.

'Come on,' Catherine said, taking her hand. Her sister led her to the single bed in the corner of the room and drew back the covers. 'Get in.' Catherine settled herself and placed a protective arm around her. The tears stopped and her breathing returned to normal. The body heat of Catherine and fatigue pulled at her eyelids.

'Mum pushed me out of the bed,' she said, moving closer into Catherine.

'Don't think about it. She just hates sharing the bed.'

'She said that the monster—'

'Shhh,' Catherine soothed, stroking her hair. 'Go back to sleep and I promise the monster won't get you tonight. I'll look after you.'

And her sister had kept the first part of her promise. But not the second.

* * *

Alex growled out loud and pushed away any thoughts of her blood ties. Her mind would not accept the word *family*.

Alex appreciated the reprieve of the girl being in the bathroom. She could feel that her facial muscles had slackened under the pressure of the memory but she needed them firm and harsh.

She readied herself for the inevitable questions before the girl finally took her leave.

'Can I take your number?' 'Will I see you again?'

Alex shook her head. Why did it have to be this way? Why couldn't people just accept a casual fuck for what it was? She resented being put in the position of having to say no and appearing heartless but inevitably it ended that way with the inexperienced type.

Her normal type was rough, energetic and gone by sunrise. On the rare occasions that she found herself in someone else's flat she made her excuses by five a.m. It was only polite.

Alex stiffened slightly as the bathroom door opened. For a few moments she had relaxed back into her own company. Her favourite place to be.

'So, can I see you tonight?'

'No.'

'At the weekend?'

'No.'

'But—'

'For fuck's sake, just piss off, will you?' Alex roared. The studio flat was tiny enough. Two people in it made her claustrophobic.

A pang of regret bit at her as the girl padded to the door carrying her shoes, but it wasn't strong enough to prompt her to change her mind. She felt bad but not that bad.

The door closed and with her domain her own again, Alex breathed a sigh of relief, wondering if it was worth it. So often, these days, the chicks wanted breakfast in bed and a lifetime commitment. She'd already been there, done that, bought the T-shirt and burned it.

'Fucking commitment,' Alex growled as she lit her first cigarette of the day. She drew in and exhaled deeply. Her first fag and coffee was something that she shared with no one, not even Nikki. Even then Alex had risen half an hour before her lover.

As she swallowed her first mouthful of coffee a gentle knock sounded on the door. 'For fuck's sake,' Alex shouted. Didn't the stupid cow have enough taxi fare? She threw the door open, her face a mask of anger. It quickly dissolved into a smile when she saw Jay, her best friend, lounging against the door frame.

'There'd better be a muffin to go with that good coffee you're carrying or you can piss off,' she said walking away from the open door.

'As if I'd grace your doorstep at this time in the morning without gifts,' he said, kicking the door shut behind him. He placed the cardboard cups on the kitchen counter and delved into his jacket pocket. 'Blueberry,' he offered.

She nodded approvingly, taking the muffin from him. The aroma of warm dough and fruit made her mouth water.

Jay retrieved a similar bag from his other pocket. 'Oh, how civilised,' he chuckled as he removed the lids from the coffee. Alex sniffed at the fresh aroma and threw her home-made instant down the sink.

Jay sniffed the air, dramatically. 'Is that the scent of a cheap tart I smell?'

'Yeah, but she's gone now.'

'I was talking about you, darling.'

Alex gave him the finger and bit into the muffin. Small crumbs broke off and tickled her chin. Suddenly, all was right with the world and if it lasted for the duration of the muffin, that was fine with her.

'Nikki came into the club after you left.'

Alex rolled her eyes. Of course it couldn't last. 'So?'

'Just thought I'd let you know, that's all. You were a gnat's bollock away from bumping into her.'

'Why should I care?' she cried at him, her voice rising.

'I just thought I'd mention it in case you were interested,' he said, flicking his non-existent hair. He'd gone for the shaved look a month earlier.

'You're so gay,' she said, laughing at his campness.

'You're right. I am a truly happy person.'

Alex chuckled as Jay tried to press a beauty spot formed of muffin crumb above his upper lip.

Thank God for her friend, she thought as she viewed his crestfallen expression when the fruity beauty spot landed on the plate. He'd been the first friend she'd made when she moved to Birmingham seven years earlier.

They'd met during her first venture into a gay bar. He was one of three males amongst a throng of females dancing and gyrating in a small airless space. Intrigued, she had asked him why he was there. He'd admitted that when he wanted a quiet drink he frequented bars full of butch lesbians who'd leave him the hell alone.

Any thoughts of meeting someone that night had been put aside as the two of them spent the whole evening chatting and laughing together. And little had changed since, she thought, as she chewed the last mouthful of dough. They both still worked part-time in different bars. He was still trying to make it as an actor and she was still content not trying to make it as anything.

'So, how did she look?' Alex asked, offhandedly.

'Gorgeous, as ever. She's put on a couple of pounds and she's got a nice tan. To be honest, if I was a lesbian I'd be all over her.'

'You're biased and you know it, so be objective for a minute.'

Jay put his finger beneath his chin and pursed his full, feminine lips in a dramatic thinking pose. 'Okay, objectively she looks fucking gorgeous.'

'Thanks for the impartiality.'

Jay shrugged. 'It's not my fault if you're too stupid to realise that she was the best thing that ever happened to you.'

Alex buried her head in her hands. 'Jay, leave it alone. You don't know anything about us or what happened in our relationship.'

'I know enough to understand that you were the happiest you've ever been when you were with Nikki. She was something special and you let her get away,' he said, accusingly.

'Back off,' she warned.

'You don't frighten me, missy. I'll say what I like; free speech and all that. You were stupid to let her go. Is it really so much better getting a quick shag now and again to ease the misery?'

'I get a quick shag 'cos I like sex,' Alex said, attempting to lighten the mood.

'You get cold sex with faceless strangers because you're lonely, and don't even pretend otherwise 'cos we both know it's true.'

'Fuck off,' she sighed, lighting a cigarette.

'And before your pride sinks any lower, I'll put you out of your misery. No, she wasn't with anyone.'

'I wasn't going to ask,' Alex said, stubbornly.

'No, you probably weren't, but it was the one question rolling around in your mind.'

'Jay, I'm warning you, if you don't shut the hell up I'll—' Alex was saved from finishing the threat by the ringing of the phone.

She traced the muffled sound to a pile of clothes on the sofa. She threw them on to the floor.

'What?' she barked into the mouthpiece.

'Is that Alex Morgan?' the voice asked, tentatively.

Alex felt a shiver trace the length of her spine. The gentle voice sounded vaguely familiar, in a way that made her immediately uncomfortable.

'Speaking.'

'Hi Alex, it's Beth.'

Alex closed her eyes as guilt rolled over her. The silence between them grew uncomfortable. Alex had no clue what to say to a sister she hadn't seen in eight years.

'Are you there?' the voice asked, softly.

Alex searched for any trace of hostility or accusation in the few words but found none. Inexplicably a lump formed in her throat. Of course, there wasn't. This was Beth.

'I'm here,' she whispered.

'I have some bad news for you,' Beth continued. Alex heard the catch in her voice.

Alex held her breath, waiting for the words to come.

'Mother died during the night.'

Alex exhaled the breath she'd been holding. She briefly listened as Beth quietly gave her the details of the funeral.

Alex said her goodbyes and gently placed the handset back in the cradle.

She turned to Jay but spoke more to herself.

'Thank God the bitch is dead.'

CHAPTER 3

Catherine

Catherine pulled into the narrow street and felt her stomach lurch. Regeneration appeared to have found other areas of the Black Country. New housing estates had sprung up in place of the foundries and steelworks that had once dominated the area.

The old corner shops that she remembered had been turned into frozen mini markets or boarded up completely. The once thriving market town of Cradley Heath had been annihilated by a shopping centre a mile up the road. Once the hub of weekend retail, it now boasted a Tesco superstore and a string of charity shops. An access road diverted traffic away, leaving room for empty buses that rarely picked up or dropped off.

But this street had barely changed at all. She travelled slowly along a road flanked by long rows of terraced houses either side. A couple of the houses were now boarded up.

A group of kids were gathered opposite her old house, their faces caked in a mixture of jam and dirt. Catherine felt no rush of fond memories as a boy aged eight or nine clad in only a vest and pants threw a smaller, weaker child to the ground to whoops of joy from onlookers. It was a street where bruises went unnoticed, as she knew only too well.

She parked the car away from the front of the house, wishing for a few minutes alone with her thoughts before she saw Beth.

She had contemplated not coming to the funeral at all but Tim had insisted that she must.

What did he know? she wondered angrily. He knew nothing of her past because she had never told him. She had never told anyone. As far as he was concerned it had been a childhood plagued with poverty and name-calling once their father had disappeared.

Christ, if only that was all it had been.

She knew she was avoiding knocking on the door for a variety of reasons. She genuinely wanted to enter that house with real emotions churning inside her, but in the days since Beth's phone call she had been unable to summon anything.

Within minutes of replacing the receiver Catherine had been smothered by a cloak of numbness that had extended beyond the feelings about her mother's death. She had functioned on remote control. An automatic pilot had taken over her faculties and guided her through the normal daily routine. She had cooked dinner, made lunch for the girls, cleaned the house and gone to work while all the time trying to work out how she was supposed to feel.

She got out of the car and locked it behind her. It was futile trying to harness genuine feelings in a few minutes when she had been unable to do so in just under a week.

The front door had been painted dark blue since her last visit, but the canary yellow paint that Catherine remembered peered through the chips left by thrown stones.

Before her hand met with the door, it opened. Catherine smiled weakly to cover her shock. For a few seconds she sensed that neither of them knew what to do. The problem was solved as Beth launched herself across the years and hugged her forcefully. Catherine returned the embrace awkwardly.

'Come in, come in,' Beth said, ushering her into the front room.

Catherine built a wall against the memories. Just being inside the house was bringing it all back to her.

Beth led her past a table laden with sandwiches stifled by cling film, to the kitchen at the rear of the house.

'I'll make tea and we can have a good chat,' Beth said, reaching for the kettle. Catherine felt the awkwardness of the situation even if Beth appeared not to. Her sister was acting as though they had met for coffee the previous week and had only a few minor facts about each other's lives to catch up on. How much catching up were they going to do to cover the fifteen-year chasm that existed between them?

Catherine swallowed the guilt that rose up and engulfed her. She half wished she could embrace Beth properly and apologise for her absence and silence over the years. She would like to tell her that she had wanted to come back and see her but she couldn't. She just couldn't.

'Sugar?' Beth asked.

Catherine shook her head, overcome with sadness that such a basic fact, such a small detail, was not known between them. It should have been second nature.

Catherine appraised her sister briefly. Her appearance added ten years to the twenty-six real ones. Her hair had been strawberry blonde as a child but it was now unkempt and dirty looking. It was tied in a severe ponytail exposing dry, flyaway strands at the temple and forehead. Her face was devoid of make-up and showed an uneven skin tone. Catherine wondered when her cheeks had last seen daylight. The brown A-line skirt was a disaster on her bony frame and was topped with a roll-neck jumper.

Catherine swallowed and looked away. She knew why Beth wore her tops that way. She would never forget, and truthfully, in the depths of her conscience, she knew that it was the reason she had never returned.

The last words ever spoken to her by her mother had kept her away initially, but she had no excuses for the years she'd been an adult, and perfectly capable of standing up to her mother. But she hadn't.

She felt a rush of anger that would be sated only by a violent act or buried until she could deal with it. How much damage had one woman done to them all?

Catherine wondered if she would be able to smile bravely at the graveside whilst extolling the virtues of her mother. Would any of them?

She faced Beth's gentle expression, full of grief. Yes, Beth would, she realised.

Impetuously, Catherine reached across the table and squeezed Beth's hand.

'I'm sorry.'

Beth patted her hand. 'She was your mother too. We just have to help each other through the pain.'

Catherine watched as Beth's eyes filled up with tears. She looked at the ceiling and prayed for the strength to maintain this façade for the rest of the day. How could she tell her sister that she couldn't find it within herself to be sorry for their mother's death? She was sorry for the years and distance that had grown between them.

'How are the girls?' Beth asked, wiping a tear from her eye.

'They're fine,' Catherine answered. How could she relay the events of all the years that had passed? Catherine had already seen the photo on the mantelpiece of her children, taken a year earlier. Her bitterness at Beth's refusal to attend the christening had long since gone, leaving only a ball of regret that her daughters had never met either of their aunts.

'I'd love you to meet—'

'Mother was very ill that day,' Beth offered. 'The doctor had changed her medication after the first stroke and she had a bad reaction to the tablets.'

'It's okay, I understand,' Catherine said, and meant it. At the time, she had known her mother's illness was contrived to prevent Beth coming to the christening. She had known and kept quiet.

Silence rested between them. Catherine could think of nothing to say. There was no way back. 'The food looks nice,' she commented, nodding towards the other room.

Beth looked anxious. 'Oh, I hope so. There won't be many people. The doctor and a few neighbours, but I still want to do Mother proud.'

Catherine nodded awkwardly. Everything about Beth travelled back to their mother. A place that Catherine did not wish to visit.

Catherine was about to say something banal about the weather when the doorbell sounded.

'I'll get it,' she offered quickly. She hurried to the door but paused as she passed the fireplace in the front room. It smelt of disuse, but Catherine remembered one occasion when the fire had been used. She closed her eyes to block out the memory but the vision of frightened faces and piercing screams reverberated around her mind. Sickness rose in her stomach and tears pierced her eyes. 'Damn that woman to hell,' she whispered vehemently.

The sound of the door brought her back to her senses.

She opened the door and it took Catherine a few long seconds to appraise the person before her. 'Alex?'

Alex nodded and smiled strangely as she entered the room. 'Fantastic that we barely recognise each other.'

Catherine opened her mouth to respond, but there was little to say.

She noticed that Alex looked her twenty-four years. Her skin was flawless and her black hair was as spiky and short as it had been back then.

Catherine followed her youngest sister through to the kitchen. Beth grabbed the new arrival and hugged her fiercely. Catherine detected the same awkwardness of feeling like strangers in the company of your siblings.

Jesus Christ, Catherine thought again, what had that damned woman done to them all?

CHAPTER 4

Alex

Alex stepped away. It wasn't the greeting she'd expected from Beth. Recriminations, bitterness, accusations – yes. A genuine heartfelt welcome – no.

She took two paces back, eager to avoid any further displays of physical affection.

As Beth moved through the rooms and she followed, Alex was conscious of not looking at anything too closely. She averted her eyes from the fireplace.

Aspects of the house were different. A fresh coat of paint covered the old patterned wallpaper that had been peeling and damp-stained, but it was still the same house. She could feel it in her bones.

'What time exactly is the funeral?' Alex asked.

'Two thirty,' Beth answered.

Alex made no attempt to hide the sigh of relief that escaped from between her lips. Only ten minutes more in this house and she could be on her way back home.

'Thank you both for coming,' Beth said, gratefully, reaching for both their hands. Alex saw that Catherine squeezed Beth's hand tightly in response.

Alex looked away. 'I'm going outside for a fag.' She opened the door and stepped outside, reaching for a pack from her jacket pocket. There was another pack of twenty in the other pocket, just in case.

She leaned against the window ledge and inhaled deeply, feeling the sting in her throat. It was the same place she'd stood eight years earlier when she'd realised that anywhere had to be better than this hell.

She remembered clasping Beth's hand and dragging her to the bedroom. She had begged her sister to run away with her but Beth had been horrified at the thought, despite being eighteen and legally old enough to do what the hell she pleased. By that time Catherine was long gone.

For once Beth had been resolute in her refusal despite Alex's urgent whispers that she would die if she stayed here. Beth had merely shaken her head and patted Alex's hand.

'You go. Go now. I'll cover for you.'

And Alex had.

At the bus station she had hesitated briefly, tempted to return and try again to persuade Beth to go with her, but she had known that it was pointless. Beth's gentleness was matched only by her stubbornness and once her mind was made up there was no changing it.

'Stupid cow,' Alex whispered as she stamped on the butt of the cigarette and instantly lit another. She glanced inside the kitchen window and saw Catherine listening earnestly to something Beth was saying. Alex could see the guilt hovering behind her eyes. And so it should, Alex thought bitterly.

Catherine had been the first to leave. Alex remembered going to sleep each night, wishing that when she woke up Catherine would be back in her single bed in the corner of the room, sitting up, watching. But she never was, Alex thought bitterly. The bed was always empty. At least she had tried to take Beth with her, unlike Catherine who had simply chosen to abandon them both.

'The cars are here,' Beth called from inside the kitchen.

Alex took one last draw on the cigarette and stamped it out. She followed her sisters out of the house and into the waiting car.

The journey to the crematorium was a silent affair. Catherine fiddled with her hands and stared at her fingernails. Beth looked straight ahead to the car carrying the body of their dead mother. Alex's only concern was the location of the alcohol for when they returned. A swift calculation told her that an hour in the house was enough for the sake of appearances and that she could spend that getting quietly pissed for the train journey home.

Alex pondered the purpose of the slow car journey. What exactly was the point? Was it a mark of respect? If so, the body in the casket deserved none. Was it to stop the body thumping against the sides of the casket? It was a picture that almost made her smile. Alex felt the relief as the cars turned into the crematorium.

She avoided meeting the gaze of the other mourners and lit a cigarette while the casket was unloaded. Catherine cast a disapproving glance in her direction but Alex turned her back, frustrated at the slow-motion speed of every handling of the casket. Why bother? Just throw the bitch in the cooker.

Alex briefly wondered if she'd feel differently if the casket held someone she actually gave a fuck about, and she could count those people on one half of her left hand.

She flicked the still burning cigarette into a clutch of shrubbery and followed her sisters into the building.

She took a hymn book that she was handed without a word or a glance and followed Beth's figure to the front pew.

Mournful music played in the background as the coffin was placed on a trolley contraption at the front of the building.

Alex felt a rush of air beside her as a male reached across her to touch Beth's hand. She watched the exchange with interest.

She guessed the male to be in his early thirties. His suit was a respectful navy blue, well cut but slightly crumpled.

'Sorry I'm late,' he offered, breathlessly, still clutching her hand.

'It's fine,' Beth said, blushing slightly and retracting her hand.

Catherine moved along the pew so the unknown male could sit down. He sat between Beth and herself. She could smell the fresh scent of pine wafting from his skin.

Beth introduced him in a low whisper as the music began to fade away. 'Doctor Wilkinson,' she clarified.

'This is Doctor Wilkinson?' Catherine said, appraising the handsome, athletic stranger.

'Doctor Wilkinson, Junior,' Beth added, with a slight flush of the cheeks.

'My father died five years ago and I took over then,' he explained, turning to address them both.

Alex found his gentle demeanour and good manners irritating. He was too nice and Alex always found herself suspicious of anyone who was too nice. It was obvious to her that the young doctor was infatuated with Beth.

Alex spent most of the service observing their body language and interaction. The kind doctor clutched Beth's hand and glanced periodically at Beth's pinched features. He handed her a tissue when she cried and held the hymn book for her to sing. Yes, but have you uncovered what lies beneath that high-necked jumper, Alex wondered viciously, and will you still be clutching her hand when you do?

Alex tore her attention from the couple as the coffin began to move through the red velvet curtains towards what Alex hoped was a fiery hell. She had the urge to run up to the casket and kick it through the curtains at a higher speed and then stand and watch her burn. She wondered if Beth saw the irony.

The coffin disappeared behind the curtain completely as the melancholy music once again filled the space. Alex was struck by the thought that the most thoughtful thing her mother had ever done was to be cremated. It meant that less of the world was to be infected by her pure and undiluted acidic body. Although Alex had quite liked the idea of insects and earth creatures feeding on her flesh within the dark, solid confines of the ground.

'I've arranged for her ashes to be scattered near the rose bushes,' Beth offered, addressing them both.

'That's fine,' Catherine answered for both of them.

Alex was amazed that Beth thought that either of them would care.

The car pulled up outside the house and Alex once again felt the suffocation stifling her.

'I'll be putting the house up for sale next week once—'

'No,' Catherine protested. 'Keep the house for yourself, or sell it and move somewhere new, but I want no part of it.'

Alex opened her mouth to protest. Unlike Catherine she wasn't rolling in money and could use all the extra cash. Then she looked at the terraced house that still rose up to haunt her in her worst nightmares.

'Me neither,' she said. 'I want nothing from this place.'

Beth appeared confused, but Catherine ushered her out of the car and into the house.

Alex hung back to observe the onlookers up and down the narrow street. Some poked their heads through the corners of net curtains while others blatantly stared from their front doors. Alex fixed them all with an icy stare before re-entering the house.

Most of the people she remembered and she felt a hostility towards them that choked her. They must have known what was going on in this very house and yet they had done nothing.

They were beneath contempt, she thought as she closed the door behind her.

Beth busied herself removing the foil and cling film jackets from an unappetising selection of banal sandwiches. Catherine placed glasses on the sideboard beside a few bottles of sherry and some soft drinks.

'I'll make a pot of tea,' Beth said.

Alex reached for a glass and poured a generous measure of whisky from the half-full bottle hiding behind the granny bottles.

'Can't you give Beth a hand with the tea?' Catherine asked sidling up beside her. 'The neighbours will be here in a minute.'

'Am I supposed to give a fuck?' Alex spat as she slugged a mouthful of whisky down her throat.

'Alex please—'

'Leave me the hell alone,' Alex cried, storming out into the back garden. She instantly lit a cigarette and slugged more of the whisky down her throat. The heat blazed a trail from her tongue to her stomach.

'Alex, will you please come inside and give Beth a hand?' Catherine said, closing the kitchen door behind her.

'You may be able to enter into this charade and pretend that we've all lost our dear sweet mother but I refuse to be a part of it.'

'Forget her. It's Beth who needs us now. It's important to her—'

'I don't give a shit. Don't you get it, Catherine? You two are nothing to me. You're strangers. I don't know either one of you.'

Alex saw the hurt that flashed over Catherine's features.

'You don't mean that,' Catherine said, uncertainly. 'We're sisters. We have to help and support each other.'

'I don't need your fucking support. I've managed quite well without it and she chose to stay here.'

Alex could see the effect her words were having on Catherine but she didn't care. Too many years had passed since any relationship between the three of them meant anything. 'We're strangers, Catherine. Accept it and stop trying to gloss over it. Let Beth play the grieving daughter and you help her along, but don't expect anything from me.'

'You came,' Catherine said gently.

'I'm here to make sure that the evil bitch is really dead at last. Now I'm sure of that I'm going to get on the next train back to Birmingham and resume my life, safe in the knowledge that I never have to give that woman another thought.'

'Do you really think it's that easy?'

'It was before today.'

'So, you never thought about it?'

'Just fuck off back in there and play the Good Samaritan. You don't want to desert Beth again like you did all those years ago.'

Alex saw Catherine's face pale and she knew she had struck a nerve.

'Is that what you think?'

Alex stuck her chin forward defiantly.

'You think I just left you both?'

'I don't give a shit what you did to me. I was fine. Beth was weaker. She needed you.' Alex felt emotion burning at the back of her throat. She swallowed the rest of the whisky to expunge it.

'But I didn't—'

'Save it for someone who cares,' Alex spat, regaining hold of the anger and bitterness that had kept her insulated for years.

'Just come inside and help Beth—'

'Fuck off and leave me alone. She chose to do the Florence Nightingale thing and stay with the evil bitch for all these years, so she can wallow in the grief now.'

'You can't mean that,' Catherine said, looking horrified.

'Of course I mean it. She reeks of martyrdom and self-sacrifice. She had plenty of opportunities to get away and she chose to stay.'

'You know full well that Mother had her first stroke within three months of you running away. Beth saw it as her duty to take care of her.'

'It was her duty to stuff a pillow over the bitch's mouth and suffocate her.'

'Don't say that,' Catherine protested, casting a glance at the kitchen window. Beth was looking out, an anxious expression on her face. The vulnerability and fear in her eyes hit Alex somewhere beneath her ribcage but she wasn't sure where.

'She hates it when we argue,' Catherine observed, reaching for Alex's cigarette. She took a draw and then stamped it out.

'Yeah, and we both know the consequences of that, don't we?'

Alex lit another cigarette and offered one to Catherine. They smoked in silence. Alex guessed that they were locked in the same memory of the devastating event that had taken place when Beth was eight. It was a day that neither of them would ever forget.

Catherine threw the cigarette into the overgrown weeds. 'Come on, let's go and give Beth a hand.'

By five thirty Alex was viewing the last few straggling grievers through an alcohol-induced haze. The whisky had built the foundations of the wall of detachment around her and the countless glasses of sherry were adding to it, brick by brick.

Fucking parasites, she thought, lighting a cigarette. Any pretence at respect had disappeared at the same speed as the mini quiches. Who the fuck was going to slap her or kick her for smoking in the house now? She had the urge to run outside and scream at the top of her voice, *Come on you fucking, heartless bitch. Come get me now.* Not that the neighbours would notice. They were too busy stuffing pork pie into their faces in the next room.

Alex made her way to the sideboard and peered into each of the bottles, shaking them vigorously to detect movement. 'Whoopee,' she muttered as the dregs of a port bottle yielded a result.

'Don't you think you've had enough?' Catherine said, taking the miniature glass from her hand.

'Fuck off,' Alex slurred, grabbing for the glass. She'd seen three and aimed for the middle one but still managed to send the dregs sloshing over Catherine's hand.

Catherine placed the empty glass on the sideboard beside the empty bottles.

'Oh well, that's that, then,' Alex said, as Catherine wiped her hand. 'Might as well fuck off home now the booze has gone.'

'For heaven's sake, Alex, get a hold of yourself. It's a funeral.'

'Not for somebody I knew, so excuse me if I amuse myself by getting quietly pissed.'

Alex headed off in the direction of the kitchen. There had to be some cooking sherry somewhere or a secret stash of something. Everyone had a secret stash.

'There's nothing left. You've drunk it all,' Catherine said, following her.

'Don't take that fucking santicim… sanctinome… fucking superior tone with me. Those bludgers drank it as well.'

'They would have if there'd been any left.'

Alex thought she heard a note of amusement in Catherine's voice, but when she turned Catherine's face was a mask of control. She'd been mistaken, she realised. Of course she had.

'That's the last of them gone,' Beth said, entering the kitchen behind them.

Despite her inebriated state, Alex could hear the fatigue in Beth's voice.

'Sit down and I'll make us a cuppa,' Catherine offered.

Beth did as she was told and smiled thankfully at Catherine. Catherine squeezed her shoulder.

Alex looked away, sickened and wishing she'd been on the train hours ago or, better still, that she hadn't come at all.

'Thanks for everything,' Beth said, squeezing Alex's hand. Alex wanted to rip her hand away and scream at this elusive stranger but one look into Beth's eyes and she couldn't. She was full of genuine warmth and gratitude. She wanted to slap the woman and scream that they weren't sisters. Just three women brought together by an accident at birth. She wanted to remind them both that they hadn't seen each other or spoken in years. They barely knew anything about each other. Alex knew that Catherine had two girls. How old were they? What were their names? What did they like and dislike?

Alex wanted to scream all these thoughts at them but the expression in Beth's eyes completely deflated her. She remembered how gentle Beth was. Poor Beth who had been born without any aggression or self-interest. Beth who had had the foresight to hide packets of biscuits for the times when their bellies burned with hunger. Alex felt the emotion rising in her throat; but that was back then and this was now and nothing was the same.

Family was an accident of blood only. Relationships needed to be fed and nurtured, looked after, built with shared experiences, laughter and love. But there'd been none of that. Despite the blood that ran through their veins, these women were strangers to her.

Alex stood. 'My train will be—'

'Please stay,' Beth said, quickly rising to her feet. 'Just for a little while.'

Alex felt her jaw tense but she sat down anyway. Beth looked so lost and forlorn, like a small animal brutally separated from the safety of familiar surroundings.

'I just want a little time with my sisters.'

Alex glanced at Catherine who shook her head slightly, warning her to keep quiet. She busied herself lighting a cigarette. Catherine reached across and took one from the box.

'Hey, here's a thought: fucking buy some,' Alex groaned.

Beth chuckled lightly. Both Alex and Catherine swiftly looked over but all too soon it was gone. Alex had seen the light in Beth briefly but now it was dark again.

Alex remembered when her foot had been in plaster. The pain had been torturous and constant but Beth had sat with her for hours, painting silly faces on the stark whiteness of the plaster and then impersonating the faces, forcing her features into almost impossible expressions. Despite the pain, Alex had never laughed so much.

'I'm just going to get changed,' Beth said, leaving the table.

'Thank you, Alex,' Catherine said as the sound of Beth's footsteps sounded above them.

'For what?'

'For not saying all of the things that are bursting to come out.'

Alex nodded. 'How did you know?'

'Because I'm feeling those things too,' Catherine admitted. 'But Beth needs to feel us close, right now. She needs to believe that…'

Catherine's words trailed off as Beth came back into the room. Alex followed her gaze, but quickly ripped her eyes to the floor. Beth had changed into a thin-strapped vest top exposing the worst of the scar that covered almost half of her body.

Alex didn't know what she'd expected, but the skin was red and mottled and rough like textured wallpaper. She looked again as Beth turned her back. Beneath the rest of her clothing, Alex knew, it stretched down and across her entire right side.

Alex's gaze met Catherine's and acceptance passed between them. Acceptance of the blame. Acceptance of the fact that indirectly they had done that to their sister.

As a child, Alex had hoped that as Beth grew, the scarred, dead tissue would remain the same size, meaning that as she aged the scar would be barely noticeable. It had never occurred to her that the scarring would grow with the skin and stretch with her.

'So, what's going on with this young doctor?' Catherine asked, breaking her gaze.

Beth turned, her face a mask of scarlet. 'He's been so good during Mother's illness. It was terrible to see her in such pain. She was a very poorly old lady and I couldn't bear to see her suffer.'

Alex saw the alarm on Catherine's face. It matched her own. Were they talking about the same woman?

'So, what's he like?' Alex pushed to get her off the subject of their mother. It was too disturbing to witness.

'He's been so helpful. I told him all about my accident and he was so supp—'

'Your ac… accident?'

'Of course,' Beth said, smiling at Catherine benevolently. 'It's very kind of you but you can't fail to notice this,' she said, pointing to the tip where the scar began. 'I told him all about the day that the fire was roaring away. I explained that the poker was on the floor and that I stumbled into the fire. Of course, you must remember,' Beth said lightly with a tone of disbelief in her voice.

'An accident?' Catherine breathed.

'You stumbled?' Alex asked, her eyes wide with amazement.

'Of course,' Beth said, frowning slightly. Her expression cleared. 'I'll just go and see if there are any salmon sandwiches left.'

'Oh my God,' Alex said, clamping a hand to her mouth. 'She doesn't remember a fucking thing.'

CHAPTER 5

Catherine

Catherine checked her emails but the one she was waiting for, hoping for, hadn't come through. The clock on the wall ticked ominously towards five. Surely if she'd won the contract she'd know by now.

She pressed the intercom button that linked her directly to her PA. 'Lisa, anything from upstairs yet?'

'Not yet,' Lisa said, impatience colouring her words.

Catherine disconnected. She'd lost count of the times she'd asked. But today should be the day.

Lisa opened the door, carrying a cup of herbal tea. 'Here, drink this. It might calm your nerves.'

Catherine ignored the drink and began to pace the room. 'For Christ's sake, surely they've decided by now. I mean, they said by Monday… '

'Will you please relax?' Lisa chided.

'It's all right for you. You have nothing invested in this. I worked night and day on that presentation to get the contract… '

Lisa huffed. 'Of course the hours that I stayed late to help mean absolutely nothing.'

'You know what I mean. It's just such a big thing for me. I've worked so hard for this promotion.'

'It's important to me also,' Lisa said with a smile. 'Although I'm sure my salary hike will be nothing compared to yours, I'll still enjoy the prestige of a title change. I can see it now,' she said, gazing up at the ceiling. 'Lisa Gordon, PA to Advertising Executive. Will I get my own office? An assistant?'

In spite of her nerves Catherine started to laugh. 'Who said I'd take you upstairs with me?'

Lisa crossed her legs dramatically. 'You'd be nothing without me. I am the power behind the throne. I am the wind beneath your wings. I am—'

'Get out and guard that phone,' Catherine ordered.

Lisa reached the door and turned. 'Hey, boss,' she paused and smiled, 'stop worrying, it'll come.'

Thank God for Lisa, Catherine thought as the girl closed the door quietly. The twenty-one-year-old possessed a bubbly personality and an unshakeable loyalty that Catherine had come to rely on.

She checked her diary for the following day. She had three meetings with prospective clients but none as big as the one she was waiting to hear about. Lisa had been right. It would catapult her from account manager to executive. A substantial pay increase but, more importantly, a move to the top floor alongside the other executives and the two directors.

There was also a pencilled note to ring Beth. She felt guilty for the fact that it was in pencil. She only marked things in pencil if they were flexible enough to be carried forward to the next day if she ran out of time. The entry had been re-written three times.

In the six days since the funeral Catherine had meant to call her sister and check that she was okay, but something had stopped her. She wasn't sure how to communicate with Beth and that had nothing to do with the years that had passed between them.

The realisation that Beth didn't remember anything had shocked her to the core. How could she not remember? Catherine had searched her expression for any clue that the truth lurked in there somewhere but she had found nothing.

Surely it wasn't healthy to be denying everything that happened in their childhood, but maybe it was a type of defence mechanism that Beth had employed to enable her to stay with their mother and take care of her. Maybe Beth was the lucky one, Catherine reasoned. If she could pay for the memories to be surgically removed she'd book the procedure tomorrow. She didn't know enough about denial to understand if Beth's total ignorance of the events of their childhood was healthy or not, but she knew it just didn't feel right.

Her thoughts turned to Alex who was a completely different story. She remembered it all, clearly. Catherine felt sadness wash over her for her youngest sister. She knew the drinking was an escape to bury the memories. Alex was still tortured by the past and remained gripped by their cycle. She wished there was something she could do. How different might Alex's life have been if her spirit and fight had been channelled in a positive direction? What could she have become? Catherine closed her eyes. Alex was drowning and Catherine didn't know how to save her.

'Catherine... Catherine... ' Lisa's voice sounded through the intercom.

'Yes,' she answered, sitting upright. Alert. Her heart pounded in her chest.

'Drinks at Brini's in half an hour.'

Shit, thought Catherine. That told her nothing. She knew people who had been fired and promoted at Brini's. It was an exclusive members' club a stone's throw from the office, in the centre of Shrewsbury. A plain door sat between a trendy boutique and health-food shop. Known only to its patrons, Catherine had been there once before when they'd head-hunted her from Pimton's.

She pressed the shortcut to Tim's mobile. He'd be on his way to the childminder to collect the girls.

'It's me,' she said as he answered. She could hear the noise of rush-hour traffic in the background. 'I've just had the call,' she said, nervously.

'Aren't you on your way home?'

'Didn't you hear me? I said I've just had the call. I'm meeting the directors in half an hour.'

The line went quiet. Catherine wondered if they'd been disconnected, but the traffic noise remained.

'Tonight?'

'Of course tonight,' she snapped. What was wrong with him? Why wasn't he excited for her?

'You'll have to postpone.'

'Are you out of your mind?' she screeched down the phone. 'Why the hell would I want to do that?'

'Because it's parents' evening for your six-year-old daughters.'

Catherine could hear the controlled rage in his voice. Shit, she had completely forgotten.

'I've been telling you for three weeks and I left a reminder on the fridge this morning.' His voice was low and barely audible.

'I can't postpone this meeting, Tim. You know how hard I've worked to get this. If I cancel now I might just as well collect my P45 in the morning.'

'That may not be such a bad thing.'

'For Christ's sake,' Catherine cried indignantly. 'It's for you and the girls that I'm doing this. The extra money could pay for a lot—'

'Please don't pretend that anything other than your need for approval and recognition drives you, Catherine,' he said, his voice loud and strong. 'The girls would much prefer you at their parents' evening.'

Catherine was stung by his words but she didn't want an argument. She needed to be focused when she met the directors.

'Listen, I'll try and hurry the meeting along and meet you at the school as soon as I can get—'

It took Catherine a few seconds to realise that the line had been disconnected. She replaced the receiver and contemplated calling Tim back. She decided against it. She'd sort it out with him later.

* * *

The low grey clouds and drizzling rain were drawing the evening in quicker than normal for a late September day. Catherine tried not to see the weather as a bad omen and fixed a bright smile on her face as she entered the wine bar.

The two directors were sitting at the same table as when they'd offered her her current position. She briefly wondered if it was reserved for them exclusively. She sat in the plush maroon velvet chair and greeted them both. A monochrome waiter appeared beside her instantly. She ordered a soft drink.

The younger Mr Leigh smiled at her but she could read nothing from his expression. He was in his early fifties, but time and millions had served him well. His hair was full and silvery and topped a healthy tanned face. His older brother had not been so fortunate and his five additional years showed in his receding hairline and growing paunch.

Mr Leigh Junior sat back in his chair. 'How's the family, Catherine?'

'They're fine, thank you.'

Catherine realised she'd just had the perfect opportunity to pave the way for leaving early had she mentioned that it was her children's parents' evening, but she'd let the moment pass.

'You know why we've asked you here this evening, Catherine?'

She nodded and despite the fact that he was smiling his expression was still indecipherable.

'How long have you been with us now?'

'Five years.'

Catherine still couldn't tell which way the meeting was going. The various permutations her mind computed had delivered three options. Her presentation had not secured the contract. Her presentation had secured the contract and she was going to head it. Or option three, which she dared not even consider: her presentation had won the contract but they were nominating someone else to head it.

'You've been with us for five years so that makes you... thirty?'

'Twenty-nine.'

Mr Leigh Junior nodded before drawing his eyebrows together in a slight frown and Catherine's heart missed a beat. Jesus, no. If they had won the contract and it was going to be awarded to someone else due to her age she seriously doubted that she could continue to work for the company any longer.

'As you know, the Finesse cosmetics presentation was one of the largest and most ambitious contracts we've ever bid for.'

She nodded, too afraid to speak. His voice was low and even, giving nothing away.

'Their annual gross profit is in the region of ninety million pounds. Fifteen million of that is spent on advertising.'

Catherine knew all that. 'But we're only tendering for the new organic line,' she said, confused. That line alone was worth just under five million and a substantial contract for the business.

Mr Leigh nodded, a slow smile spreading across his face. 'You're right. That's in the bag, but they were so blown away by your presentation that they'd like to see what we could do with the entire product range.'

'Jesus Christ,' Catherine said and then coloured. The other, quieter, Mr Leigh was a good Christian man. Luckily he was smiling, too. Catherine could barely believe it. She knew the presentation had been good. She'd spent months on it, neglecting her other contracts at times, and it was something she was incredibly proud of. The late nights and early mornings had paid off. Relief flooded through her body.

She wanted to hug and kiss everyone in the room but a niggling thought silenced the fanfare in her mind. They hadn't yet ruled out option number three: that although her presentation had won the contract, someone with more experience would be drafted in to head it.

'Well?' he prompted.

'It's fantastic news. Better than I could have hoped for but...'

'Your new title will be Senior Executive, which incidentally is a new position and answers directly to myself.'

'Oh my... Oh Jesus... Oh my Lord!' she exclaimed.

Both Mr Leighs laughed out loud. 'You'll need to choose a team, starting with a project manager.'

'Lisa Gordon.'

Mr Leigh looked a little doubtful but shrugged. 'I'll trust your judgement on the support that you choose and we'll discuss the finer details of the promotion tomorrow.'

Catherine knew that he was talking about the salary but she didn't care. The point was that she'd got it. Finally, recognition for her hard work, for the time and effort she'd put into the project. At last, she was being recognised.

'Obviously your other contracts will be redistributed amongst the other account managers, leaving you free to focus on the Finesse range alone.'

Catherine nodded gratefully. They chatted for a while longer but she barely heard a word. Her mind was already making plans to secure the other lines. Her brain was buzzing with ideas.

The two brothers congratulated her once again and excused themselves for a dinner appointment.

Catherine finished her Perrier and floated to where she'd parked the car.

* * *

As she pulled into the school playground the digital display told her it was almost eight. She was nearly an hour late. She grabbed her bag and hurriedly followed the directions to the classroom. Thank God for the signs. Although she'd dropped the girls off at school a couple of times she had no idea where their actual classroom was.

The room was almost empty. Two women were sitting at the teacher's desk and Tim was in the far corner amongst colourful toys and the girls. A boy was showing Jess something in a pop-up book.

'Thank goodness. I'm not too late, am I?' Catherine asked, smiling at Tim.

'I waited until last,' Tim said, rising to his feet. 'Show Jamie how that toy works,' he instructed Jess, ruffling her hair. He moved to the other corner of the room, away from the children.

Catherine tried to pre-empt his words. 'Tim, I'm sorry. I know how important tonight is but you'll never guess what's happened.'

'And it's still all about you, isn't it?' he hissed. 'We've been here for two hours. Miss Whitney has called us twice. We should have been home ages ago. The girls are tired and restless. They want to go to bed and the only thing you're bothered about is your damn promotion.'

Catherine tried to keep a rein on her anger. Her feelings during the drive from the wine bar had alternated. Her indignation at Tim's lack of support for her career had fought with her wish to smooth over the troubled waters, prompting the immediate apology.

'I've explained why I had to—'

'Save it, Catherine. I'm not interested. Take a look at that woman sitting at the desk. She's twenty-four years of age and that's her six-year-old son. She's a single mother and has three part-time jobs to support him. And guess what? She got here on time.'

Catherine opened her mouth to retort but Tim was heading towards the desk where the two women were now standing. He shook the woman's hand and ruffled the head of the young boy before they left the classroom.

'Would you like to come over?' the teacher asked, smiling kindly.

She took her seat beside Tim and though they were only separated by inches Catherine could feel the gaping chasm between them.

Miss Whitney smiled at them both, her green eyes friendly and open. 'I'd like to congratulate you both on your lovely daughters.'

Catherine felt Tim's chest expand slightly with pride, whereas despite Miss Whitney's best efforts to put them at ease she still felt as though she was back at school.

'They're both very bright young girls but I do have one or two concerns. Lucy is the quieter of the two and her interaction with the other children is often reserved. I'm not saying that there's a major problem, but she only really likes to partake in activities that don't include being part of a group. Singular activities such as painting she absolutely excels at but she struggles to take part in group games.'

'She's just shy,' Catherine defended.

'There are other shy children in the class, Mrs Richards, but none quite so isolated as Lucy. Jess, on the other hand, is the complete opposite, umm… too much so if I can be honest.'

Despite the teacher's smile, Catherine felt her heckles rising. Who the hell was this woman to start judging her children?

'Jess is constantly in the mix of everything that's going on. Unlike Lucy she hates the solitary activities. She has a lot of energy and a need for attention—'

'She is not spoilt,' Catherine exploded. Tim cast a warning glance in her direction.

Miss Whitney shook her head. 'I'm not inferring that she is. It is often the case with twins that their personalities can be extreme, but Jess does seem to demand a lot of attention, be it positive or otherwise, and sometimes she can be a disruptive influence on the rest of the class.'

'So, you're saying that she's naughty?'

Miss Whitney frowned, as though somehow her words were changing into something else once they'd left her mouth.

'Jess isn't a naughty child. She has lots of energy and I'm sure if it was channelled in the right direction she'd be a much—'

'Miss Whitney, I am not going to listen to any more of this rubbish. My children are not dysfunctional. They are completely normal six-year-olds,' she said rising out of the chair.

Miss Whitney looked towards Tim beseechingly. Catherine saw that her raised voice had caught the attention of the girls.

'Sit down,' Tim ordered, with steel in his voice. Catherine sat.

'As I said before, both Lucy and Jess are wonderful girls and a delight to teach. My only concern is that their social skills are quite limited.' Seeing the granite look on Catherine's face she moved on swiftly. 'On a more positive note, Jess absolutely excels in physical activity. She loves to run and play games and invariably beats the rest hands down.'

Tim nodded knowingly and shared a smile with the young teacher. Catherine felt annoyed and excluded.

'She has a particular love of gymnastics and it's something I'd like her to pursue during this new school year.'

'She's the same at home. She can form herself into all sorts of shapes,' Tim replied.

Catherine smiled despite the fact that she hadn't seen any of these shapes.

'Now, on to Lucy.'

Catherine heard a subtle change in the teacher's voice. Almost like she'd presented the starter and it was time for the main course.

'I'd like to show you something.' She reached in her drawer and extracted an exercise book. She opened it a few pages in and turned the book to face them.

'What is it?' Catherine asked.

'I asked the class to paint a picture of the planet earth. As you can see from Lucy's picture she went much further than that. She looked at the picture on the wall and produced the entire solar system.'

'She copied a picture?' Catherine asked, trying to understand the teacher's excitement.

'She did much more than that. Look at how she managed to emulate the subtle shades of the colours. She would have needed to mix colours to achieve that – something far in excess of normal capabilities for this age group. Look at the detail she put into the placement of the stars. The fact that everything within the picture is in proportion to each other.'

'But ultimately, you're telling me that she copied a picture?'

Tim shot daggers in her direction as he looked towards the girls. Lucy had moved slightly closer and her face looked flushed and crestfallen. She returned to her place beside Jess on the play mat.

'What I'm trying to demonstrate is that this painting is an exceptional piece of work, and would be for a child twice her age.'

'She's six years old and she copied a picture,' Catherine exclaimed, ignoring Tim's warning glance. Catherine was concerned about the ideas this teacher might be putting into a young girl's head. What she saw on the page was a mixture of balls daubed with pretty colours.

'What I'm trying to say, Mrs Richards, is that Lucy is an incredibly talented and gifted child and this talent should be nurtured and encouraged.'

The woman continued to drone on as Catherine found herself transported back to a similar room many years earlier.

* * *

'Catherine, that is absolutely beautiful,' Mrs Tromans had said to her.

Catherine had liked Mrs Tromans. She was big and warm with woolly cardigans and feather earrings. She smelled of flowery perfume, smiled a lot and patted her on the head.

'I love the way you've used green glitter to form the branches of the Christmas tree.'

The teacher took the card from her. 'Truly, Catherine, this is a very skilful piece of work.'

Catherine glowed with pride as Mrs Tromans touched the sparkly glitter. 'Is this for your mum?'

Catherine nodded.

'I think she'll love it and give it pride of place above the fire. Go and write a nice message inside so that you can take it home today.'

Catherine returned to the table and sat silently for a moment. She picked up a crayon but she didn't know what to write. She glanced at Becky's card and saw that it was filled with hearts and kisses and stars. She had a good look and then copied what Becky had done.

The finished card filled her with pride. The hearts were better than Becky's because they were coloured in. The stars were prettier because she'd done them in different colours. Mrs Tromans was right, Catherine decided. Her mum was sure to love it.

She placed the card at the back of her exercise book to protect it from the plimsolls in her bag. The covers of the book would keep it flat and clean.

She skipped home, imagining her mum putting up the Christmas tree. All of her school friends were already filled with wonder at the glistening baubles and colourful tinsel of their own trees, but hers wasn't up yet.

The house was as bare as when she'd left it. No bright Christmas tree with colourful lights or red and white candy canes. Her mum was at the table spreading jam sandwiches for tea, a grim look on her face. Beth stood solemnly beside her cutting the sandwiches into smaller squares. Alex was waving her potty around her head in the living room.

Catherine took the card from the supermarket carrier bag that served as her school bag. She handed the card to her mum who opened it and started laughing. For a moment, just a brief moment, Catherine thought that she had done something good. But then the smile turned into a sneer and cold eyes rested upon her.

'What the bloody hell is this?'

'A Christmas card.'

Her mum turned it over and looked at every surface. 'You could have fooled me. It's a scrap of shitty paper with some cheap glitter thrown on it.'

'I made it for you,' Catherine tried to explain, thinking it would make a difference. 'I wrote in the middle—'

'You spelt Christmas wrong.' Her mum smiled again, the corners of her mouth twisting. 'I've got enough fucking rubbish to get rid of. I don't need no more,' she laughed, tossing it into the bin amongst the stale bread and used tea bags.

Catherine felt the tears sting the backs of her eyes. The card, so colourful and bright, in the bin.

'But Mrs Tromans said—'

'Fuck, Mrs Tromans. Teachers will say anything to get you to behave. It's no fucking masterpiece, I can tell you that much.'

Beth moved to retrieve it but her mother was faster and poured the dregs from the teapot into the bin.

Catherine backed out of the room, desperate not to let the tears fall over her cheeks. Making the card had taken her into a world of her own. She had become oblivious to the rest of the classroom. She had been transported into a parallel universe where it was just her and the picture in her head. And she'd thought it was good.

She had never picked up a paintbrush again.

* * *

Catherine shook herself back to the present. She'd heard enough. She had no idea how this girl, who was hardly out of college herself, had the gall to fill the heads of her children with outlandish claims.

Catherine stood and offered her hand. 'Thank you for your time, Miss Whitney, but it's late and the girls are tired.'

Having no choice, Tim followed suit before calling the girls over. Catherine felt the awkwardness between them as they left the classroom but she didn't care. That teacher had no right filling anyone's head with unrealistic expectations. 'Honestly, who does that…?'

'Catherine,' Tim said, indicating the girls walking between them. She sighed. She would explain her point once the girls were in bed.

Tim ushered the girls into his car and she followed behind in hers. When she pulled on to the drive she saw that the gentle hum of the drive home had lulled the girls to sleep.

Tim opened the back door and his face softened. He nodded for her to take a look at the girls lolled against each other in the back seat.

'It's a shame to wake them. I'll carry Jess, you get Lucy.'

Catherine watched as he carefully released the seatbelt and gently placed one arm beneath Jess's legs, the other supporting her neck. She stirred slightly but turned her face into Tim's jacket, her eyes firmly closed. He expertly opened the front door without disturbing the sleeping form in his arms.

Catherine knelt beside Lucy and shook her arm gently. 'Lucy, wake up, we're home. Come on, get out of the car.'

Lucy opened her eyes with effort but they drooped closed again. Catherine shook her again. 'Lucy, it's late, wake up and go inside the house, now,' she said, her voice sterner.

The child did as she was told and climbed out of the car.

Catherine followed Lucy into the house. Her daughter looked like a drunk, swaying from side to side, hitting both the wall and the banister on her way up the stairs.

Catherine headed for the kitchen and opened a bottle of wine. She took a cigarette and stood just outside the kitchen door. Oh, how she wished she'd been able to hold on to the euphoria she'd felt as she'd left the wine bar, but it had been kicked, trampled and left for dead.

She drew deeply on the cigarette and hoped that when Tim had finished putting the girls to bed he would congratulate her on the promotion and help her celebrate. Maybe they could order in a nice meal, drink a few glasses of wine while planning what they'd do with the extra money.

Perhaps, once he saw how hard she'd worked and that tonight had been unavoidable, their celebrations could continue in the bedroom.

She extinguished the cigarette as Tim entered the kitchen. He had removed his tie and opened the top button of his shirt. Despite his tired, pinched expression, Catherine thought he had never looked sexier.

She sidled up to him and placed her arms around his neck. 'Sweetheart, I'm sorry about earlier but now it's just the two of us—'

'Stop it, Catherine,' he said, removing her arms from around his neck. He stepped away from her and poured himself a glass of wine.

'Sit down,' he instructed. 'We need to talk and I don't think you're going to like what I have to say.'

Catherine sat and refilled her wine glass. The rejection of her advances stung a bit but she realised that Tim had to have his say before the rest of the night could go the way she wanted.

'I can even tell what you're thinking,' Tim said, looking at her evenly. 'You're already thinking that this is one of my rants and then everything will return to normal.'

Catherine blushed but shook her head in protest.

'It doesn't matter what you think, but I am going to say what's on my mind.' He took a deep breath. 'A fog cleared tonight and I've got to be honest, I don't like what I see.'

'But it—'

'Please don't interrupt me. I need to say some things. I spent quite a while talking to that girl you saw when you first came in. She's a single parent struggling to bring up her little boy alone. Many of the things she said to me while describing some of the hurdles she has to overcome seemed a little too familiar, uncomfortably so.' He shook his head and looked at her directly. 'This is a single-parent family, Catherine, and you're the one that's missing.'

Catherine looked back at him, horrified. How could he say something so cruel?

'I get up at six every morning to make sure—'

'Don't embarrass yourself by listing the things that you do. You'll make yourself sound like the hired help.'

Catherine was incensed. 'Now hang on one—'

'No, you hang on. Did you even recognise your own children in the things that their teacher said about them or did it feel like she was discussing the personalities of two strangers?'

'She was inferring that there was something wrong with our children,' Catherine cried. She lit a cigarette with trembling hands.

Tim thumped the table, his eyes blazing. 'Are you so blind that you can't see what she was saying? She was telling us that our children are not getting enough attention. Lucy has disappeared within herself and Jess is starving for recognition of her individuality.'

'That teacher thinks she knows our daughters better than we do.'

'For fuck's sake, Catherine, wake up. She knows the girls better than you do. You were a complete embarrassment tonight. I seriously wish you'd never made it at all.'

'I was defending the girls,' Catherine screamed at the injustice. Where had his arguments been? He had been too happy to just listen to the teacher's accusations.

'That argument doesn't work because you ridiculed her when she tried to tell you how talented Lucy was. Where was your pride in your daughter's achievements? Where was your total agreement that she is special, unique and talented?'

'I will not fill her head with—'

'It's not about the damn picture. You should have those feelings for her regardless. She's your bloody daughter.'

Tim was standing, leaning on the table bellowing at her. She stared back at him. The anger seemed to drain out of him and he fell wearily back on to the chair. 'We both looked at that picture tonight and saw totally different things. I saw a talented painting by my oldest daughter which filled me with pride. You saw some balls daubed on a piece of paper. You spoke of Lucy as though she was a stranger and what's worse is that she heard you.'

Catherine waved away his concerns. 'She's a child.'

'She's your child but it certainly didn't feel like that tonight.'

'I'll speak to her tomorrow,' Catherine offered, hoping to repair the damage between them. Despite the thought that he was over-reacting she didn't like the weary, hopeless look on his face.

'Just leave it. I don't want you making it worse.'

Catherine nodded but his eyes were cast downwards. She hoped that the argument was over but sensed that it wasn't. Something was different this time. Tim was different and there was more that he wanted to say.

'Tim?' she whispered, reaching for his hand. He pulled it away. Catherine felt the panic churn her stomach. Usually once Tim had made his point they kissed and hugged and everything returned to normal.

When he finally looked up his eyes were tired and haunted. When he spoke his voice was low and controlled.

'I can see that you haven't really listened to anything I've said, which saddens me. Your coldness towards the girls is tearing me apart because I don't understand it and I know they can feel it. I've hidden from the fact that it's hurting them for too long.' He paused and Catherine's heart missed a beat. He smiled sadly. 'Surprisingly, I still love you more than life but you're damaging our children. I know that your own childhood was less than ideal but you've never even shared it with me.'

'It's the past, Tim. It has nothing to do with now.'

His smile disappeared, leaving only despair in its place. 'Catherine, you need help. You need to talk to someone about what happened to you all those years ago. You say it's the past and it's over, but it's not. It's affecting the present and it's hurting the girls.'

'Don't be so ridiculous,' Catherine cried. 'I don't need to see a bloody shrink. My past has nothing to do with us now. Get a grip, Tim. We have a nice house, good jobs and two lovely girls. What the hell is wrong with you?'

'That's the illusion, Catherine. It's what you like to think we have, but name one conversation you've had with either of our children since the day you buried your mother.'

'Don't be so damned pedantic. I can't just pull one out of my head and you know it. You're just trying to trap me—'

'Catherine, stop it. I'm not arguing about this any more.' He finished his wine and headed for the door. 'Either get help or I'll take the girls away for good.'

CHAPTER 6

Alex

Alex turned her head to look at the clock and instantly regretted it. Whoever was swinging an iron bar around her head was invisible but no less effective because of it.

The red LED display told her that it was 7.45 but her clock wasn't twenty-four-hour, so she had no idea if it was morning or evening and she certainly had no idea what day it was.

She laid her head back down on the pillow, which felt like a concrete slab, and listened for clues in the sounds outside. There was a faint tapping against the window that she recognised as rain. The sound of traffic was constant and gave her no help. It was light outside so that was useless also. She considered getting out of bed and switching on the TV but realised that she didn't care enough to bother.

She turned over and pulled the covers over her head to block the light that was trespassing through her closed eyelids. The density of the blackness comforted her and reduced the wrecking ball in her head to a pneumatic drill. She prepared to return to oblivion but her bladder had other ideas.

'Fuck,' she whispered as she realised what the journey to the bathroom was going to do to her. She eased herself up to a sitting position and cringed as her skull shrunk around her brain.

She shuffled her feet around until she found a bare piece of carpet and forced her eyes open to navigate safe passage to the bathroom.

Alex negotiated through the empty whisky bottles and beer cans until she reached the safety of the bathroom. She collapsed on to the toilet and fell against the wall.

She stood and washed her hands, catching a brief glimpse of her reflection. Red, puffy eyes glared back at her. Blotchy skin sat beneath short, black unruly spikes.

She lunged for the toothpaste and cleaned her teeth in an effort to evict the dead farmyard from her mouth and threw cold water at her face. There, that was her grooming regime for another day.

She headed back to the bed. 'Hair of the dog,' she murmured, tipping up the bottles on route. They were all empty. She headed for the kitchen and opened all the doors, throwing the contents onto the counter top. Maybe during her drunken state she had seen fit to hide a bottle of something, anything, from herself for a rainy day. 'Well, it's fucking raining now,' she cried, as the washing machine yielded no alcohol.

She struggled to the sofa and aimed the remote control at the TV. The opening credits of *EastEnders* blared out at her. Thank God it was evening and she could go out and restock.

She guessed it was probably Tuesday, partly because she vaguely remembered Monday, and *EastEnders* aired on a Tuesday. And most other days of the bloody week. She switched channels and caught the end of the local news. She stared, stunned, at the television screen. Fucking Thursday, they said. How could it be Thursday? What had happened to Wednesday?

Shit. She vaguely remembered the phone ringing incessantly and then Jay appearing in front of her but she'd thought that was a dream. Surely Jay hadn't held her under the shower and then put her to bed? The memory returned to her in fragmented pieces. She had pretended to be asleep until he went and then she had dressed and nipped to the off-licence.

'Oh Jesus,' she sighed and buried her head in her hands. He had returned the following day but her mind couldn't piece together exactly what day that had been. She vaguely recalled calling him some horrible names and telling him to fuck off.

'Oh, Lord,' she whined again. She hauled herself into the kitchen and searched for the effervescent tablets that she'd thrown somewhere. She located them underneath an upturned box of rice. She added water and swallowed the bitter-tasting liquid.

A shower and a change of clothes later, Alex was feeling alive if not human. She locked the flat and headed for the bar where Jay worked five nights out of seven.

As she passed a greasy chip shop the tantalising smell of fish and chips lured her in. She wasn't sure when she'd last eaten. She made a hole in the layers of paper and delved in, retrieving a clump of greasy batter and grey fish. The first mouthful made her feel nauseous and she threw them away.

The bar on Broad Street was rich with bodies and laughter and Alex had to fight her way to the bar. Most of the activity swarmed towards the DJ, leaving a couple of bar stools free. She perched herself on one and waited for Jay to notice her. When he saw her his face tightened and he looked away.

'Jay, please,' she called across the bar, struggling to make herself heard. At first he refused to turn around but Marcus, a friend to them both, nudged Jay and pointed in her direction. He moved towards her end of the bar, his face hard. She stood and shouted in his ear. 'I'm sorry, Jay. I've only just remembered but I'm really sorry.'

'For calling me an old worn-out queer or a fucking failure?'

'Both,' she cried, battling to make herself heard above the noise. She could see from the hurt on his face that her insults had affected him deeply. She felt sick to her stomach and it had nothing to do with her hangover.

'You know that I'm a total bitch when I get like that and I didn't mean a word I said,' she offered, sincerely.

'I didn't know you had so many friends that you could afford to discard one quite so easily.'

'I don't,' she said, honestly. Jay was the only person she cared about in the world and the thought of losing him brought tears to her eyes.

Jay surveyed her for a second, chewing his lip. He reached across the bar. 'Come here you silly old dyke.'

Alex accepted the embrace, relieved that she hadn't damaged their friendship irreparably.

He released her and pointed a wagging finger in her direction. 'And no more fucking benders, eh?'

Despite the humour in his words she could see the seriousness in his eyes.

She nodded. 'No more benders.'

He turned and poured her a Coke. 'Here, this one's on the house.'

'Fuck off, I'm not turning into Mary Poppins.'

He laughed and added a measure of brandy.

'The wagon will still be there tomorrow,' she said, slugging the drink down in one go.

'Promise?' Jay asked, real concern shaping his eyes.

She nodded and meant it.

'Mike was in here yesterday.'

'Oh shit,' she said, lighting a cigarette.

'I told him you'd contracted that summer flu and you'd probably be back at the weekend.'

Alex felt a rush of love and gratitude. Despite her treatment of him he had still saved her bacon. Thanks to him she still had a job.

Jay headed for the other end of the bar, which was becoming congested.

Alex sipped her second drink more leisurely than the first, savouring the warm sensation as it travelled the journey from her throat into her stomach. Already the comfort blanket was cloaking itself around her. The memories unearthed by the funeral were travelling further away into a long black tunnel.

She didn't want to remember how Beth had gained that scar. She didn't want to relive other painful events from all those years ago. She didn't want to consider the repercussions of Beth's repressed memories, but most of all she didn't want to remember how close the three of them had once been.

She was surprised at the speed of the effect the alcohol was having on her system. Only two drinks and her head was feeling pleasantly woozy. She supposed it was like a top-up effect as the previous binge of alcohol was still in her system. Fantastic, she decided, pleased that less effort and money was required to restore her to her very own plateau of contentment.

The third drink slid down easily and within seconds she was jigging on the stool in time to the music. Her arms waved madly in the air. The deep thudding sound of the trance mix worked its way up the stool and into her brain until all she could feel and hear was the incessant pounding of the beat.

She felt a tap on her shoulder and turned to find Jay appraising her with concern. She smiled widely at all three of him and mouthed 'Tomorrow' at the top of her voice to show him that she had not forgotten her promise. The word sounded amusing on her lips.

'Tomorrow, tomorrow, the sun'll come out tomorrow,' she sang to Jay, but he wasn't listening. He had the phone to his ear.

She spluttered with laughter. Who the hell would try and make a phone call with all this noise?

'If that's the Samaritans for me, tell 'em I'll call at my normal time,' she shouted across the bar before dissolving into fits of laughter. She signalled to Marcus to fix her another drink. He looked doubtful but shrugged and put another one before her.

'Thank you very much, thank you very much, that's the nicest thing that anyone's ever done for me,' she sang to his retreating back.

She responded to the voice in her head that urged her to down it in one go. The alcohol travelled straight to her eyesight and the whole dance floor tipped on its own axis. She turned her head sideways so that it was straight again. The motion prompted the telltale rush of bile into her mouth.

Oh shit, she thought cheerfully, as she weaved in and out of the crowd on her way to the toilets. She pushed past the waiting queue and collapsed beside the toilet. She kicked the door shut behind her and threw up. She watched as the diluted black liquid of the Coke filled the toilet bowl. Angry knocks sounded on the cubicle door and between heaves she politely told the party poopers to go fuck themselves.

The acid in her throat had brought salty tears to her eyes and her whole body began to tremble with cold and weakness. She reached for the toilet paper to stem the mucus dribbling from her nose but found the holder empty.

She felt another rush of nausea and threw up again, barely aware of the cubicle door caving in behind her.

Alex felt a presence beside her.

'Come on, I think it's about time I got you home,' said a soft voice that she recognised. A gentle hand rubbed her back. She turned and looked into the sweet face of an angel.

'Hello Nikki, what the fuck are you doing here?'

* * *

Alex was barely aware of the journey. Her head fell against the window and rattled against it every time the car hit a pothole or stopped at lights. The mist in her mind was clearing and it annoyed her. It meant she had to think, explain, justify, when all she really wanted to do was exchange one form of anaesthetic for another by moving straight from being pissed to falling asleep.

She stared out of the window, seeing in the reflection of the glass the concerned glances occasionally cast by Nikki.

The car stopped in front of the flat they had shared until six months ago and which had been Nikki's before that and was Nikki's again now. Alex was surprised at the stab of nostalgia she felt on seeing the converted Victorian house.

'Come on, sweet, let's get you inside,' Nikki said, helping her out of the passenger-side door. Alex's natural instinct was to push aside the assistance and get out of the car by herself. Nikki stood to the side as Alex swayed and almost collapsed in the gutter.

Nikki took her arm forcefully. 'No arguments,' she said.

Alex allowed herself to be assisted up the stairs to the front door of the first-floor flat. Nikki managed to support her and open the front door at the same time. It occurred to Alex that the flat had barely changed since she'd left. And, she realised, from when she'd moved in as well. She saw just how little impact she'd had on the place either by moving into it or moving out.

It seemed to have grown since she'd seen it last or maybe it was just in her head. She had quickly acclimatised to a studio flat where everything except going to the toilet was done in one room. She remembered now what it was like to move from room to room to perform different functions.

'How are you feeling?' Nikki asked, as she eased Alex on to the sofa.

'Like my stomach just got ripped through my throat.'

'I'll make some black coffee.'

'Why?'

'To sober you up.'

'Don't bother,' Alex instructed, allowing her head to loll back against the fabric of the sofa. 'It's a myth. Black coffee does nothing. I'll have some water.'

Nikki nodded and headed for the kitchen.

'And throw a double measure of whisky in with it,' she called, but Nikki ignored her. If she knew Nikki, any alcohol in the place would have been tipped away before she left to come and get her. Damn Jay, she thought angrily. Why did he have to be so damned interfering? If she'd been left alone she would have thrown up some more and then started drinking again. It was a vicious cycle and she loved it.

'When was the last time you ate?' Nikki asked, placing the water on the coffee table that separated the two sofas. The one she was sitting on now had always been hers. At times they had shared and cuddled up on both, but when they had been doing separate things this sofa had been hers. She could almost feel the outline that her body had sculpted in the fabric during their two years together.

'I can't think about food,' Alex groaned as her stomach began to roll.

'I bet it's been a while since you gave it a thought at all. How long was this one?'

Alex shrugged. 'A couple of days.'

'That's not what Jay said.'

'Then why fucking ask?' Alex exploded. If Jay had already filled her in why was she getting the third degree?

'Because I wanted to see if you'd lie. And you did. Why?'

'I d... don't know,' Alex said, beginning to dither. The heat inside the car had been close and suffocating but now her body began to react.

Nikki went to the bedroom and returned with a patchwork quilt that she had made from scraps of material. Alex had always loved that quilt because despite being a mismatch of fabric there was an order, a theme to it, that was so Nikki.

Alex had always called it 'Nikki's Worry Quilt'. She had only worked on it when she had things on her mind that she needed to think through. Nikki draped it over her and pulled it up around her shoulders so that no skin was exposed.

'Jay said that your mother died,' Nikki said, as she turned up the heating.

Alex shrugged. 'So?'

'Is that all you have to say about it?'

'What do you want me to say?'

Nikki sighed and smiled sadly. 'You still won't let me in, will you?'

'We've been through this,' Alex said, reaching for her cigarettes.

'But that's the point, Alex. We never really went through anything, did we?'

Alex drew on the cigarette, hating the fact that Nikki finished almost every sentence with a question. 'You were the one who made an issue of it.'

'Because we weren't communicating. You didn't trust me enough to confide in me. The only thing you ever said was that it was rough.'

'I didn't ask you to tell me everything about your childhood,' Alex said. She could almost recite the lines word for word.

'Because there was nothing to tell, but I would have told you everything. You wouldn't even say if you had brothers or sisters.

We were together for two years and I didn't even know that much about you.'

'It wasn't important.'

'It was to me.'

'Why?' Alex asked, meeting her gaze for the first time. She was shocked at the love and concern she found staring back at her. She looked away.

'Because I loved you,' she said quietly.

Alex noticed the use of the past tense and an inexplicable wave of panic coursed through her, but what could she expect? It had been six months since they split. Nikki had carried on with her life and Alex accepted that she was no longer the centre of it. She also knew that it had been her choice.

'And I loved you,' Alex said, quietly. For some reason it was important to her that Nikki knew that.

'As much as you could.'

'Don't demean what I felt for you,' Alex raged. It was something Nikki had said to her on the day of their final argument. The one where they had both said things that they couldn't unsay. Things that no amount of apologising would ever erase.

'It's true, Alex, whether you like it or not. There are things that you need to work through and until you do you will be unable to give yourself properly to anyone.'

'Glad to see the eight-week psychology course paid off,' Alex said, nastily. She didn't like the fact that Nikki felt that in some way she was unable to love properly. That she was incomplete, somehow. That she was damaged.

'I don't need my psychology degree to see that. Anyone who's ever spent more than ten minutes with you would agree.' Nikki held her hands up to Alex's protestations. 'What I'm trying to say is that I'm flattered. I'm flattered that it was with me you tried your hardest.'

Alex snorted derisively. Why couldn't Nikki accept that it just hadn't worked out? They'd had some good times but ultimately they were just not meant to be together. It happened to couples all the time. Why did she have to apply some deep and meaningful reason to the fact that they had just separated?

'I'll be back in a minute,' Nikki said, heading off to the kitchen.

Alex finished her cigarette and took a long drink of the water. Her head was beginning to clear more every minute and she didn't like it at all. A wave of irritation rolled over her at Nikki's attitude towards her. Even when they'd been together Alex had despaired at Nikki's constant equilibrium.

She remembered the night they'd met in Jay's club. One glance at the woman with the golden hair had stopped her in her tracks. Nikki wasn't the sort of girl that Alex usually went for. She was far too feminine and girly. Hell, the woman even wore make-up.

She'd been dancing with a casual acquaintance with whom she'd hoped the night would end but the crowd had parted to reveal a tall, slim woman standing at the bar drinking a pint of lager. Alex had been struck by how out of place the drink had looked. The woman should have been holding the stem of a wine glass or sipping a daiquiri. Corny as it was, their eyes had met and both the music and Alex's partner had disappeared. The woman had stared back at her, a silent challenge in her eyes, but Alex had refused the battle.

As her senses returned to her, Alex realised the woman was probably part of a hen party frequenting the gay bars for the good music and a bit of a laugh. Disgusted at the thought, Alex had headed for the other end of the bar and tried to push the memory of those piercing green eyes away.

'You gonna ask me to dance or what?' the woman asked, sidling up beside her.

Surprised at the advance, Alex made a decision that she didn't know would change her life. She accepted the invitation and decided to give this straight girl a night to remember for trying to make a fool of her in front of her straight, girly friends. She guided Nikki on to the dance floor and held her in a close embrace.

Her hands caressed Nikki's back as her pelvis ground against Nikki's. Alex had been surprised to feel hardened nipples against her chest, so she had turned up the heat. Her hands wandered down to the small of Nikki's back and lower. She didn't grab or clutch at Nikki's buttocks but made slow, tantalising movements over the curve that led down to her leg, before bringing her hands round to rest on her hips.

Alex forced Nikki's head up so that their eyes met. She was expecting to find fear and uncertainty as the girl realised that the game had gone too far. What she did see stunned her. Nikki's eyes were filled with desire and longing. They danced some more and Alex knew that Nikki was hers. It was something she could feel in the movement of their bodies together. But Alex didn't want a quick shag with this woman. It felt wrong and she knew it. Five minutes later Alex excused herself and went home. She'd briefly considered trying to find her previous partner but she didn't want hamburger. She wanted steak, but she wanted it cooked properly.

A month later Alex had moved her belongings into Nikki's flat.

'Here, try and eat some of this,' Nikki said, placing a dish on her legs. Alex could smell the overpowering aroma of chicken soup.

She turned her head away. 'I can't, honestly.'

'Alex, for once trust me. Your body is reacting so badly to the alcohol because you've eaten nothing for days.'

'But I feel—'

'Now you're whining and sounding like a child,' Nikki said, smiling. 'Just try a little bit and then I'll stop nagging.'

Alex lifted the spoon to her mouth. It was worth it just for that. The soup was thick and creamy, strewn with pieces of chicken. The first mouthful travelled down her throat and plummeted to her stomach with a resounding thud. Alex tried to push it away but Nikki was quick to push it back. 'Try some more. It's just your body reacting to food after having none for a while.'

Alex swallowed another mouthful, enjoying the taste on her tongue but hating the uncomfortable feeling of it falling into the oblivion of her empty stomach. Mouthful by mouthful the sensation lessened until the last spoonful seemed to work its way through her intestines properly.

'That was delicious,' Alex admitted. 'Did you make it yourself?'

'Yeah, me and Campbell's,' Nikki chuckled, reaching for the dish. She went to the kitchen and returned with the bowl refilled.

Alex groaned good-naturedly, but now her system had been woken she felt ravenous. She reached for the half of French loaf and dipped it into the soup so that it was sodden and yellow.

'Sorry to see that your appetite is still suffering,' Nikki said, taking the empty dish from her.

Alex chuckled and lit a cigarette. Nikki had always been able to make her laugh. She had a dry, acerbic wit that often matched her own. Some of their bantering sessions had lasted for hours, reducing them both to childish fits of laughter that had made them cry.

Nikki disappeared to the kitchen once again and returned with two mugs of steaming hot chocolate.

'Can you make it?' Nikki asked, with a smile.

Alex tried to stand and found that although a little wobbly she could make it to the balcony. Nikki followed with the mugs of hot chocolate and the blanket. The reclining patio chairs stood as she remembered them. Facing outwards towards the view of two rows of rooftops, yet the chairs were turned in towards each other slightly. Alex sat in the one that had been hers. Nikki draped the blanket around her and handed her a mug of hot chocolate.

Nikki sat and they remained in silence as they had done hundreds of times before. It had been part of their nightly ritual to come on to the balcony with either a whisky and lemonade or hot chocolate, as dictated by the weather.

'Do you remember some of the stuff we used to talk about out here?' Nikki asked.

Alex nodded. 'We'd discuss our evening out, the music, the food, the atmosphere. Sometimes you'd tell me the events of your day.'

'Sometimes you'd tell me about something you were working on. An idea for a story or a character that you wanted to write about. Your eyes would light up with excitement as though you'd suddenly uncovered a secret, hidden world,' Nikki added, wistfully.

Alex looked away. Of all the things Nikki had done during their time together, the most beautiful had been to reawaken in her a dream that had been murdered when she was eight years old.

One of her most vivid childhood memories played in her head as though she was watching it on stage.

* * *

'Did you get me some?' Alex had asked, hopefully, as Catherine placed her school bag beside the bed. She inspected the outside to see if the shape gave her any clues.

Catherine shook her head. 'I'm sorry, Alex, I couldn't get any today. Mrs Gibson didn't leave the classroom for a minute. I tried to sneak one out but she just wouldn't go away.'

Alex was distraught. She'd just used the last page that Catherine had got for her yesterday.

'Ooooh, Aleeeeex,' Catherine called from behind her.

Alex turned to see her oldest sister waving two brand-new exercise books in the air.

Alex chuckled and lunged for the books, but Catherine dodged expertly out of her way and Alex landed face down on the bed.

'You're not having them,' Catherine sang, as she climbed on to the top bunk.

'Give them to me,' Alex cried, scaling the ladder. Catherine jumped over the other side, landing with bended knees.

'Catch me and you can have them,' Catherine teased, heading back towards her own bed.

Alex climbed back down the ladder, puffing with laughter. 'Please, Catherine, give them to me,' she begged, realising that her own chasing skills were far outweighed by those of her sister.

'No pain, no gain,' Catherine cried, her eyes alight with amusement.

Alex forced her face into a solemn expression. 'Okay, have it your own way. I'm not going to play this stupid game any longer,' she said, pouting. She headed for the door but at the last second changed direction and took Catherine by surprise. They fell on to the bed, hysterical with laughter as they fought over the exercise books being held aloft by Catherine. Alex reached and reached but couldn't quite grasp the treasure.

A plan formed in Alex's mind. She pinned Catherine's legs to the bed and tore her shoes from her feet.

'No, no,' Catherine protested as she realised what Alex was planning to do, but it was too late. Soon her socks were resting in a pile on the floor. Alex pinned Catherine's ankles down and drew shapes on her soles.

Catherine's laughter became manic. She threw the books at Alex but her sister was having too much fun. She tickled and tickled until Catherine forced her legs free and turned on her. She pinned her younger sister on the bed and tickled her sides until Alex cried with the pain in her stomach from laughter.

They collapsed in a heap, exhausted and still giggling. Once she'd recovered, Alex leaned over and kissed Catherine on the cheek. 'Thanks,' she said, before bounding off the side of the bed and retrieving the exercise books from the floor.

She returned to her position of kneeling at the lower bunk and began sharpening her pencils. Now she'd got more paper she could carry on with the ideas that had been plaguing her all day at school. Incey, her character, had just met the fairies at the bottom of the garden. They were living in plant pots and sleeping in the flowers, sliding down the stems into the soil if they heard anyone coming.

'How many of those have you filled?' Catherine asked, lying on the bed, facing in her direction.

Alex shrugged. It didn't matter. They were all in her bottom drawer. She reached in and pulled them all out. She counted them. Twelve exercise books filled with Incey's tales and adventures.

'Is it ever going to be finished?'

'Dunno,' Alex said, absently, concentrating on her story. She hoped not. She could live in Incey's world for ever.

Catherine changed out of her school clothes and headed for the door. She hesitated and turned back. 'Don't forget to put those books back in the drawer.'

'Okay,' Alex said, waving away her sister's words. She just wanted to be on her own to write stories about the fairies and the elves that lived under the shed. For the next two hours Alex was transported to another world, away from her own, where children had fun and laughed all the time. Incey's mummy took care of her and hugged her and helped her with her homework. Incey's mummy read her stories at bedtime and kissed her goodnight.

'Alex, tea,' her mum shouted from the bottom of the stairs.

Alex rushed to write down the last few lines of the story in her head. The beginning of Incey's next adventure. She scribbled quickly, misspelling many words in her haste to get them on paper.

'Alex, I'll come and get you in a minute,' her mum shouted again.

Alex could hear the anger in her voice and jumped to her feet. She launched herself down the stairs and landed beside Beth. She viewed the plate disinterestedly. Cheese sandwiches, again.

Her mother passed behind her and slapped her around the head, hard.

'Next time you'll come first fucking time I tell you.'

She left the room and they all ate silently for a minute. Catherine reached across and rubbed her head. Alex looked at her, determined not to cry. Catherine blew air into her cheeks and forced her eyeballs into the corners, making her laugh. They took it in turns to pull faces. Alex started to chuckle but Beth looked worriedly at the door and told them both to shush.

'Oh my God,' their mum called from upstairs. 'Quickly, run outside. It's only fucking snowing.'

They looked at each other in wonder. It was the beginning of May. They all headed for the door at the same time and jostled each other to get through first.

Alex was the first to make it outside into the back garden, below their shared bedroom. She looked up in wonder. It was, indeed, snowing: tiny white pieces of exercise book.

* * *

On the balcony with Nikki, Alex swallowed, hard.

'Where did you go just then?' Nikki asked, gently.

'Nowhere important,' Alex said, without meeting her gaze.

'Then why have you started to cry?'

Alex rubbed at her cheek, surprised to find it wet.

This situation was beginning to feel far too familiar for her liking. It was surprising how easily they had slipped into their previous roles, the roles they'd had before it all went wrong.

'Listen Nikki—'

'I know it's over, Alex. I'm seeing someone else, but it doesn't mean that I can't still be a friend when you need one.'

Alex focused on the cigarette that was glowing brightly in the breeze. The fact that Nikki had moved on stung her. She wanted to ask if it was serious but it wasn't her business. She'd lost count of the girls she'd had sex with in the six months since they'd split up, but she had not yet been 'seeing someone'.

Alex finished the hot chocolate and rose to her feet. 'I'll just call a taxi and—'

'Don't be ridiculous. Who on earth is going to look after you when you get back?'

'Don't you mean who is going to stop me drinking when I get back?' Alex asked, knowingly.

Nikki shrugged. 'If the cap fits… '

Alex protested. 'Honestly, I'll be fine. I'll go straight to bed and off to sleep in no time.'

Nikki put her finger to her chin in a mock pose. 'Hmmm… my sources tell me that you've tried that one already on Jay and he fell for it.'

'For fuck's sake. Is there anything that Jay didn't tell you?'

Nikki thought for a moment. 'I don't think so. But even if he hadn't, I know you well enough to hazard a guess at the type of tricks you'll pull.'

Alex chuckled. 'For God's sake, you make me sound evil.'

'As I said before, if the cap—'

'All right, don't get clever. I can see that I'm not going to win this one so I'll kip on the sofa…'

'You take the bed. You need the sleep more than I do.'

Alex shook her head vehemently.

Nikki held up her hand with finality. 'Alex, for once do as you're bloody well told and go to bed.'

'Ooh, I like it when you get all masterful.'

Their joined laughter turned to embarrassment and unease as they both realised how that had sounded. It was too much like past times.

'Well… Goodnight, then,' Alex said, weaving towards the bedroom door. Despite the food and rest, her legs still felt wobbly.

'Goodnight, Alex, sleep well,' Nikki said, turning towards the window.

Alex had the urge to take Nikki in her arms and hold her close. For a moment she wanted to feel Nikki's body against her own. She wanted to nestle her face in the warm confines of her reassuring closeness. The realisation that Nikki was seeing someone else surged through her. That place in Nikki's life had been taken and didn't belong to her any more. The knowledge hurt her. She turned and closed the bedroom door.

The room had barely changed. The photos of them together on holiday had been removed and watercolour prints hung in their place. The scent of lavender still permeated the air. Clutches of church candles littered the room. Nikki had always been entranced by the romance of candlelight.

Alex threw off her clothes and snuggled into the bed that she had shared with Nikki for two years. She lay on Nikki's side but then changed the thought. They were both Nikki's sides. The whole bed was hers now. Hers and whoever she chose to share it with. Alex didn't like that thought any better.

The familiarity of the room and the comfort of the bed pulled at her eyelids. She fell into a deep sleep, fighting the memories of their nights together.

The ship had well and truly sailed on that one.

* * *

Alex woke at five thirty with a start. The nightmares had been vicious and insistent. They were based on fact but distorted in her mind. She shook herself awake despite the hour. She didn't want to return. For a while, in her dream, she had been that powerless little girl again.

Memories of the previous night assaulted her. The events in the club were blurred but she remembered clearly from the moment she'd seen Nikki's face peering down at her within the toilet cubicle. She recalled the mixture of feelings she'd experienced being back in her old home and suddenly she wanted to return to the safety of her bedsit.

She stood and dressed quickly. The effects of the previous night had worn off and she felt solid and whole again.

She opened the door to the living room quietly, not wishing to disturb Nikki, who would insist that she return to bed and get more sleep.

She tiptoed into the room and slipped on her boots, leaving the zips undone and headed for the door. As her hand met with the door handle, she felt overcome with curiosity about the spare bedroom. She hesitated for a few moments, unsure as to whether it was wise to satisfy the urge to look. Her hand moved away from the door handle and she padded quietly past Nikki, asleep on the sofa, towards the room.

She opened the door quietly and stepped inside. She closed the door behind her and reached for the light switch. She was stunned at what she saw.

The corner desk, crafted from mahogany, stood in the same position, with the second-hand computer and printer on top. The pile of lined notepads remained neatly stacked to the side of the printer. The pencils she'd used stood proudly in the desk tidy that Nikki had made for her from an old jam jar. The embroidery above her desk still hung there. It was a picture of an owl wearing a mortarboard holding an oversize book open in front of him. The wording below read 'I believe in you'. Every stitch had been sewn by Nikki.

The desk, computer and printer had all been gifts from Nikki. Nikki had made it possible for her to live her dream, or at least take a stab at it. Nikki had been the one driving her forward, insisting that she had a talent that she should nurture and develop. It was Nikki who had cried with joy when Alex had won a short story competition in a local newspaper.

Alex felt the tears sting her eyes. She had spent the happiest moments of her life in here creating stories and characters and living within her own fantasy dream world. The art of turning words into pictures had consumed her for days and nights and all the time Nikki had supplied her with coffee and encouragement. She had handwritten hundreds of pages of paper until her hand cramped up with pain.

Alex backed out of the room, the bittersweet memories too much for her to endure. She covered her mouth as she darted across the room and out of the front door. Once outside the tears came. They rolled from her eyes freely and she made no attempt to stop them.

She glanced up at the window, behind which Nikki lay sleeping.

'Why, oh why, did you demand something from me that I just didn't have to give?'

CHAPTER 7

Catherine

Catherine couldn't help the swell of pride as she looked around her new office. Not only was it on the highest floor of the building, but it was situated on the east corner, affording her a view of the river and the morning sun. Her desk was formed of polished French mahogany and was wide enough to land small aircraft.

The space to the left of her desk was occupied by two leather sofas and a drinks cabinet.

She had fashioned the walls with prints of her favourite paintings.

Luxury came at a price, she thought, remembering her meeting with Mr Leigh Senior the previous day. Although the conversation had seemed innocuous, Catherine had caught the underlying meaning in every word he'd spoken.

'Is the office comfortable enough for you?'

Because you'll be spending most of your life here.

'Have personnel contacted you about the salary increase?'

I'm reminding you that we're paying you a lot of money to deliver.

'We're sure we made the right decision in asking you to head the project.'

There were others who would have killed a close relative to get this position.

'You've chosen a very different artistic theme to Jonathan Adkins.'

The office belonged to someone else before and it can do again.

And so far he had not been wrong about the amount of time she'd spend in the office. She'd moved in on Monday and in the four days since had not switched the lights off before eight o'clock.

Not that the atmosphere at home was anything to rush back for. By the time she got in, the girls were in bed and Tim was working in the study. So far this week she'd spent the rest of her evenings alone in the kitchen, sipping a glass of wine.

After the ultimatum Catherine had been in shock at the severity of his feelings. She was stunned that he thought that she needed to speak to a therapist to deal with feelings that she didn't have. The hurt had come later.

When she was with Tim she sensed that he had withdrawn from her completely. She still saw him and the girls each morning and he was polite and courteous to her, but she didn't want that. She felt like a casual acquaintance with whom he was being forced to communicate.

His face, so animated when he was talking to the girls, could harden within a second when she asked him a question. Seeing that change in his face cooled her blood. He'd said that he still loved her but how could he look at her with such distance in his eyes?

She sighed and checked the clock. 'Lisa, I'm going out. I'll be back in an hour or so,' she said, via the intercom. The appointment was for four thirty but she would have to return to work afterwards.

As she exited the underground car park, Catherine wondered at what point she would pass Tim's test. Would she be required to make up stories about her non-existent feelings about her mother to satisfy his concern? Or would simply attending the appointment suffice?

* * *

The office was located in a Georgian building in a residential area of Much Wenlock. The street was quiet and fashionable, littered with luxurious cars. Catherine resented the fact that her hard-earned money was contributing to this phoney doctor's lifestyle.

Catherine didn't class psychotherapists as doctors. She classed them as people who charged extortionate sums of money to listen. Something the Samaritans did for free.

The office into which she walked was nothing like Catherine had expected. It was decorated in warm pastel colours with simple watercolour prints on the wall. Her appraising eye noted that they were all signed by the same artist but he wasn't one she had ever heard of.

She approached an empty desk that housed a switched-off computer and an A4 diary. The door that led off the reception area was slightly ajar. Not sure what to do, Catherine coughed loudly.

The door opened wider and a woman Catherine guessed to be in her early fifties appeared. Her hair was completely white and spectacles hung around her neck. She was dressed smartly in a chocolate-brown trouser suit. She offered her hand with a smile.

'Emily Dunn. Please call me Emily,' she instructed, moving to the other side of the desk. As she opened the diary Catherine noted that names were entered in almost all of the spaces and that her name was in green.

'You're busy,' Catherine said, nodding towards the diary as the doctor closed it.

'Those names may be fictional, placed there just to reassure you that I'm good at what I do.' She smiled disarmingly. 'Of course, that joke was inappropriate if you're suffering from some type of paranoia.' She put on her glasses and peered at Catherine closely. 'You're not, are you?'

Catherine shook her head. 'Why am I listed in green ink?'

The doctor smiled. 'Because you're new,' she said as she indicated for Catherine to follow her through to the inner sanctum. She motioned towards two leather chairs that faced each other across a coffee table.

'So I'm green?'

'At the moment you are. It's a system I have to chart how people are progressing through therapy.'

'What colours come after green?' Catherine asked, as the doctor sat opposite.

'Catherine – may I call you Catherine?' she asked without pausing to acknowledge any response. 'We can spend the entire hour talking about my colour-coding system or my filing system or even refusal to conform to the twenty-first century and buy a smartphone but that's not why you agreed to my fees.'

'What exactly am I paying you for?' Catherine said, honestly. Her instincts told her that this woman was intelligent and perceptive and would appraise her within minutes.

'Yes,' she said, crossing one leg over the other. 'I thought you were a non-believer but I would like to correct your question. What exactly have you *paid* me for? I ran your credit card details before the session in case you can't pay.'

Catherine was shocked. So already her bank balance was lighter and she'd barely said a word. 'That seems a little…'

'Sensible?' the doctor completed.

Catherine shrugged. She supposed so, but what if someone who was in desperate need of help was a little overdrawn and couldn't pay? Would this woman just turn them away? Actually, she suspected not.

'Nice art,' Catherine complimented, nodding towards the east wall where the watercolour prints continued.

Emily's face flushed with pride. 'The artist is my daughter and, yes, she's very talented.'

Catherine felt an inexplicable sickness in her stomach. She was relieved when the doctor rearranged her expression and glanced at her questioningly. She held up a shorthand notebook and pencil. 'Do you mind? I prefer the old-fashioned way.'

No response was necessary from Catherine as Emily had already scrawled a couple of notes on the first page.

'I'm not sure what I'm supposed to say,' Catherine admitted, feeling self-conscious. She felt responsibility for all the pauses as the purpose was for her to talk.

'Start by telling me why you're here, and don't lie.'

'I'm not really sure what…'

'I said, don't lie.'

Catherine thought for a moment. 'My husband forced me to make an appointment.'

'Why?' Emily asked, registering no surprise at her admission. Catherine shrugged.

'Why does your husband think this is a good idea?'

Catherine looked down at her feet. She didn't want to say the words. It hurt her to have to admit to a stranger that her husband thought she was incapable of being a mother.

'Would you like some coffee?' Emily asked.

In an effort to play for time, Catherine answered that she would.

'I've added a good measure of truth serum,' the doctor said as she placed mugs on the table. Catherine noted they were emblazoned with the emblem of Shrewsbury Town football club.

'I'm uncomfortable with this… situation,' Catherine admitted.

Emily put her notebook aside. 'What exactly do you mean by this situation?'

'Sitting here talking to a stranger who has been paid to listen to me. It feels unnecessary.'

Emily nodded. 'Of course it does. I'd expect nothing less from someone who had not come to me of their own volition. What you're feeling is understandable. Within this room you can say as much or as little to me as you like. I have plenty of thoughts in my head to fill the silences, such as do I prefer pasta or a sandwich for my dinner. I can think about how poorly my favourite football team played last night or – now listen here because it's important – I could actually be thinking of the best way of helping you overcome your problems. It's your choice.'

Despite herself, Catherine smiled. Emily's manner was somewhere between abrupt and firm, yet she found herself warming to her forthright attitude and kindly eyes.

'So, tell me what event prompted your husband to decide that you need help?'

That was easy enough, Catherine decided. Maybe if she relayed the story precisely Emily would understand exactly why this was a waste of time for both of them and money for her. She relayed the whole episode, detailing their fight, word for word, in the kitchen.

Emily was thoughtful for a minute.

Catherine filled the silence as she felt inclined to do. 'Do you see how unreasonable he's being?'

'Your husband seems to feel that you need help in two areas. He feels that you need to come to terms with what happened in your childhood and he feels that you have no connection to your children.'

'That's right,' Catherine said, mortified at the absurdity of his accusations.

'And you think he's wrong?'

'Of course.'

'Why?'

Catherine suddenly felt frustrated. She had just explained the whole situation. She'd explained about her work and how important the promotion was.

'You're already siding with him,' she said, defensively.

'I'm not siding with anyone. You've explained the catalyst for your husband's feelings and concerns but you disagree with him, so I'm only asking for your side of the argument. Why are his observations unfounded?'

'Because I love my children.'

'Be specific,' Emily instructed. 'You've given me an actual event from your husband's viewpoint but a generalisation from your own. Give me an example.'

'Well, I cook the breakfast, iron their clothes. I make sure that their gym bags are ready for school, I—'

'I'm after something a little bit more but we'll leave it for now. If you had to rate your achievements so far in your life from one to ten, where would you fall?'

Catherine thought about the question and decided to answer honestly. 'Probably around an eight.'

Emily nodded. 'When you visualised what your life would be as an adult, what did you see?'

Catherine remembered her dreams. 'A husband, children, a good job, a nice home.'

'So that would be your ten in achievement?'

'Yes,' Catherine nodded.

'So why isn't it?' Emily asked, frowning.

'I don't understand.'

'Everything that you dreamed of you already have, so if that was your ideal dream, why isn't your current achievement rate ten instead of eight? What's missing from the picture you had in your head?'

'I don't know,' Catherine admitted. 'I have everything that I ever wanted, everything that I vowed I would have, and everything that she said I'd never… I'm happy. I don't understand. It's Tim who wanted me to come here,' she said, feeling the words fall out of her mouth.

'It may have been Tim's idea but there's a shortfall between the image of how the dream would be and the actuality of it in real life. It's one of the things we need to find out about.'

'But my children don't suffer,' she protested.

'By your standards that may be true,' Emily offered, kindly.

'But— '

'I'm not here to judge you, Catherine. I'm here to help you. You provide for your daughters but… '

'I love my children,' Catherine protested hotly. 'I work hard to make sure that they want for nothing. I get up early and work late to ensure that…'

'Okay, thank you. That's very interesting but it's not where I want to start work.'

'You think there's work to be done?' Catherine asked, dumbfounded.

Emily smiled kindly. 'Yes, Catherine, I think there's a lot of work to be done.'

CHAPTER 8

Alex

Alex leaned across the sink to get closer to the mirror. The scissors were poised high above her head while she tried to gauge the angle of the reflective hand cutting her hair. The half bottle of vodka was doing little to assist her.

As she aimed the scissors at the section just behind her fringe the phone started to ring, startling her. She cursed and repositioned her hand, with no intention of answering the phone. It was probably Jay and she didn't want to talk to him.

She'd successfully avoided him since the day after she'd stayed at Nikki's. Since the moment she'd popped to the supermarket and refilled her alcohol supply. At the bottom of the first bottle she'd found the vague memory of a promise to her friend.

The realisation that it was already broken had forced her to open another bottle. Halfway through that she had resolved that it really hadn't been a firm promise anyway. It was like the pact she'd made with Catherine as a child. She remembered when they'd both pricked a thumb and held the blood together, promising that they would always take care of each other. It was that kind of promise. The type you meant at the time but had no hope of keeping. Empty.

The phone stopped ringing and then started again. Her jaws clenched with irritation. Why the fuck did people do that? She obviously wasn't home, so why keep bugging her?

She held out the sides of her hair, stretching locks to the middle of her ear. Perfect. Another couple of snips and her hair was exactly how she liked it. Short.

The sink was full of black, pin-like debris. She looked back to the mirror half expecting her mother to be standing behind her, a murderous look on her face as she had when Alex was seven years old.

* * *

She'd only wanted to trim her fringe. All her friends had sported shorter, tidier styles, ideal for running and gymnastics.

It was a school day so Mummy would brush it again with the silver comb that stabbed her head like a hundred pins. She'd tried not to turn too many times in the night so that it wouldn't get so tangled, but she could see the knots running from close to her head to where her hair was resting against her upper arm.

Mummy refused to cut it, however much she begged. Catherine and Beth had shorter hair so why couldn't she?

Alex had tiptoed into the bathroom, an idea occurring to her. She closed the toilet lid and stood on it to stretch to the bathroom cabinet. Behind the mirrored panel was a pair of black-handled scissors.

Alex jumped off the toilet and hurried to the dressing table in the bedroom. She smiled at her reflection as she clutched a handful of hair. If she cut out the knots it wouldn't hurt to have it brushed. The sound of the scissors crunching along the hair close to her ears was followed by the length of hair falling to the ground.

Alex was pleased to see that it was a section of hair that contained a knot.

'Oh no, Alex,' Beth cried from the doorway. 'Oh no, oh no, oh no, what have you done?' she cried, clutching the severed hair.

'It's tangled,' Alex offered, confused at Beth's concern.

'Oh Alex, you shouldn't have done—'

'Shouldn't have done what?' her mum asked from the doorway. Alex saw Beth pale as she dropped the hair to the ground.

'She didn't mean to do it, Mum,' Beth said, standing in front of Alex. Her mum slapped Beth around the face, sending her sideways to the ground.

Alex felt herself being dragged by the hair out of the room. She felt the pull on her hair and tried to keep up as her mum dragged her down the stairs and dropped her in the middle of the room.

'So, you want to hack off your hair and look like a little fucking boy? Well, Mummy's got a much easier way of doing it for you,' she screeched as she opened the door that led to the kitchen. She moved the single armchair so that it was against the open door. She studied it for a moment.

'Sit,' she ordered.

Alex was confused. She'd thought Mummy would be pleased that she had got rid of the knots but now she wasn't so sure. She'd seen this look on her mummy's face before and now she was scared.

'Sit,' she said again, her eyes glazed and huge.

Alex sat.

She felt strands of her hair being pulled from the front of her head, not bunches of hair like she had clutched herself but thinner strands from the top of her forehead. Alex relaxed. This didn't feel too bad. It wasn't hurting as much as the daily combing did.

Beth appeared in the doorway, a red welt on the side of her face. The horror that formed her expression caused Alex to turn around.

The motion caused the thin strands of hair on her forehead to pinch painfully. The brief glimpse had shown her mum securing small thin clutches of hair to the handle of the open door with the elastic bands from her wrist, normally used for tying her hair into a tight ponytail.

Alex didn't understand why her mum was tying her hair to the door handle.

'Mum… please don't… ' Beth pleaded from the other side of the room. Alex realised that Beth had turned deathly white and the left hand that covered her mouth was trembling.

From the corner of her eye, Alex saw her mum stand back and study what she'd done. Alex tried to turn but her head was being held firmly in position facing forward.

'Sit still and don't move,' her mum instructed before turning to Beth. 'And you make sure that you watch.'

For a few seconds Alex had no idea what was happening as her mum's figure went out of sight.

She glanced sideways at Beth who sat where she had been instructed. She had pulled her legs up in front of her and tears rolled over her cheeks. Alex wanted to ask her what was wrong but then three things happened all at once.

The door slammed behind her.

Clutches of hair were ripped from her scalp.

She passed out.

* * *

Alex closed her eyes against the memory and the nausea that came with it. She stared long and hard into the mirror, willing her mother to appear.

'Come on, bitch,' she whispered. 'Do it to me now.'

As she re-entered the room the phone disturbed her again. She swore at it and proceeded to the kitchen area to get another drink. It was probably her boss wondering if she was going to make it into work this evening.

'Highly unlikely, so fuck off,' she bellowed as the ringing stopped again.

Alex had a sudden thought. What if there was something wrong with Jay? Maybe he was in trouble. Perhaps he was hurt.

She snatched at the handpiece when it began ringing again.

'It lives,' Jay cried, forcing her to move the earpiece two inches away from her ear. With the dull ache reverberating around her skull she wasn't so sure his statement was completely accurate.

'Meet me in an hour,' he barked. 'You know where.'

Alex replaced the receiver and marvelled at the brevity of the conversation. If it could be called that when she hadn't uttered one single word.

On her way to Birmingham Bull Ring she picked up some of the fruit bonbons that Jay loved so much, though she had the feeling it would take more than his favourite sweets to butter him up.

She entered the outdoor market from the street entrance and any hope she'd had of ingratiating herself further by having a large latte ready for his arrival were dashed as she spied him sitting at their usual table with two frothy drinks before him.

'Hey gorgeous,' she said, bending to kiss his cheek.

Jay evaded her touch expertly and Alex realised that her efforts to act normally were not going to work.

She sighed as she sat opposite him thinking that denial was a wonderful place to be, if only people would let her stay there.

'Take your glasses off,' Jay instructed, frowning.

Alex growled and removed them. The day was fresh and bright, and it pierced her eyes.

'You're like some type of fucking vampire and you look like shit.'

'Cheers, pal, I appreciate your tact. Don't beat about the bush and just tell me how—'

'You lied to me,' he said, fixing her with a direct glare.

Alex swallowed. She could tell by his face that he was not going to be easily placated.

'Look, Jay, it's not serious. I'm really going to stop. It's just a difficult time with my mother—'

'That's a cop-out, Alex. You hadn't seen the woman for years. There was no love lost between the two of you.'

'She was my mother,' Alex offered weakly. Jay knew little of her past, but Alex regretted telling him anything at all. It proved her life philosophy: don't let anyone know anything because they'll just end up using it against you.

'I don't accept that. It was getting bad before your mother died. It's just that now you think you have a reason.'

'Come on, Jay. It's really not that serious. I like to have a couple of drinks now and again.'

'No, you like to have a lot of drinks during the hours that you're upright, which incidentally are getting less and less.'

'See, it must be getting better,' she said, brightly.

Jay didn't respond. He stirred the frothy liquid and placed the spoon in the saucer.

'You lied to me,' he said, quietly. The words punched her in the gut. It was the disappointment in his voice. She reached for his hand but he withdrew it.

'Jay, I meant it but I was just… ' Her words trailed off. She was just what? She had no excuse and Jay knew it. That's why he was so hurt. He knew that she'd never really taken the promise seriously.

She lit a cigarette, wondering how to make Jay forgive her. Life was shit and empty as it was but without Jay it would be intolerable. He was the only person she had.

'Look, I'll try. Really try. I promise—'

'Don't,' he said, thumping the table. The drinks clattered in the saucers.

Alex was startled. She'd never seen him like this. Her stomach began to churn.

'Don't promise something that you just can't do. It weakens you.' He paused and then fixed her with a stare. Alex realised that there was more going on here than her broken promise. He looked drawn. Dark circles were evident beneath his eyes. His skin was pinched.

'Have you had a drink today?' he asked.

'Of course not. It's only half past ten.'

'I thought not. Your hands are trembling.'

'They're not,' she said, placing them out of view in her lap.

'It's a bit late now. It took two attempts for that lighter flame to find the end of your cigarette.'

Alex was hoping that he hadn't noticed. 'Jay, what's wrong?' she asked, gently. There was a leaden quality to his voice. It was deadened as though all the joy had been sucked out of him.

'You need help,' he said, finishing the cappuccino. 'You need to see someone about your problem. You need something like AA.'

'You have to be fucking joking,' she exploded.

Jay shook his head. 'It's getting worse and you can't do anything about it until you get help.'

'Jay, I love you dearly but you are talking serious shit. I like a few drinks and I've had a rough couple of weeks. I'm not a fucking loser.'

Jay shook his head and smiled wryly, as though he'd expected her response.

'You forget that I've seen it before.'

'I'm not your father.'

He winced at her words. She knew his childhood had been painful because of alcohol, but she wasn't like that. She knew she could stop if she wanted to, but at the moment she just didn't want to.

'You're exactly like my father. He pulled away from the people who loved him because he was ashamed. He distanced himself from his family so that he became a stranger. He had no involvement in the lives of his children. He had no knowledge of important events in their lives.'

Jay's voice had grown wistful and Alex knew he was clamouring, knee-deep, through memories of the past.

'But I'm not like that,' she said, touching his hand. For a brief moment he left it there as he travelled back to the present. His eyes filled with tears and he gently let go of her hand.

'Nicolas left me last week for a middle-aged banker.'

'Oh God, Jay. I'm so sorry. I don't know—'

Jay stood and tossed a note on to the table. 'Thanks for being around, friend.'

Alex watched in horror as Jay walked away and disappeared from view. She lit a cigarette and replayed their conversation in her head. She'd lost the only person that she gave a shit about and he'd accused her of being an alcoholic.

Fuck, now she needed a drink.

CHAPTER 9

Catherine

The collared doves were out early, Catherine realised as she stood at the door. She watched as they stood on the fence, necks stretched, heads bobbing, looking around all the time.

The morning breeze brushed past her cheek. The movement disturbed the conifer in which they were nesting, and the couple disappeared from sight.

She closed the door and poured more coffee, hoping it would take effect soon. She had ground more beans than usual in the hope that the extra caffeine would infuse life and energy into her dormant muscles.

Maybe the third cup would ignite her mind so that she could return to the folders still strewn across the dining table. If only her brain would kick in she could work for another hour or so before Tim and the girls woke.

Her stomach churned at the thought of Tim and the expression on his face the previous evening. He'd been less than thrilled when she'd cried off the reservation he'd made for them all at her favourite restaurant, but she'd consoled him with the promise of a late-night takeaway in front of the TV with the girls, giving her a little extra time to work.

He had not been overjoyed with the idea but had conceded anyway. Three hours later, when she showed no signs of joining them, he ordered pizza for the three of them. The sound of their laughter while watching a Disney film had reached her ears.

She'd been tempted to join them but she knew she couldn't sit by idly watching the television with so much work still to be done. So she quietly closed the glass doors that separated the two rooms.

Tim had come to stand beside her, silent but with folded arms.

'I know, I know,' she defended, without looking at him.

'You've missed Saturday night with your family. It's now the early hours of Sunday morning.'

'I have to finish this,' she said tersely, preparing herself for the battle, but it hadn't come. Tim had simply looked at her, shaken his head and gone to bed.

'I had to finish it,' she explained to the morning sun. The weeks were slipping by and she didn't feel as though she was on schedule. The majority of the working week was being swallowed by progress meetings, team meetings and brainstorming. Meetings with press, radio and television people to programme adverts.

She was arranging the filming of the first commercial to launch the new brand of cosmetics. She was meeting with her team to work on the campaign to secure the rest of their product lines. And that was the part that was worrying her. The presentation needed her input but she was barely around to offer it, and when she was she felt too strung out from meetings to offer anything remotely creative.

The whole of last night she'd spent analysing the presentation word for word, reviewing the storyboards, trying to refine the language, but her worst fears had been realised. Something was missing.

This presentation didn't have the same tone or energy or drive of the first one, the one that had won the contract. She could feel the pressure from her bosses to land this second contract. She was sure they had already ordered newer, faster cars, larger, more luxurious houses on the back of it.

In short, there was no room for failure on this and she knew it. She had won the initial contract, so as far as her bosses were concerned, the rest was merely a formality. If only she could be so sure, Catherine thought as she circled the dining table, moving from one brightly painted storyboard to the next. The pitch was right, she knew.

She started moving the boards around in the hope that inspiration would strike and melt the ice block in her mind. Her brain had been so saturated with the minutiae of details that the creative urge had gone to ground.

'No luck?' Tim asked, coming to stand beside her. She hadn't heard him approach.

She shook her head. 'It's just not working.'

He moved along the storyboards, sipping coffee as he appraised the ideas.

Catherine followed his eyes, trying to gauge what he might be thinking. His forehead furrowed occasionally and a slight smile tugged at his lips when he reached a section that she had inserted as an afterthought.

'Well?' she asked, holding her breath. Even now his opinion meant everything.

'It's good.'

'But?' she pushed, hearing the unspoken word in his voice.

'It reminds me of a thousand similar campaigns already running.'

Catherine didn't take offence at his words. He was only confirming what she'd already been thinking.

'It's restrained and safe. A gorgeous model wearing the lipstick, a fresh-faced teenager modelling the skin cream. Nothing new.'

'I know.'

'I can't see much of you in it. It's unlike you to settle for something like this. I can pick out the parts that are yours but it's not enough to lift the whole thing.'

Catherine nodded her agreement. 'I know that it's missing something but we only have two months left to make the presentation. Trying to rework the whole idea is impossible.'

'Why?' he asked, moving back into the kitchen to refill his cup. Catherine followed.

'Because there's too much work involved. There's no way I could pull it off. We'd end up with nothing to present.'

Tim shrugged. 'It wouldn't hurt to throw some ideas around.'

'Really?' Catherine asked, surprised. It had been so long since Tim had taken an interest in her work that she rarely expected it any more.

'I can't pretend I agree with the job you're doing.' He held his hands up in defence as Catherine opened her mouth. 'Wait a minute. It's not because of the long hours or the work that you bring home each night. It's not even because I'm forced to watch you work yourself into the ground or because you now spend zero time with the girls. It's because it's not the right job for you.'

'Tim, please,' Catherine pleaded. It was too early in the day for an argument.

'I'm not arguing, honestly. I understand your reasons for wanting promotion and I think you worked hard to get it. You deserved the opportunity but I think you should have turned it down.'

'Are you mad?'

Tim nodded and smiled. 'Probably by your standards, I am. The job you did before suited you. It gave you an opportunity to be creative, to think about throwing a different light on something. You loved to push the boundaries and throw unique ideas into the pot. If seven people said yes, then you said no.

'In your old job you had the chance to dream up scenarios and make them work. You could use your initiative and creativity, your ideas and your thoughts, but it seems to me that you can't do that any more. You've been penned in to the small print of the business. You're attending meetings all day that are sucking the lifeblood from you. Your brain is too mashed to—'

'Enough,' she said, smiling, despite his words. He wasn't getting at her; he was merely trying to explain his point of view. She understood what he was trying to say, but ultimately the only way was up and much as she had enjoyed her previous job, promotion had been offered to her and she'd had no choice but to accept.

'Despite that,' Tim continued. 'I think if you allow yourself to try and find the ideas that still lurk in the back of your mind you may be able to salvage something and have a serious attempt at landing the contract.'

'Do you think?' Catherine asked, hopefully. At this point she was willing to believe anything.

'Just talk,' he instructed. 'Tell me about the sessions that led to this campaign and we'll see if there's anything there that was overlooked.'

Catherine sat at the table with a fresh cup of coffee and began telling him about the meetings. Two hours later, with her feet resting comfortably in Tim's lap, Catherine realised that she had filled seven pages with notes. A familiar bubbling began in her stomach. It was the excitement of trying something new.

Tim had helped her turn the old idea on its head. She felt renewed, energetic and desperate to start, but she knew better. The new ideas needed time to circulate around her head and grow into something she truly loved before she set them in concrete. This was the best time. Sowing a seed of something new and observing what it became within the fertile earth of her mind.

'I love you,' she said, impetuously, reaching across and snaking her arms around Tim's shoulders. She raised her head for a lingering kiss. Tim planted a peck on the top of her head and tapped her feet lightly.

'I'll go and rouse the girls. It's almost nine thirty. They'll never sleep tonight.'

For a brief time it had been like the old days. She acknowledged the wave of resentment that washed over her and tried to hide from the guilt. She loved the girls. She knew she did, but sometimes…

She prepared the breakfast bowls ready for their arrival. As usual Lucy entered the kitchen serenely and placed herself at the kitchen table. Jess wasn't far behind and then Tim followed, sitting at the head of the table so that he was between the girls. Instantly he was chatting and joking with them about the wrestling match they'd all had the previous day. Catherine envied his ability to do that. Ten minutes ago he had been helpful, supportive partner. Now he was a loving, nurturing father. How did he manage to become another person in such a short space of time, without even a costume change?

'What are your plans for the day?' Tim asked, as she placed bowls of muesli on the table for the two of them.

'I thought I might go and see Beth,' she said, startling herself. The words hadn't formed in her head before they exited her mouth. It had been on her mind since Beth had called two days ago inviting her to choose a keepsake from their mother's possessions.

The only thing she wanted from her mother was a copy of the death certificate but she did want to see her sisters again. Both of them.

'Really?' Tim asked, looking surprised but pleased.

'There's no reason for me to stay away any more. I just want to make sure Beth's okay.'

'The girls would enjoy meeting their Aunty Beth,' Tim said, ruffling Jess's hair.

Catherine blanched. Both girls looked at her excitedly at the prospect of meeting a new relative.

'But... '

'I did tell you about the match,' Tim said.

Jesus, she had forgotten all about it. Tim had told her last week that he was playing rugby in a match two hundred miles away. Damn, she wished she'd never said a word. Otherwise she could have settled the girls down with some toys and got back to work.

'Catherine... ' Tim said, gently.

The girls were still eyeing her with muted interest.

Catherine desperately wanted to refuse – she couldn't recall the last time she was alone with them – but the hopeful expression on Tim's face stopped her. How could she refuse after the help and support he had given her earlier? He had taken the time to encourage and assist her despite his feelings about what she was trying to do.

She wiped her mouth with the cotton napkin. 'I'll be ready to go in one hour.'

* * *

'For goodness' sake, Jess, I asked you if you'd been to the toilet before we got into the car,' Catherine growled as Jess began squirming in the rear passenger seat.

'I did, Mummy, honest.'

'You couldn't have or you wouldn't be so desperate to go now, would you?'

Catherine was already regretting bringing the girls. She should have insisted that they went to visit Tim's mother for a couple of hours. Jess had already thrown half a packet of sweets over the seat and floor and removed her seatbelt twice.

'Stop it,' Lucy hissed at her sister in the back seat. 'Don't make her angry.'

Catherine smiled at the sensible attitude of her oldest child. She was suddenly struck by a thought. How many times, as a child, had she said those same words to Alex? She shook herself, filled with horror. She wasn't her mother and this situation was completely different.

'Jess, sit still,' she ordered. 'We only have a few miles to go and then you can go to the toilet.'

'But I need to go now,' she cried, desperation in her voice.

'Well, you're just going to have to wait,' she snapped.

'Don't wanna go, anyway,' Jess said, kicking the back of Catherine's seat.

'Stop it,' Catherine snapped.

Another thud caught her in the small of her back.

'Jess, I'm not joking. Stop it right now.'

'Won't,' she said, kicking out again.

'Jess, so help me I'll smack your bottom once we get out of this car.'

'Stop it,' Lucy said, tapping Jess's left leg lightly.

Jess ignored her and did it again. Catherine realised that she was playing into Jess's hands by reacting. She clenched her jaws and ignored the blows to her back, hoping the child would get bored.

'Why don't you colour a picture?' Catherine suggested when the blows continued to land.

Lucy reached for the books from the bag of toys that Catherine had packed to keep them quiet. She passed one to Jess before opening a page and beginning to colour a picture.

Jess threw the book on the floor and used the crayons to daub marks on to the upholstery of the back seat.

'What on earth are you doing?' Catherine screamed, viewing Jess's antics through the mirror.

Jess met her eyes in the mirror.

'Doing what you said, Mummy. I'm colouring a picture.'

CHAPTER 10

Alex

Ker chunk, ker chunk, ker chunk. Alex tried to focus on the sounds of the train but Jay's face wouldn't leave her mind.

It had been a week since she'd seen him, since he'd walked away from her. She remembered little of the four days that had followed but on the fifth she'd woken up with a sick feeling of regret in her stomach. During that brief period of lucidity she had replayed their conversation over and over again like rewinding the part of a movie that you just don't understand. She kept pausing on the section where Jay had insisted she needed help.

During day four she had resolved to go and have it out with him. How dare he say such things to her? Who the hell was he to tell her how to live her life? She'd proved his accusations wrong when she'd waited until eight o'clock before having a drink. The first two she remembered toasting to her absent friend and then, two days later, she could recall little else.

But today she had determined that she would not have a drink. Today, she had planned to clean the flat and seek forgiveness for her absence from her boss. But then she'd had the call. Somehow, as the ringing had punctuated her consciousness she had known it was Beth and, despite Alex's repeated protestations that she wanted nothing from the house, Beth had begged her to come and take a look.

Alex sighed again and all will to resist temptation disappeared. She headed for the buffet car and bought two cans of lager. The circle on the first can pinged with satisfaction. She took a slug that ended halfway down the can. She sat back aware that the trembling in her fingers was beginning to abate. Her stomach broke loose of the knots that had been tightening inside her. Her muscles began to relax.

It was a difficult day today, she reasoned. It was no problem. She'd stop drinking tomorrow.

The second can kept her company until she disembarked at Cradley Heath station. A smoke accompanied her to the street, but as she turned the corner her stomach lurched.

Fuck, she wished she'd never agreed to this. Why had she? She knew why. Beth had asked her. Beth. And the guilt for Beth's life would never leave her.

She smiled wryly as she spotted Catherine's car outside the house. Its bright, shiny newness glared its exclusion in the narrow, dingy street.

Alex knocked on the door, already eager for the moment she'd be leaving the house. Damn the Sunday-service trains. The first one back to Birmingham was two hours away.

Beth opened the door and hugged her tightly. Alex accepted the embrace but made no move to return it. If Beth noticed she didn't comment.

'Oh, I'm so pleased you're here. Catherine has brought the girls.'

Alex nodded, unsure if she was expected to whip pom-poms from behind her back and perform some sort of dance. It meant nothing. Her nieces were as alien to her as their mother.

Alex followed Beth through to the lounge, beyond the front room. As she travelled deeper into the house her senses were assaulted by the aroma of cooking. It was a mixture of smells that she remembered. A cheap cut of fatty pork belly, mixed with the sickly smell of cabbage and waterlogged sprouts. The stench made her want to heave, so synonymous was it with her childhood. For a brief second she felt like she was a child again. Fear filled her stomach and her knees weakened.

Two girls were sitting in front of the fire, with colouring books and anxious expressions.

Alex's knees began to buckle. She was back. She was a child again and she was trapped in this house unable to get away. Any minute her mother…

'Alex, are you okay?' Beth asked from the other side of the room.

Alex tore her gaze from the girls on the floor. She focused on Beth who was looking at her anxiously. Her vision cleared and her eyes rested on Catherine, the adult Catherine, who was staring fixedly out of the window. Safety rested around her as she lowered herself into the single chair.

'I'll make some tea,' Beth said, leaving the room.

Alex felt an awkwardness sweep into the room. It was the same as she'd felt at parties when the mutual friend suddenly went to the toilet.

'So, lunch is provided in this madhouse?'

Catherine shrugged. 'Just be polite, Alex. It won't kill you. She's trying to make an effort.'

'An effort for what? I don't want any of the old bitch's things, do you?'

'Alex,' Catherine said warningly, indicating the children with her eyes.

Alex rolled her eyes. She was sure the girls had heard worse in the school playground.

'Bitch is a naughty word,' the fair-haired one whispered without looking up.

'Bitch, bitch, bitch, bitch, bitch,' the other one cried, looking directly at Alex with a devilish glint in her eye. Alex hid a smile. She could quite get to like that one.

'Thanks Alex,' Catherine said, shooting daggers in her direction. 'That's Jess by the way. The other one is Lucy.'

'I'm so pleased that you're both here,' Beth said, placing the tea set on the coffee table, which was the only new addition to the room. 'Mother would be so pleased.'

'Of course she would,' Catherine said, quickly, sending a glance over Beth's head in Alex's direction.

Alex gritted her teeth, unable to believe that the charade was continuing. On what level did Catherine think it was healthy to aid Beth in her complete denial of their mother's saintliness? It was obscene. All of this was obscene. The three of them drinking tea in the house that had been a loveless, soulless prison for their entire childhood.

There was Catherine sitting with her back straight and her legs crossed, her children sitting on the floor. How could she bring her own girls into the house that still breathed with hatred? Her very stance said that she was poised to escape at the earliest opportunity.

And Alex herself had not bothered to remove her jacket.

Beth handed out tea and then juice to the girls. Silence reverberated around the room. Alex noticed that the child called Lucy was keeping her head down focusing on her picture, whereas Jess was studying them all one by one.

'I sorted through Mother's jewellery. There's not much. A couple of nice pieces. She'd have loved you to have them.'

'Beth, you should keep it,' Catherine said, gently. 'You took care of her for all these years. She'd want you to have them.'

Beth shook her head. 'She didn't talk much towards the end but she would have liked to see both of you.'

There was no accusation in the words, just a deep sadness as though Beth regretted the time they had both missed with their mother.

Catherine stared into the fire. 'Honestly, Beth, you should keep—'

'Let me go and get them and you can choose whichever piece you'd like.'

Beth tore from the room.

'This is not healthy. She's living in cloud cuckoo land and you're helping her furnish the house.'

'What do you suppose I do?' Catherine hissed at her. She looked at her daughters. 'Lucy, take Jess and play outside for a while.'

Lucy stood but Jess remained sitting. 'It's cold outside.'

'Just go, Jess. Your coat is in the kitchen.'

'Don't wanna go,' she said stubbornly.

'Jess, I'm warning you… '

'Come on, Jess,' Lucy said, offering her hand and guiding her sister out of the room.

An inexplicable feeling of sadness washed over Alex and she had no idea why.

'Do you wonder at the reasons why Beth can't remember?' Catherine hissed.

'She's blocked it out but it's not healthy. She thinks our mother was a warm, loving woman who wanted us to have her jewellery and I'm not sure how much longer I can keep my mouth shut.'

'You'll keep your mouth shut until you're out of this house. The memories will come back when she's strong enough to handle them. It'll be hard enough for her then. She can do without the knowledge being forced on her. So just zip it.'

A memory surfaced of Catherine speaking to her in a similar manner when they were children. With the memory came a flash of anger that Alex couldn't control.

'Don't tell me what to do. You gave up that right when you ran away and left us.'

Catherine paled before her eyes. 'Is that what you think?'

'Don't give me that,' Alex growled, finding solace in her rage. It was a tangible emotion that strengthened her. 'The first chance you got you legged it with no thought of leaving us behind. You didn't give two shits about what happened to us just as long as you were okay.'

'It was the hardest time of my—'

'Bollocks, Catherine. Tell that to your fancy colleagues with their nice posh cars and their fancy houses. Oh yes, Catherine, it sure looks like you've suffered.'

'I was forced to—'

'Just remember,' Alex spat, unwilling to listen to anything Catherine had to say. 'Just remember that you're partly responsible for the state that Beth's in today. If you hadn't left us when—'

'I had no choice, Alex. I never had the chance—'

'Don't you remember how Mother's punishment worked?' Alex spat. 'You fucked off and guess what, it didn't turn into fucking Disneyland.'

'Of course I remember. I remember when it changed.'

Alex closed her eyes and shook her head, battling to keep the memory away. But it was no use. Suddenly she saw herself gasping for breath as she ran home from school.

* * *

She'd known what would be waiting for her when she got home. Her mother had said no more netball but Miss Totney had asked her to play. Miss Totney had wanted *her* to play goal attack.

Her legs had faltered as she approached the house but she forced them to carry her forward. Maybe if she wasn't too late her mother would be content with a tongue-lashing. Especially if she could see the effort that Alex had put into getting home quickly.

She entered the semi-darkness of the covered entry between the two houses. Her breath caught in her throat as a dark figure loomed before her.

'So, you little bitch, you're finally here,' her mother said as Alex felt her arm being yanked and her feet leaving the ground.

'I'm sorry… I just played—'

Alex felt the stinging slap around her face. The thick wedding band pierced her skin, close to the eye. The area began to swell immediately.

She tried to steady herself on the ground but she was being pulled through the entrance to the house. The fatigue in her legs won out and she toppled to her knees. They scraped painfully against the brick floor, grazing her flesh.

Her mother dragged her into the lounge where Catherine and Beth were sitting on the sofa, with pained expressions. Any hope of a reduced punishment dissolved. Alex knew that her sisters had been assembled to witness the beating to teach them all a lesson.

She was deposited in front of the fire and her mother stood before her.

'So, you ignore everything I fucking say?'

Alex shook her head, miserably. Her face was stinging from the blow and her knees were raw and painful.

'You ignored me when I told you there was no more netball practice.'

'But I—'

'I don't give a shit what you've got to say. I said you couldn't and you chose to disobey me.'

Alex said nothing. She was resigned to the fact that she was not going to get off lightly. She attempted to brace her body for the impact. The last thing she saw before she closed her eyes was the fear on the faces of her sisters.

Waiting for the first blow was always the worst part. Once the pain started she could almost lose herself in it, aware that she was just waiting for it to end. The waiting became unbearable, the fear rising in her stomach, making it hard for her to breathe.

Alex suspected that this was just another of her mother's cruel games. Prolonging the terror for as long as she could, but when Alex opened one eye tentatively her mother was regarding her with a puzzled look.

'You expected this, didn't you, you devious little bitch?'

Alex shook her head.

Her mother nodded knowingly. 'Oh yes you did. You knew what would happen to you if you disobeyed me but you did it anyway.'

'No… I didn't—'

'Shut the fuck up. The fact that you knew I'd beat you didn't stop you from doing whatever the hell you liked. You were happy to take the shit for it.'

Alex dared not move a muscle as she saw a veil come down over her mother's face. And she was right, Alex realised. She had known that she was going to get a beating for her actions and she'd taken the risk.

Inevitably, the blows began to land. There was a split lip, a black eye, the crunch of a rib cracking. There were slaps and a broken little finger.

Alex felt every punch, kick and slap as it rained down. The pain of what she'd done haunted her as the final blow landed on Catherine's head and she crumpled to the ground.

* * *

'What about your blame, Alex? Where was your concern for your sister when you ran away?' Catherine said, jolting her back to the present.

Alex turned away, sickness rolling around her stomach. 'Look, we both failed her so let's leave it at that. Just don't tell me what to do, Catherine. You no longer have that right.'

'Here we are,' Beth said, bringing a cheap shell jewellery box into the room. She opened the lid and pulled out a simple string of pearls, yellow in their cheapness. 'I thought these would bring out the slenderness of your neck, Catherine. You always did have a wonderful, regal posture.' Catherine touched the beads and said nothing.

'And these earrings would bring out the beauty of your eyes, Alex.'

Alex wasn't even looking at the earrings. Her gaze was fixed on the pearls. A single tear fell from Catherine's eyes on to the beads and Alex knew they were sharing the same memory.

'I dressed you up in all this stuff,' Catherine whispered. 'I put all Mother's jewellery on you and painted your face,' she said, without taking her eyes from the item in her hand.

'The lipstick was cherry red,' Alex said, recalling the day she'd sat on Catherine's bed, being painted and dressed up. 'You got a chiffon scarf and wrapped it around my waist. You said I looked like a movie star.' The words caught in her throat as she remembered the two of them laughing and prancing around the room while Beth sat on the other bed, telling them to stop before Mother came home.

'We were so close, the three of us,' Catherine murmured.

'No, just you two,' Beth offered gently.

'Don't be silly,' Catherine said, wiping her eyes and then reaching for Beth's hand.

'It's okay,' Beth said, patting Catherine's hand. 'I didn't mind. I was just happy to see you two having fun. It made me laugh.'

Alex heard a wistfulness in Beth's voice and realised that she was right. Beth had always kept herself slightly on the outside.

'Dinner should be ready,' Beth said, going to the kitchen.

Catherine said something about needing some air and avoided Alex's eyes as she left the room. Alex fought back the tears that threatened her. She didn't want them or what they represented. Other memories came back to haunt her and every single one involved Catherine. Catherine reading her stories, Catherine tickling her on the bed. Catherine making her laugh. Catherine holding her while she ran from the monsters in her nightmares.

She wiped her eyes, unsure what to do with the memories that were assaulting her mind. She wanted to slope away to a dark room and reclaim her anger. She wanted to disappear beneath the safety of her rage. The accusation of the day when Catherine had left them.

The tears began to subside and the rage returned to niggle away at her belly. She would never forgive Catherine for that.

Beth's voice reached her from the kitchen. Alex blindly reacted to the instruction that dinner was ready. Every instinct inside begged her to run away and reach the safety of the train that would return her to the anonymity of her life in Birmingham. Yet, she couldn't hurt Beth. She'd done enough of that over the years and Beth didn't deserve her bad manners.

Poor sweet Beth who had always been the cautious one, the timid one, permanently terrified that they'd get into trouble. Poor sweet Beth who had suffered far worse than either of them. Who even now after so much of her life had been taken away only wanted to give to her sisters. For that Alex could manage one lunch.

The small table in the kitchen was cramped with the five of them. Alex smiled at Beth and thanked her for going to so much effort. She paused as she looked at the plate before her. It could have landed from a time machine. The pork was fatty and a sickly shade of grey. Large boiled potatoes were struggling to stay cohesive after an hour in the pan and a green mushy mass represented two different vegetables that were impossible to detect, name or separate.

Alex sprinkled salt on to the food in an effort to disguise the taste.

The meal started in silence and as Alex took her first bite she realised that there was very little warmth between Catherine and her daughters.

'Jess, stop that,' Catherine warned, as Jess kicked her beneath the table from the opposite end.

Alex watched Jess's pleasure in getting a reaction from her mother. Lucy nudged her sister and Alex wondered if the irony of the relationship between her daughters was lost on her. Jess kicked again and laughed out loud.

'Jess, I won't tell you again,' Catherine said, without looking up.

Alex watched the exchange with interest. She noted that Catherine had not exchanged one warm word with either of her children since she had walked into the house.

Alex saw the defiance rising in Jess's eyes and wondered if Catherine had any idea of how desperate this child was for attention.

Jess started rocking on the chair, which caused the table to shudder.

'You'll know about it if that juice goes over, young lady,' Catherine warned.

With one almighty effort, the child kicked the table and sent both beakers of juice crashing down. Purple liquid spread and soaked into the tablecloth. With lightning speed, Catherine was on her feet and around the other side of the table.

She yanked Jess from behind the table and stood the child before her. 'You've tested me and pushed me all day. You've been expecting this, haven't you?' Catherine screamed as she raised her hand.

Beth whimpered and Alex looked on in shock as Catherine hesitated, her hand in the air. The sound of the slap rendered them all dumb. Beth clasped her hand to her mouth in horror.

Alex jumped to her feet and grabbed the offending hand.

'Catherine,' she said, turning her sister to face her. 'Do you even realise that you just slapped the wrong child?'

CHAPTER 11

Catherine

Catherine sat in the cover of darkness. The scene at Beth's still circling in her mind. The rage inside, so strong that it had consumed her, had frightened her also. And not just her. She felt sick as she remembered the looks on the faces of her sisters and children.

Tim's key turned in the door. Catherine pulled her coat tightly around her. He called out gently and she asked him to leave the light off. He dropped his gym bag and sat beside her on the sofa.

'Sweetheart, what's wrong?'

Catherine had sat in the dark for two hours trying to find the words and still they eluded her.

'Where are the girls?'

'They're in bed,' she answered. 'They're fine.'

She could see his profile, illuminated from an outside light in someone's garden. She reached for his hand and the tears that she'd held in check began to flow over her cheeks.

'What is it, Catherine, what's wrong?' he asked, panic filling his voice.

She squeezed his hand. 'I'm so sorry.'

He turned her to face him but she couldn't meet his gaze. 'I've done something terrible and I can't take it back.'

'Whatever it is, we'll sort it out. You don't need to worry about anything. I love you and there's nothing that we can't face together. You know that.'

Catherine lowered her head, shame coursing through her.

'Please, sweetheart, tell me what's wrong. Whatever it is we'll talk about it and find some way to resolve it. You can share anything with me. There's nothing you can say that will make me love you any less than—'

'I slapped Lucy.'

Although she couldn't see his face clearly she felt the tension enter his body. Silence fell between them and Catherine knew that following the shock of her admission he would instantly be trying to excuse her actions.

'Did you say Lucy?'

Catherine nodded in the darkness and closed her eyes. How could she possibly explain what had happened? How could she translate the lightning-quick thought process that had led her to that inexcusable action? She knew that Tim was wondering how Lucy could have done anything to deserve such treatment. It was inexcusable with either of their children, but whereas Jess had the spirit to test the patience of a saint Lucy did nothing wrong. Ever.

'Was she being naughty?' Tim asked, doubtfully.

'No,' Catherine whispered.

'Then why?' Tim asked, turning to face her.

'It's complicated, Tim. I can't explain except to say that it was wrong and that I am the only person to blame. It was Jess who was playing up but—'

'Did you hit Lucy by accident?' Tim asked. Catherine could hear faint hope in his words and she realised that this was her opportunity to backtrack. She could tell Tim that Jess had been playing up and she'd lost control for a moment and lashed out, smacking Lucy accidentally. She could do that and Tim would take her in his arms and help her through the guilt. This was her chance to make it all go away.

'No, Tim, I didn't.'

'But I don't understand,' he said, loosing her hand and running his fingers through his hair.

Catherine scrunched her eyes in the darkness, pained by his confusion. She wanted to explain it to him but it wasn't straight in her own mind.

She took a deep breath. 'Tim, I have to leave.'

His head shot up. 'What do you mean, leave?'

'For the sake of the girls I have to get away. It's not fair to them and it's not fair to you.'

'But why? I mean, I don't get what...'

'Tim, I hit the wrong girl on purpose to teach Jess a lesson.' It hurt her to say the words but she had to be honest with him. 'I can't explain the significance of that right now until I understand it better in my own mind, but I have to get away from them for their own safety. Next time it might be worse.'

She could tell that Tim was struggling to comprehend what she'd said to him. He was torn by his anger at her actions and his resolve to persuade her to stay and work the problems out.

An emptiness was beginning to form in her stomach at leaving her family, but in her heart she knew it was the right thing to do. It was the right thing for her children.

'I love you, Tim, and in my own way I love the girls. I just have to work out if that's good enough.'

She stood and retrieved the suitcase that she'd packed earlier. Tim remained immobile on the sofa. Catherine bent and kissed the top of his head. She let herself out of the front door soundlessly.

She pulled out of the drive and parked a few doors down, her visibility hindered by the tears streaming from her eyes. She watched the house for a few moments before pulling away and still the light didn't go on.

* * *

'Are you ready?' Lisa asked from the doorway.

'For what?'

'The monthly meeting.'

Catherine glanced at her diary. 'There's nothing in here about a monthly meeting.'

Lisa rolled her eyes. 'I put it on your scheduler.'

Shit, Catherine thought as she realised that she hadn't even checked her calendar for the day.

She grabbed her daybook and headed for the door. The daybook was a system that she'd recently reintroduced for herself. It consisted of listing everything that she had to do and ranged from making simple phone calls to arranging promotion time for the products. The system was simplistic and relied on regular updating. Each night she would go through the list striking off items that she'd achieved and then rewrite the list adding new tasks. An old boss had told her that once the list went on to two pages it signalled too much work. Her list currently stood at three and a quarter pages.

The team was already assembled when she entered the room. Lisa poured coffee for them both and took her seat. Catherine worked through the minutes of the previous meeting, ticking off the things that had been achieved and setting new targets for the items that hadn't.

'Any other business?' Catherine asked, twenty minutes into the meeting. She desperately hoped not as her attention span was being seriously hampered by the lack of sleep of the previous night amidst the unfamiliarity of the hotel room.

She started with Laura, the creative consultant and the only person around the table that Catherine envied. Laura's job consisted of imagination, storyboards, concepts; unlike Catherine's, which prioritised schedules, deadlines and budgets

'The models,' she stated. 'Two of the original choices are no longer available. One is pregnant and the other has an epidermal cyst or something on the bridge of her nose.'

'Well, go to list B,' Catherine instructed. When choosing the models they had drawn up two lists so that if one list became exhausted they would start on the second.

Laura shrugged her shoulders. 'These girls *are* from list B.'

Catherine groaned. That meant getting on to the agencies and finding a new batch of models that fitted the criteria. Something she would have to supervise herself.

'I'll contact the agencies,' Catherine said, making a note at the end of her list.

She moved on to Mitchell but Laura coughed. 'Umm, the make-up artist that we booked for the preliminary shoot is playing up. She's hiked her prices up after a film that she worked on got nominated for an award or something.'

'So is there any Oscar in her immediate future?' Catherine said, dryly.

'Nothing that glamorous but she's in demand and she's making the most of it.'

'Tell her that she'll do it for the agreed sum or...'

'I've tried that and it didn't work. She won't talk to anyone but you and the preliminary shoot is only—'

'Two weeks away. Yes, I know that, Laura. I'll talk to her once we're out of this meeting.' Catherine made another note.

'Mitchell?' Catherine asked, feeling a gnawing sensation begin to bite at the backs of her eyes.

Mitchell shook his head and she moved on to Victor, in charge of design.

''Fraid so,' he said, smiling. 'There's a problem with the size of the lettering on the smaller bottles of the hand cream.'

Catherine frowned. It was the first she'd heard of this. 'What type of problem?'

'Well, the font size on the larger bottle works well with the size of the bottle. The name fits perfectly without going around the curves of the shape. On the smaller bottle it's not working. The font has been scaled down to match the reduction of the bottle but the lettering is hardly legible. It's partly due to the lettering that the client insisted on. In a smaller font it just doesn't work.'

Catherine sighed. 'Give me a little time with that one.' That was a problem not so easily rectified and would result in another three product meetings including one with the client. She made a note on her list.

Only Jasper was left and she could tell that he had something from the slightly nervous look on his face.

'I'm just waiting for the go-ahead to book the programming.'

Catherine hid her discomfort. 'Of course, Jasper, I'll let you have that as soon as possible.' Damn, she had forgotten to balance the budgets at the weekend. Jasper had given her a provisional figure for the television and radio costs and she had to confirm that it was within budget, which it was sure not to be. That was when the negotiations with the TV and radio stations would begin.

She nodded to signal the end of the meeting and checked her list. She knew there was a note about the budgets somewhere. Her eyes searched each page until she found it at the bottom of page two.

'Well done,' she said to Lisa when they were alone. 'That wasn't too bad. You're doing a good job of heading the weekly meetings.'

Lisa smiled but her expression faltered.

'What's wrong?'

'Look, it's really nothing, but there were a couple of comments earlier about things being missed. Victor said he sent you a memo and two emails about the packaging problem last week. I explained how busy you were… '

'Don't worry about it,' Catherine said, sensing Lisa's discomfort. She was doing a great job and she didn't want the project to fail. Catherine respected that. 'I hear what you're saying and I'll be on top of it by the end of the day.'

'And you still haven't replaced me. I know that you've got a lot of things to do at the moment and I'm happy to struggle on for a while longer because I'm loving what I'm doing, but I'm just getting this vibe that you're not.'

'Of course I am,' Catherine said, mechanically. 'I love what I do. It's just a bit hectic at the moment.'

She smiled brightly, the expression belying the feelings in her stomach, but Lisa deserved her full attention. The girl had been stretching herself between two jobs since the beginning of the project. If Catherine was truthful she'd deliberately put off replacing Lisa as her PA because she felt reassured having Lisa around. 'Okay, ring around the agencies and get me some prospective replacements. Oh, and before you do that, get that bloody make-up artist on the phone.'

Two minutes later Catherine was talking to Joyce Patterson.

'We had an agreement, Joyce. You were our first choice for this photo shoot. Our girls are beautiful and our product is spectacular but your skills are invaluable,' Catherine said, blowing up the woman's butt. It was worth a first attempt.

'Thank you for that, Catherine, and you know how much I'd like to do this shoot but things have become very hectic for me since the nomination.'

Catherine admired how quickly the shrewd woman managed to get that into the conversation. 'Yes, I heard about that and I'd like to congratulate you on the accolade, but obviously we made an agreement with you before any of this happened and it would be only fair to have that agreement honoured.'

'It's not that I don't want to do it, but I have to make a living and I'm being offered the same money for half a day's work on a television documentary about makeovers for the rich and—'

'I understand that, Joyce, but we had an agreement.'

'Well, it was more of an informal thing really, wasn't it? I mean there was nothing in writing, so I assumed it was just a hypothetical chat.'

Catherine felt her insides igniting. The woman was just plain lying now. It had been a verbal exchange and the formulation of the contract was on her list of things to get done.

'Joyce, that idle conversation was a verbal contract and you know it. You committed to working on this photo shoot and now you've reneged on the agreement.'

'Verbal contracts do not pay my bills, honey,' she said, sweetly. 'And I haven't reneged. I've given you an opportunity to pay me the appropriate fee for my services. If you choose not to take me up on that then that's your choice.'

Catherine was incensed at the woman's lack of morals. 'Thank you for your time, Joyce and I wish to inform you that we will not be taking you up on your offer. Goodbye.'

Catherine slammed down the phone.

Line 2 rang. 'What?' she barked.

'Sweetheart?'

Catherine closed her eyes at the sound of Tim's voice. His voice around her name was gentle, caring, like a caress.

'How are the girls?' she asked. Only one night away from them but she missed the reassurance of having them near. The knowledge surprised her. She'd been away from them before when attending business meetings but she'd never missed them the way she had the previous night. Maybe it was because she always knew she was going back to them, she thought, unlike now.

'Jess is a bit subdued. They're both asking about you. I asked Lucy what happened and she insists that you struck her by accident.'

Catherine's heart lurched in her chest. Dear, sweet Lucy who knew the truth and was trying to protect her. She felt an unfamiliar rush of warmth surge through her.

'She's wrong, Tim,' Catherine said, sadly. 'I knew what I was doing and it was wrong on so many levels.'

'Can't we meet and talk about it?'

Catherine shook her head but said nothing. The part of her that wanted to return to the safety of her old life screamed out for her to say yes. The temptation to meet Tim and give him enough of an explanation for him to understand was overwhelming. She knew that he would try and forgive her. But she had always been a realist and she knew that she could never go back. Not until she understood.

'I'm not ready to talk to you.'

How could she make Tim understand all the emotions running riot in her mind? Her life had suddenly imploded. The death of her mother, meeting her sisters again and finally seeing the truth about her relationship with her daughters. How could he understand the fears that had destroyed the veil of security behind which she'd hidden?

She'd thought that her perfect life with her successful career and happy family façade would protect her from the person she really was and had always been destined to become.

'Then at least talk to someone you can trust.'

Catherine realised that that particular list was non-existent. There was no one who would understand. Late last night, she'd considered calling Alex but at the last minute had changed her mind. Alex was too busy hiding at the bottom of a bottle to admit that their childhood experiences were having any effect on her in adulthood. Catherine realised that Alex was suffering as acute a case of denial as Beth, only she wasn't prepared to admit that either.

'There's no one.'

'What about that therapist?'

Catherine realised that he meant Emily. She couldn't go back now. She'd refused to go back a second time after Emily had told her that they had a lot of work to do. She couldn't do that.

'Please, Catherine. I don't know what's wrong. You won't tell me and you won't come home. Whatever it is you need to understand it.'

'I'll think about it,' she said, begrudgingly.

'I'll call you tomorrow.'

'No, Tim, please don't. The only hope I have of being able to sort this out is if you stay away from me.'

'Catherine, I love you.'

Catherine could hear the torment in his voice. He was powerless to help her and it pained him. As it did her. 'I love you too,' she said, replacing the receiver.

Lines 1 and 2 lit up as soon as she put the phone down but Catherine transferred the calls to voicemail. Immediately the light went on and started flashing to indicate that she had a message.

She allowed her head to fall into her hands. Somehow she had to try and quell the distraction of the emotions causing havoc inside her like a virus. Feelings that she'd never had before were surfacing from nowhere and she didn't know how to control them.

She took a plain piece of paper and named the feelings and her reasons for them.

Disillusionment with the job I'm doing.
Guilt at abandoning my sisters.
Despair at how lonely my life was without them.
Terror that I can never be with my family again, and
Fear of what I've become.

Catherine read the list back and realised that Tim was right. She needed to speak to someone.

CHAPTER 12

Alex

Alex surveyed the chaos of her flat. Every drawer and cupboard had been turned out. Clothes and cutlery claimed equal amounts of space on the floor. Half an hour ago she'd given up the hope of finding any forgotten money hiding in an unwashed pair of jeans or a jacket that she hadn't worn for a while. Now she was looking for things to sell and her shortlist had been slung on to the bed.

Her first option was the leather biker's jacket that had taken her months to save for and was probably her biggest asset. Second was an iPod Touch gifted to her by Jay last Christmas. Third were the sapphire earrings Beth had insisted she take from the house.

She viewed her net worth critically. Which of the three items would give her the best return? In the back of her mind she hoped that she wouldn't need much cash, just enough to buy the courage she needed to be able to speak to Mike and then she was sure that everything would be okay. He would roll his eyes and order her behind the bar before she lost any more time. He would give her the job back. She was sure.

Her eyes settled on the earrings. She viewed them from the other side of the room. She had no idea of their value and tried to view them dispassionately as a piece of jewellery that meant nothing to her. She approached them cautiously and picked them up. She expected to locate a distant memory of her mother wearing the earrings, which would have sealed their fate immediately, but the only face intertwined with the blue stones was that of her sister, Catherine.

The memory of the day that Catherine had dressed her up was as clear in her mind as though it had happened yesterday. She remembered Catherine's mischievous smile as she had applied blusher, lipstick and mascara to Alex's face. It had been a day of realisation for her. It was the day she realised that without Catherine she would die. But that had been before Catherine had deserted them.

Her hand closed around the earrings. The small stones dug into her palms. She dropped them and reached to the other side of the bed. The jacket it was.

Ten minutes and fifty quid later Alex rubbed at her arms viciously as she made the ten-minute walk to the club. The heat of writhing bodies hit her as soon as she opened the door. She took a deep breath and edged her way through the dance floor to the bar. Mike spotted her almost immediately. His eyebrows moved towards each other and his jaw visibly tightened. Alex followed him along the length of the bar, trying to catch him before he disappeared into the office at the rear of the building.

'Please, Mike, just a minute,' she begged, placing her hand on his forearm.

He viewed her grip with distaste and shook himself free.

'I know how much I've let you down,' Alex said, launching into her speech before he had a chance to speak. 'But I'm better now. I've just had a lot of illness over the last few weeks but I've got it together now and—'

'Save it, Alex. It just ain't happening. You've let me down too many times.'

Alex realised that this was going to be harder than she'd thought. Mike's arms were crossed firmly in front of him. His stance was rigid.

'But it's true. I promise. I'll be here on time and I'll work hard and I'll be in for every single shift.'

'What's happened to you, Alex? Your clothes are creased, your hair is greasy. Your skin is blotchy and dry.'

Alex detected a note of concern in his voice and decided to make the most of it. 'I've had a virus and I just couldn't shake it. I was taking antibiotics and I had some sort of reaction to them. I'll be completely better in a couple of days. The doctor said—'

'You just can't stop, can you?'

'It's the truth, Mike, I promise. Please believe me.'

Mike shook his head and when his eyes met hers they were filled with disgust.

'I've been fair to you for eight years. I've overlooked your occasional transgression because you were always good at your job, but this is too much. You're an alcoholic who can't even tell the truth any more.'

Alex was shocked at his words. Yes, she liked a few drinks and maybe she had been drinking excessively over the last few weeks but she could stop any time she chose. She wanted to argue the point with him but there was still begging to do.

'But I've changed, Mike. I've stopped drinking and I want to come back to work. You just said yourself that I can do the job, so why not give me another chance?' She offered her best winning smile.

'You're a fucking alcoholic. I'm not giving you a job in a bar.' He sighed heavily. 'It's too late. I've filled the vacancy.'

Alex felt desperation biting at her heels. 'Oh come on, Mike. You can soon get rid of them. Just pay them for the night and put me back in my old job. I've told you that I won't let you down. I promise—'

'Stop it, Alex,' Mike said, holding his hand up and looking away. 'It's too late. You blew it.'

She sagged against the wall. 'Maybe just for a week or two so I can sort out some of my bills. I've got stuff that's way overdue and no way to pay for it.' Alex felt sick to her stomach. Never before had she begged so blatantly for anything in her life but if she didn't get some cash soon she'd be thrown out of her bedsit.

'Here, take this,' Mike said, holding a few purple notes towards her. 'Call it redundancy pay,' he said, closing his wallet.

Alex wished she was in a position to refuse but she was desperate and Mike knew it.

She took the money from his hands and mumbled some incoherent words of thanks without meeting his eyes. She stopped to speak to no one and headed straight for the door. Once outside the cold wind drove long sharp needles of rain into the skin on her bare arms. The money from Mike together with the funds from her jacket would pay the electricity bill or half of her rent arrears with a little bit left over.

The bright lights of Mellie's Bar called to her as though with a beckoning finger. She felt powerless to resist.

Sultry, thumping music greeted her as she entered the club. She pushed herself through gyrating female bodies to get to the bar. Mellie's was always packed full on a Thursday night and Alex felt the tension begin to leave her body. This was just what she needed. A few cold drinks, a nice warm body and she'd worry about her money problems tomorrow.

She squeezed into a seat at the bar and ordered a double vodka. The heat of the liquid left a trail of fire from her tongue to her stomach as she downed it in a single swallow. She ordered two more, which went the same way. The familiar sensation of well-being began to cloak her as she sipped the fourth drink more slowly.

She cast her eye around the heaving bar, unconcerned about the worries that had troubled her earlier. They were quietly dissolving in vodka. She'd worry about them tomorrow with a clear head.

She smiled to herself, content that everything would be fine. She'd find another job within a couple of days and her landlord wouldn't pursue his threat to evict her at the weekend. She'd talk to him tomorrow and straighten everything out. She'd have the money for him soon and he'd understand that. She sighed deeply, content that she had been worrying for nothing.

She continued to gaze around the bar. Her eyes met those of a woman with short bleached, spiky hair who had a half-smile on her face. Alex held the gaze for a moment and by doing so indicated her interest. The woman looked a little butch but Alex wasn't fussed. Tonight she was in the mood for some mindless sex with a good-looking stranger and the girl who was approaching through the crowds fitted that bill perfectly.

'Buy you a drink?' the woman asked.

'Vodka.'

'Hmm… A woman with expensive tastes.'

Alex smiled and said nothing as the woman ordered a pint of lager and a double vodka. Alex decided she could get to like this one. She took the drink and downed half of it. Her head began to swim and she welcomed the sensation.

'Dana,' the woman said, offering her hand.

Alex downed the last of her drink.

'Can I get you another?'

Alex nodded.

'So, do you come here often?'

Alex almost laughed at the absurdity of such a stupid question but something about the woman's expression stopped her. There was a glint in her hard blue eyes that Alex found a little dangerous and erotic at the same time.

'Stop working so hard. It's a done deal, okay?'

'Your place or mine?'

Alex decided that this butch beauty was in danger of spoiling the whole mood with phrases like that.

'Neither, I'll meet you outside in a few minutes,' she said, negotiating her way off the bar stool. She headed for the toilets and threw some cold water on to her face. The effects of the vodka were catching up with her and she wanted to be sober enough to enjoy what was about to happen. She dried her face on a rough paper towel and headed outside. There was an alley between the bar and an Indian takeaway next door, which didn't normally get busy until throwing-out time.

The cold air hit her and caused her to weave into the alleyway. Although the rain had stopped, the air still held a dampness around her bare skin. She saw a shadow halfway into the alley and headed for it. As her eyes adjusted to the reduced light she immediately recognised the Amazonian stature of Dana.

No words passed between them as Alex reached the substance of the shadow. Immediately she felt lips on her own and the hard, muscled body of the woman pressing her against the wall. Heat surged through her as the rough lips pressed down on her.

Dana took hold of her wrists and raised them above her head, forcing her bare arms against the rough, hard brick. Alex winced at the pain. With her hands above her head and her whole body exposed to Dana, Alex felt vulnerable and powerless to act.

The feeling sent a shiver of anticipation through her body. Dana used her free hand to caress Alex's breast and Alex gasped with pleasure as her nipple began to harden. She wanted to free her arms to roam the uncharted territory of a fresh new body but Dana held her arms firm as she pulled up Alex's T-shirt and covered her breast with her hand. Ripples of desire shot through

Alex as Dana's mouth fixed on her breast, her warm tongue manipulating her aroused nipple to hardness.

Alex felt a spear of regret when Dana's mouth began to move away, but was rewarded when she felt Dana's free hand unbuttoning her waistband. She heard the grating noise as her zipper was undone. A strong hand worked inside her panties and Alex groaned out loud. She stroked gently, bringing Alex to a state of frenzy. Her body began to arch towards Dana, willing her to work faster and satisfy the need within her.

Dana pulled back slightly and her hand moved up and rested on Alex's hip. 'I wondered where you'd got to,' she said, turning her head to the left.

Alex hadn't noticed anyone approaching, but she turned to see a small Chinese girl with dyed orange hair. She gently stroked Dana's arm.

'Well, I'm here now so quit hogging all the fun.'

'Hang on a minute,' Alex protested, unsure just what they had in mind. A threesome had never been part of her plans.

Dana held her wrists above her head. The danger that Alex had seen hovering in her eyes earlier was now blatantly apparent within the voraciously hungry expression on her face.

'Don't tell me you've never been spit roasted?'

Alex again struggled to get her arms back down from above her head but Dana was strong and held her easily.

'Awww... don't be like that,' Dana said, moving her away from the wall so that Dana was behind her and the Chinese girl in front.

'I'm not fucking into this,' Alex growled, struggling to get free.

Dana brought her arms down and fixed them behind her back, getting a better grip on her wrists and holding her tight. She used her right foot to kick Alex's right foot as far as it would go and then did the same with her left so that her feet held Alex's feet imprisoned against the two sides of the wall with her legs wide open.

'Pull 'em down,' Dana instructed the Chinese girl.

Alex felt real panic in the pit of her stomach, the effects of the alcohol long gone. She was no longer a willing party.

'Let me fucking go,' she screamed. 'I've told you I'm not into this.'

'Like we give a fuck, sweetie. You're hardly in a position to argue.'

Alex writhed as the Chinese girl began pulling her jeans down. The girl looked at her body with desire and licked her lips suggestively. Alex felt sick.

The Chinese girl moved in closer, checking that Alex was being forcibly enough restrained. She touched Alex's breast and Alex tried to move away from the touch. All traces of desire had long since departed, leaving behind a feeling of terror deep within her.

'Get the fuck off me,' she cried, trying to wriggle out of the hold.

Dana laughed uproariously. 'You're going nowhere, bitch, so just keep still and enjoy it. We've got a long night ahead.'

Alex felt the nausea rise in her stomach. The Chinese girl caressed her breast and her hand travelled down. At the same time Dana's free hand reached down from behind into the back of her panties. Their hands met in the middle and fondled her roughly. Alex felt their hands link as though they were about to hold hands and she knew what was about to happen. Horror and fear coursed through her. She'd heard about it before and the act could cause serious internal damage.

She spat at the Chinese girl in front of her, which caused enough of a distraction for her to gather every ounce of strength to rip her arms from Dana's grip. Dana made a grab for her arm but Alex turned and kicked the hand away. She heard bones crunch as the hand smashed against the wall. Dana was still behind her and the Chinese girl was in front. Alex attempted to dodge around the Chinese girl to get away. For a brief second she thought she had escaped but she felt a strong hand clutching at her hair. She felt herself being pulled backwards against Dana.

'Come here, you fucking tease.'

Alex struggled to get Dana's hand out of her hair while being yanked backwards. Her legs grew unsteady beneath her and she fell to the ground, a clutch of hair ripped from her scalp.

Her view from the ground was of legs and feet but she didn't know which ones belonged to who. The first kick to her eye obscured her vision completely, sending her reeling into a world of blackness. She fought blindly against the blows to her body that rained down like boulders being dropped all over her.

As the punches and kicks continued to dent her body she gave up any attempt at fighting back and accepted the vicious blows to her flesh.

Alex had no perception of how long the beating continued. All she knew was that different parts of her body were being torn apart slowly and she welcomed the final blow that would end it and give her some peace. Finally the beating stopped and footsteps faded into the distance but the peace never came. Pain wracked her body and blood mixed with the rain and ran in channels all over her. She couldn't move. She had no wish to move and hoped that the pain would claim her body and guide her to peace.

She heard a flurry of activity at the end of the alley. She steeled herself for the tormentors' return and tensed her body in anticipation, unable to defend herself in any other way. Someone leaned down and shouted something into her ear but she lost consciousness. She faded in and out as she felt herself being raised on to a stretcher. Her body screamed out in pain but her mouth remained shut. She felt the movement of a vehicle and the distant sound of a siren. Suddenly everything was white, and bright and busy and noisy. She wanted to escape it all and go somewhere better. Her mind had left but her body was refusing to let go.

So many people, prodding her and moving her limbs around, injecting her. She felt drugs surging around her body and a beckoning wave of light waiting to take her somewhere calm.

As she headed towards the brightness she whispered one solitary word.

'Catherine.'

CHAPTER 13

Catherine

'Get out of the fucking way,' Catherine screamed at a transit van. She couldn't go around it as the traffic lights were on red. She pummelled the steering wheel with her fists, ordering the lights to change. After what seemed like a lifetime they did, but Catherine couldn't resist a quick blast on her horn to the transit van as she overtook it on the dual carriageway.

She pulled into the car park of a grey, concrete building and ignored the countless instructions to pay and display. They could goddamn clamp the car for all she cared. She headed past the smokers outside the entrance and caught the lift to the first floor. She was out of surgery, the doctor had said on the phone and in the Nightingale ward.

Catherine found it and headed for the nurses' station. Two females in differing shades of blue glanced at her disinterestedly.

'Alex Morgan?'

The younger nurse in the light blue uniform stood. 'Doctor Thurlow would like to see you first. If you'd follow me.'

The nurse headed out of the ward, frustrating Catherine. She was being taken further away from her sister.

'He's just in here,' she said, knocking on the door of a room in the corridor that she'd just passed.

A gruff voice instructed her to enter. She found an elderly man with a mass of grey hair and a beard. He smiled with kindly eyes. 'You must be Alex Morgan's sister?'

'I'd like to see her,' Catherine said, remaining by the door.

He nodded his understanding. 'I won't keep you long but you need to be prepared for what you're about to see.'

'I understand that she's been badly beaten,' Catherine answered, wishing the doctor would just take her to Alex.

'That she has. You must prepare yourself for a shock. She has seven broken bones including one in her face. She's bruised and swollen all over and she has sustained injury to her kidneys. She has stitches across her forehead and her left eyelid won't open. It's not a pretty sight.'

'Is she going to be all right?' Catherine asked, fear pounding at her heart.

'She should be okay as long as she allows her body to recover from the trauma. Another twenty minutes in that alleyway and this would be a completely different conversation.'

'I just want to see her.'

'I understand that, but there's one other thing.'

Catherine closed her eyes. What else could there possibly be?

'Your sister hasn't uttered a word since she whispered your name. We know that she's conscious, occasionally she opens her right eye, but so far she's refused to speak to anyone.'

'Why would that be?'

The doctor shrugged. 'It could be the shock of what's happened but I sense that your sister is retreating into herself. It's not uncommon for victims of this type of attack to withdraw, as they find some sort of safe place during the incident itself and find it difficult to return.'

'Will she be okay?' Catherine asked for the second time.

'In most cases, victims are back with us within a couple of days but if it goes on much longer, well… '

'What?'

'Let's just say that they begin to feel more comfortable where they are and are loath to leave that place of safety.'

Catherine nodded her understanding. 'May I see her now?'

'I'll take you to her.'

Catherine followed the doctor to a side ward with the blinds closed. 'Not too long,' he said as he opened the door for her to enter.

Catherine stepped into the room and almost cried out loud. The only part of Alex visible was her head but that was enough. The swollen lump of flesh barely looked like a head at all. Her left eye was completely lost beneath the swelling, her flesh was rising to the colour of beetroot with a shade of cranberry thrown in. A track of stitches ran across her forehead.

'Oh, Jesus,' Catherine whispered, taking steps towards the bed.

The form offered no movement and Catherine was pleased that Alex could not witness the horror on her face. She moved closer until she was standing at the head of the bed.

'Alex, it's Catherine. I'm here.'

There was no response.

Catherine ached to hold her sister close. To put her arms around her and form a barrier against the world. She wanted to protect her from whatever it was that had led her to this, but Catherine knew she could not protect Alex from herself.

'I'm here, sweetheart,' Catherine said, fighting back the tears. Without the acidic tongue and hardened expression her sister looked exactly what she was: lost and alone.

It had always been the same. Alex the rebel. Alex the mouthy one. Alex the tough kid. Alex, the youngest who had probably needed their mother the most. And Catherine had always known that, had always tried to protect her fragile heart from the pain.

Catherine gently touched the top of her head, wishing to make contact with an inch that wasn't painful. She stroked gently at the coarsely cut hair. The tears spilled from her eyes and Catherine made no attempt to stop them. 'I'm so sorry, Alex. So very sorry.' Catherine wasn't sure what she was apologising for. All she knew was that she felt sorry to the depths of her heart for this battered, broken soul.

She moved closer and held her sister close. Bitter, frightened tears ran over her cheeks and on to her sister's head. She stroked Alex's hair gently.

'I'll never leave you again, I swear.'

* * *

Half an hour later Catherine's head rested on the steering wheel of her car. The tears fell unashamedly and in those moments she knew hatred she had never felt before. The fire consumed her whole being.

Their mother had done this to Alex. If Catherine knew nothing else then she knew that. Their mother's cruelty had damaged them all and only she was responsible for the condition in which Alex now lay in a hospital bed. She was loath to drive away, wishing she could return to Alex's side, but the ward sister had made it clear that Alex needed her rest and that Catherine had visited for long enough.

Catherine took deep breaths to stem the emotions raging through her. She wanted revenge. She wanted her mother before her now. For the first time in her life Catherine felt capable of murder.

She fought the tears away, pushing the image of Alex's battered body to the back of her mind. She needed to talk to someone and there was only one person who could help. She reached for her mobile phone and rang the number on the card in her purse.

The call transferred to an answering machine and a wave of hopelessness settled around her. Never had she felt so alone.

'Emily, it's Catherine Richards. If you're there please pick up. I need to talk to someone. I think I'm going mad. My sister has been beaten to within an inch of her life and—'

'Catherine?' Emily's voice was warm and concerned and a relief to Catherine as the darkness stole around her stationary car.

'Please help me. It's all falling apart. I don't know what to do.'

Silence met her ears.

'Please,' she whispered in desperation. She could understand the woman's reticence. It was almost ten at night.

'Okay, you know where I am.'

Catherine almost cried with relief. 'Thank you, thank—'

'And, Catherine, drive carefully.'

Catherine ended the call.

She left the city centre with Emily's words ringing in her ears. The winding country lanes were filled with visions of her sister lying silent and hurting on a hospital bed. The car lurched forward as anger reached into every cell of her being. She clenched the steering wheel hard, afraid of the intensity of her emotions.

Relief flooded her body as she pulled up outside the house of the therapist, but she was dismayed when she realised that she could barely recall the journey.

Emily had the door open before she'd left the confines of the car.

'I'm sorry for calling you so late,' Catherine said. 'But I just didn't know who else I could talk to.'

Emily waved away her apology and guided her past the closed door of the office. Beyond a heavy wooden door was a kitchen fashioned of light pinewood and glass panels displaying kitchen wares. Illumination was provided by lights that shone from beneath the cabinets. Two football mugs steamed on a small wicker table.

Catherine instantly began to relax.

'Don't worry. I was watching a re-run of *Frost* on my own. So what's happened?'

Catherine told her about the phone call from the hospital and described Alex in detail. Her voice cracked and salty tears stung her red-raw eyelids.

The woman looked horrified and paused for a moment when Catherine finished.

'I'm sorry for your sister, Catherine, but what can I do for you? You never came back after I told you we had a lot of work to do. Did it scare you?'

Catherine weighed the question and answered honestly. 'Partly, but to be honest I thought you were wrong.'

'So how's the family?'

'It's fallen apart,' Catherine admitted. There was no point holding anything back or even trying to lie to Emily. She had asked for the woman's help and truth was the only thing she had to offer.

Emily nodded. 'That must be hard for you but it's not the most pressing point at this time of night, is it?'

Catherine wasn't sure what prompted her to recount every detail she could remember of her childhood, but once she started she couldn't stop. It was like a vacuum storage bag. Once released everything fell out.

She told Emily about the cruelty and the beatings and the fear and the hunger and the pain and every other negative emotion that had formed her childhood years. Finally, she sat back, exhausted.

'Jeez, I can see no good reason why you'd have problems later in life at all. Hardly *The Waltons*, is it?'

'Catherine, you have to understand that you've just given me enough material to work through for the next few years and that's before we even start on your current family situation. Every single thing you've just told me has gone some way to shaping the person you are today. It's going to be a long process to unearth and face a lot of your feelings, but if you want to work through it you have to commit to letting me help you.'

'Can you help us all?' Catherine asked, weakly.

'I can try, but first you have to understand a few things. Although you remember the events of your childhood you recite them with the cool detachment of a disinterested onlooker.

'You've done this to guard yourself from the pain, but during the healing process that will change and you will see yourself in those situations and you're going to feel a lot of painful emotion. You'll want revenge and I can't give it to you. You'll want cast-iron understanding of why it happened and I can't necessarily give that to you either, but eventually there will be real acceptance and a positive way that you can move forward. I'm not going to lie to you, anything more is a bonus. We can talk generally about your sisters but unless they come to me for help my priority is in helping you.'

Catherine thought for a moment and nodded her head. She understood what Emily was telling her. She understood that she wasn't going to wake up one morning having dreamt her childhood. It was always going to be part of her but maybe she could learn to live with it. She only knew that she had to get help and she had to get help for all of them.

'You said we could talk generally about my sisters?'

'We can, but my focus has to be on you.'

'The middle sister, Beth, doesn't remember anything. She suffered the most horrific injury of us all yet she still talks of our mother fondly.'

'From what you've said, Beth never got the chance to leave home. You were forced out and your youngest sister ran away as soon as she could, leaving Beth at home with your mother. It sounds as though she's in complete denial because she had to make her own situation as acceptable as she could. Did you say your mother became ill shortly after Alex left?'

'She suffered a stroke.'

'So, Beth really had no place to go. She was scarred badly, afraid of the world and how it would treat her, and suddenly her mother is now dependent on her. It was a coping mechanism that helped her deal with a life from which she had no escape.'

Catherine understood Emily's words but she was still unsure. 'But, even now, after all this time, she still talks as if the woman was some kind of saint.'

'Her mind will let her remember when it thinks she is strong enough.' Emily frowned.

'What?'

'After so many years of denial it's going to be tough for her when she does remember. Half her life has been spent glorifying a woman who doesn't exist. She's going to need some help when the façade comes crashing down.'

Catherine's head fell into her hands as she thought about the three of them. Alex was lying in a hospital bed having retreated to God knew where. Beth was hovering on the precipice of discovering that her whole life was a lie and she herself felt as though she was hanging on to sanity by a thread.

'Why?' she asked, wearily.

'I can't answer that, Catherine. I didn't know your mother and can't begin to understand her motivations. There may have been some form of mental illness involved but I can't speculate. We can only deal with the effects of abuse on the people who are left.' Emily took a deep breath. 'There are four types of abuse: physical, neglect, sexual and emotional.'

'Well, three out of four ain't bad,' Catherine muttered, with a weak attempt at humour.

'People who have been physically abused may suffer from poor self-image, aggressive behaviour and often drug or alcohol abuse.'

Catherine's thoughts drifted right back to Alex. Although they'd all suffered physically at the hands of their mother, Alex had seemed to get the most beatings. She was the one who just wouldn't stay down.

'Neglect is normally categorised as refusal or delay in seeking healthcare, abandonment or expulsion from the home. Typically people have an inability to trust or love others and become passive and withdrawn. Of course, there's also psychological neglect. Emotional abuse can be psychological, verbal and cause mental injury. Things like scapegoating, belittling and rejection.'

Catherine shook her head, bewildered. 'Jeez, it's complicated.'

'That's just a brief overview to help you get a basic understanding of the types of abuse and neglect that you've all suffered. Remember, children are the only people in this society that anybody is allowed to hit. The rest of us are legally protected.'

Catherine thought about that. Society sure was fucked up.

'So, you can see that we have a lot of work to do,' Emily said, stifling a yawn.

Catherine was surprised to find that it was after midnight and they'd been talking for almost two hours. One question burned the tip of Catherine's tongue: 'How much is my mother to blame for the way I feel about my children?'

'Phew, that's a hard one,' Emily said, fixing her gaze on a point somewhere above Catherine's head. Catherine was starting to realise that Emily did this whilst thinking about her answer.

'Every single thing we do leaves a mark on us in some way. Everything we experience has an effect. In a reasonably normal childhood, whatever that is,' she said with a smile, 'the average positive to negative ratio of comments is one to four; so for every time a child is told, "Well done", there will be four negative comments. All that information gets stored in the subconscious part of the mind, which is like the typical iceberg. The conscious part is the bit above the water but the subconscious is much bigger.'

'I don't get the difference.'

'Okay, think about touching a hot cooker. It's your conscious, immediate mind that knows it is hot and that it hurts. But it's your subconscious mind that stores the information so that you won't do it again. It's the same with negative comments. If someone tells you enough times that you're stupid, your subconscious mind will allow you to believe it and your actions will alter accordingly.'

Catherine shook her head, confused. 'But take Alex and me. We both got similar treatment as children but I received all the things my mother said that I wouldn't and Alex didn't.'

Emily nodded. 'Absolutely, you used your conscious mind to get those things. Always, your focus was on proving your mother wrong. But what we have to find out is whether or not you really believe that you deserve those things. Do you see the difference?'

Catherine nodded her understanding, new thoughts clouding her mind. 'So, you're saying that Alex has known all along that she didn't deserve anything better and therefore played into the hands of her subconscious mind?'

'Yes. She never hid from her subconscious thoughts. They were with her all the time so she rarely tried for anything better, whereas you got the things your mother said you would never have but there's still something that prevents you from enjoying them.'

'Christ, my mind is spinning.'

'Is that your conscious or subconscious mind?' Emily asked, with a smile.

'Both.'

'Do you now agree that we have quite a lot of work to do?'

'Where do we start?' Catherine asked, daunted by the task ahead.

'We start with bite-size chunks. Tonight I've given you an overview of different situations to give you something to think about, but our sessions will be very different. The hard work will be coming from you and you'll begin to answer your own questions with me just guiding you along.'

Catherine sighed with relief. She felt as though a great weight had been lifted from her shoulders.

She thanked Emily profusely for agreeing to meet with her at such a late hour and promised to contact her the following day to schedule appointments. This time Catherine knew she'd keep that promise.

Exhausted, she made the journey to the hotel and tried to sleep whilst battling to rid herself of the vision of her battered and torn sister lying motionless in hospital.

* * *

Catherine glanced at the clock over Mr Leigh's shoulder, trying not to be too obvious about it. It was a safer bet than rolling up her coat sleeve and checking her watch. The minute hand was just peeping out from behind her boss's ear, saying it was after six thirty. Visiting started at seven and although she hadn't been late yet, one evening she'd cut it fine, and even though Alex still hadn't spoken, she had punished her by spending the whole two hours with her eyes firmly closed. Catherine didn't want to be late again.

'It's not that I don't think you can handle the workload, Catherine. I just feel that you may be a little distracted at the moment.'

'My sister is—'

'I understand that,' he said, holding his hand up. Catherine knew that he didn't wish for the finer details. 'But this contract is very important to the company and you assured us that you could see it through. I know that you have personal problems at the moment but they have to be put aside. You were placed in a position of trust with this project.'

Catherine fought the urge to place her hands around his sanctimonious throat, clenching her fists to her sides. 'I accept your point, Mr Leigh, and I can promise you that things are going to run smoothly. I will do whatever it takes to deliver this contract on time.'

The muscles in his face visibly relaxed and Catherine hoped that she'd said enough to get him out of the office before the long hand hit the eight.

'I have every faith in you, my dear.'

Catherine nodded as he turned and left the room. How quickly she had changed from Catherine to 'my dear' following a few clichéd platitudes. The second he disappeared into the elevator, Catherine grabbed her overcoat and headed for the stairs. Three flights and a couple of calls from her mobile phone and she was ready for the journey.

During the drive Mr Leigh's comments returned to her and brought with them a surge of anger. She was receiving an impromptu performance review based on her activities over the last five days. She'd been seated at her desk every morning by six thirty to make sure the contract didn't suffer due to her hospital visits.

She'd juggled make-up artists with glamour models, shoot locations, packaging problems and media coverage, not to mention budgets and team management. She'd worked twelve-hour days and still taken work back to the hotel to fill the short hours between the end of visiting time and falling into bed exhausted. The phrase 'Be careful what you wish for' floated through her mind but she pushed it away as she parked the car and bought a ticket.

'Any change?' Catherine asked Linda, the ward sister, as she passed the nurses' station.

Linda smiled but shook her head.

Catherine hadn't really expected anything different but it was beginning to worry her. The doctor had said that the longer Alex refused to speak the further into her own world she was retreating. And the harder it would be to get her back.

'Hi Alex,' Catherine said, with forced cheer. She didn't expect any answer and wasn't disappointed when none came. 'The weather's taken a turn for the worse. There's a cold snap coming, apparently.'

Catherine placed the magazines she'd brought on top of the ones she'd brought the previous day. A whole stack of them remained untouched, as did the fruit that was overflowing from the basket. Only the flowers still looked in reasonable shape. The swelling had reduced considerably since that first night, but Alex's skin still bore the colours of a sunset.

Catherine began to weed out the old fruit and dropped it into the bag beside Alex's bed. She kept her back to her sister, not wishing for Alex to see the concern that shaped her features.

On day three Alex had opened her eyes. They hadn't looked around the room or made contact with anybody. She hadn't registered any activity or presence. She had simply stared straight ahead.

Doctor Thurlow had been waiting for Catherine at the end of her visit the previous evening. He had explained that physically Alex was healing well and that they had to now consider discharging her. But, to where, was the problem. The psychiatrists who met with Alex had both proposed she be transferred to a local institution for further evaluation. Doctor Thurlow had placed his hand gently on Catherine's arm and told her that as the next of kin she would have to consider committing her sister for her own good.

Come back to me, Alex, Catherine pleaded silently. How could she give the order for Alex to be thrown into a place like that? Hadn't she suffered enough? But what if the doctor was right? What if Alex would benefit from specialist attention?

Catherine wanted to do what was right for Alex but she didn't know what was for the best. 'These plums are growing jackets,' she said, lamely, just to fill the room.

As she wrapped them in paper towels, Catherine felt her mobile vibrate in her pocket. She knew she should turn it off upon entering the hospital – she could read the signs that told her so – but Alex wasn't hooked up to a heart monitor and she really needed to be contactable for work and the girls.

Catherine looked at the phone but didn't recognise the number. It couldn't be Tim.

She put the phone back into her pocket and finished sorting through the fruit.

'I've sorted the rent arrears on your flat and paid one month in advance,' Catherine said, hoping that it might put Alex's mind at rest. Her landlord had turned up at the hospital two days ago demanding back payment or he'd throw Alex's possessions onto the pavement. Catherine hadn't liked him one little bit but she'd settled the debt so that Alex had a home to go back to.

Alex moved on the bed and Catherine thought she saw a trace of fiery emotion in the deep hazel eyes, but just as soon it was gone and Alex's gaze resumed its steady concentration on an invisible point beyond her eye line.

Catherine took the seat beside her sister's bed. She ached to take her hand or touch her arm but she couldn't. Somehow she just knew that a faint distaste would pass over her sister's features. And that was something she couldn't bear. It was an expression she'd experienced enough from her mother.

As her body settled into the chair, Catherine felt exhaustion seep into every fibre of her being. The long days and sleepless nights were beginning to take their toll. She rested her head in her hands.

'Alex, please come back to me,' she whispered. 'I don't know what to do.' A silent tear fell from her eye and landed on her hand. She wiped it away quickly and berated herself. Displays of emotion were not going to help her sister get well.

She felt her phone begin to vibrate again and reached for it. This time she did recognise the number. 'I'll be back in a minute,' she told Alex, who didn't respond.

Catherine went into the visitors' toilet area just outside the entrance to the ward.

'Hello,' she answered, breathlessly.

'Catherine, thank goodness—'

'Are the girls okay?' she interrupted as the fear balled up in her stomach.

'The girls are fine, sweetheart. They miss you and want you to come home but other than that they're okay. It's Beth... she's been calling for you.'

Catherine leaned back against the cubicle door. 'Did she say what she wanted?'

'She just needs to speak to you right away. She tried your mobile but got no answer so she tried here. Umm… Catherine, she didn't sound good.'

Catherine rubbed at her forehead. 'I'll give her a call.'

She would have liked to stay on the phone to Tim and let his voice soothe and comfort her for a while longer but she needed to speak to Beth.

She found the missed call on her phone register and hit the recall button. The phone was answered on the first ring.

'Catherine, is that you?'

Catherine could hear the panic and fear in her sister's voice. 'Beth, what's wrong? What's happened?'

'Catherine, I need you. I've remembered. I've remembered it all.'

CHAPTER 14

Alex

Alex hovered at the edge of something but she wasn't sure what. Sometimes it was a precipice that led into blackness. Other times it was a tunnel that led into the same darkness. Same result but with different ways of getting there. It was a big decision to make. The dense, comforting blackness was the same whichever way she looked, but she had to decide whether to trust the fall into the unknown or walk into it herself.

She had spent hours considering each option, searching the darkness for the answers. Did the same blackness take her to different places? She suspected not. It was all about the choice. Either way she had to face the darkness that was imminent, but it was all about the choice. She knew that it was important.

So many times she'd been poised at the edge of her decision when Catherine had arrived and distracted her from the task. During that time Alex was forced to deal with strong emotions of hate and anger. When Catherine left she felt exhausted and weary but relieved that she could mute the feelings once more and return to the most important decision of her life. How to enter the darkness.

Only once had Alex been tempted to leave the safety of her ledge on the cliff face. Just once, when Catherine's head had fallen into her hands, a small part of Alex had wanted to reach across and touch her hair. Just once and that feeling had been quickly extinguished.

Alex had felt the vibration of the phone and had known that Catherine would have to go and answer it. Nothing ever changed. There was always something more important to Catherine than her. Everything was more important to Catherine than her. That's why she had left all those years ago.

Alex stamped on the thought and ground it out with her heel like an extinguished cigarette butt. She would not think of things like that. It was gone. It was in the past. It was over, her mind screamed, but her heart knew better.

Catherine stormed back into the room, her face fixed in a frown.

Alex took the opportunity to appraise her as she reached for her coat from the back of the chair. Her face looked pale, her skin pasty, but the thing that struck Alex most was the fear around her eyes.

'I have to go,' Catherine said, as she shuffled into her jacket.

Some sort of problem at work, Alex thought, angrily.

'You know I'd stay if it wasn't urgent but I have to…'

Catherine's voice trailed off as it began to shake.

Alex realised that this was more serious than work. She felt a stab of concern that there might be a problem with Catherine's children. The concern was quickly quashed by the feeling that Catherine was leaving her again.

She sensed Catherine hovering by the door. Her sister turned and lowered herself onto the chair, gently.

'Alex, it's important to me that you know that I love you and that I wouldn't be leaving unless I absolutely had to. Beth needs me.'

Fear coursed through Alex's body. Her mind woke up and became alert at the mention of her sister's name. Beth, their poor sister who had probably suffered more than either of them.

'She needs me, Alex, I have to go to her now. She's remembered what happened.'

Alex felt her hand being squeezed. A blinding panic raged through her body. Beth needed them both.

Catherine's hand was on the door handle when Alex swallowed deeply to moisten her unused vocal chords.

'Wait,' she muttered, hoarsely. 'I'm coming with you.'

* * *

The effort of covering the distance from the bed to the car was evident in the pain that coursed around her body. Catherine had tried to help but Alex had pushed her away.

After giving Catherine directions to her home to pick up some clothes, Alex remained silent during the journey. She'd spent the last few days in hospital in pyjamas that Catherine had bought for her, but her clothes from the night of the attack were ruined.

To Alex's regret, Catherine followed her into the building. For some reason unknown to her, Alex didn't want Catherine to see where she lived.

'It's, umm… cosy,' Catherine said, as they entered.

Alex could hear the distaste in her voice and reacted. 'Yeah, well, this is just while the penthouse is being redecorated.'

Alex felt winded as Catherine encased her in a huge embrace. 'Thank God, you've come back to me. Alex, I was so worried. I thought I'd never reach you. It's so good to hear your voice properly and you sound so much like yourself.'

Alex pulled away from Catherine's arms. 'Don't touch me,' she growled. She saw the hurt that passed through Catherine's eyes but she didn't care. Her only priority was Beth. Both the tunnel and the cliff edge had faded into the distance but she could still see them and they still beckoned.

Alex changed as quickly as she could into black jeans and a ripped T-shirt. She briefly looked around for her jacket before remembering that she'd sold it. She grabbed a thick grey fleece from the floor beside the bed, then followed Catherine back to the car and focused her gaze into the glare of oncoming head-lights on the other side of the carriageway.

'You know, Alex, some day, you're going to have to find a way to forgive me.'

The words filled the interior of the car and while it was moving Alex had no escape. 'Why?'

'Because you're angrier with me than you are with our moth-er and that's messed up.'

'I don't want to talk about it.'

'You have to. For your own sake.'

Alex could hear the frustration in Catherine's voice and felt a small stab of triumph. 'I don't have to talk about it. It won't change anything that happened. It's not like we're ever going to be close. This is the plan. We'll go see Beth and try to help her as best we can. Then we'll all go our own separate ways and get on with our lives.'

As she said the words, Alex had no idea what that entailed for her. It hit her that she had no friends, no family, no job, and very soon would have no place to live.

'So, it's back to the bottle for you then?'

'Shut the fuck up.'

Alex didn't need reminding that she hadn't touched a drop of alcohol for days. Her body craved the warm embrace of vodka. She was honest enough to admit that the moment she could get her hands on something she would.

'So tell me why you hate me so much?'

'Leave it, Catherine,' Alex spat, feeling the rage build inside her stomach.

'I have a right to defend myself against your hostility. Explain it.'

'I'm warning you.'

'I'm not backing off. Let me have it. Give the rage somewhere to go. Aim it my way but at least do it honestly and tell me the truth instead of hiding behind your silence.'

'Just shut up,' Alex screamed. If she wanted to cloak herself and protect herself inside of the hatred she felt for her sister then it was her choice to do so.

'Come on, Alex. Just say it. I'm an adult; I can take your accusations and rage. I've lived with them in my head for years. Just get the words out so that we both know. Tell me why you hate me so much.'

'Because you fucking left me.'

The words exploded out of Alex's mouth so quickly that she couldn't stop them. They hung heavily between them. Alex stared ahead but could see that Catherine swallowed deeply and her hands tightened on the steering wheel.

'When did I leave you, Alex?'

Catherine's tone was gently probing. Not what Alex had expected at all. In the few seconds since the words had escaped she had anticipated strong defences and arguments that would boil down to a whole lot of excuses. Alex was ready to deflect them.

'The night of Beth's accident.'

'Don't call it an accident, Alex. We both know that it wasn't. What do you remember of that night?'

'You ran away.'

Alex used the least number of words for each thought deliberately. She always avoided reliving that night and the realisation that Catherine had left her.

'Tell me exactly what you remember. It's important.'

Alex didn't want to remember. There was no point to it. 'I can't…'

'For fuck's sake, Alex, just do something for someone else for a change.'

Catherine's words shook Alex to the core. She recognised the tone from when they were children.

'I remember the sirens of the ambulance and then being taken away somewhere. It's a bit blurry but I do remember that night when I waited for you to come back. I couldn't sleep because you weren't in the bed opposite, watching me. I waited all night for you to come home but you never did,' Alex said, accusingly. 'And the next day Mother told me that you'd run away and left me.'

'And you believed her?'

'I had no choice. You weren't there for me to fucking ask.'

Catherine shook her head in the darkness. 'How is it that you can remember some of the night so clearly yet completely blank out the rest of it?'

'What are you talking about?'

'The sirens came from the police as well as the ambulance. They took us to a children's home while Mother was at the hospital with Beth. They were trying to get us to tell them what had happened, but we'd been so well trained that we wouldn't say a thing. We just sat there, clinging to each other in a small white room while different people tried to question us.'

Alex shook her head. 'No, I don't remember…' But she did remember something. She remembered white walls. She couldn't recall exactly where she had been during that time but she did have a vision of plain white walls.

'Mother came to fetch us,' Catherine continued, as she overtook a juggernaut that was moving slowly in the left-hand lane.

'But she only took you. You didn't want to go. You clung to me and screamed the place down. It took Mother and two orderlies to get you off me. I could hear your cries as they took you away.'

Alex dared to glance at her sister, hearing the pain in her voice, but her eyes were fixed on the road ahead. She didn't want to hear any more. She wished she was a child again and that covering her ears would block out anything painful, but she felt compelled to listen.

'I didn't know where they'd taken you but Mother came back. She had told the police that it was all my fault. She persuaded them that the family would be better off if I was taken into care so that I couldn't harm either of you again. She signed me over to the state, Alex.'

Alex stared straight ahead, her vision blurred by the emotion in her sister's voice and a startling revelation that everything Catherine said to her was true.

Catherine pulled the car onto the hard shoulder and flicked on the hazard lights. Alex felt herself being turned towards Catherine whose face was haunted by the memories that she was being forced to share.

'It broke my heart being torn away from the two of you. You were my whole life, but it wasn't my fault. I tried to see you but Mother threatened that she would make your lives unbearable if I came anywhere near you. She promised to treat you both better if I stayed away. I had to try and protect you even if I wasn't right there. Don't you understand? I had no choice.'

Anger-filled tears rushed over Alex's cheeks, cleansing her of the hatred that had driven her for so long. She had no memory of the time that Catherine recalled but she also knew that Catherine had no reason to lie.

'I loved you both so much,' Catherine said, reaching for her hand. Alex allowed her to take it. 'My life was empty without you but I had to try and make something of what I had. If only to prove her wrong.'

'Yeah, I did a great job of that, didn't I? I managed to turn into everything she said that I would.'

'But it doesn't have to stay that way, Alex,' Catherine murmured, as Alex felt herself being drawn into the protective circle of her sister's embrace.

* * *

'Are you ready for this?' Catherine asked as the comforting hum of the car engine faded away.

Alex looked at her sister. 'Are you?'

Catherine shook her head. 'No, but we owe it to her to listen. It's the least we can do.'

Beth opened the door and immediately balked at Alex's appearance.

'Oh my goodness, what happened to you?'

Alex waved away the question. 'Nothing, it's not important. And, anyway, you should see the other guy,' she joked weakly.

Beth ushered them all in the front door and through to the lounge.

'I'll make tea. You must be—'

'No, Beth, no tea,' Catherine said, blocking her path to the kitchen. She gently guided Beth to the sofa and sat beside her. Alex took the single chair.

'What happened?' Catherine asked, taking Beth's hand and holding it tightly.

'I picked up the poker to dust underneath it but I couldn't put it down.'

Alex noted that the dark metal instrument lay on the hearth.

'I wanted to put it back but I just couldn't let it go and then it was like I was back there, seeing it, reliving it.'

Catherine moved closer and looked at Alex who desperately wanted to look away, run away, but she didn't. Beth had to face this and so did they.

'What did you see?' Catherine asked, gently.

A tolerant smile formed on Beth's lips as her eyes wandered to the poker. 'The two girls were arguing about something. It wasn't serious but Catherine was telling Alex that the plates she had wiped were sopping wet. Alex was doing a cheeky dance and pulling faces.'

Alex noticed that Beth recited the memory as though for the benefit of two strangers and not for the two people in front of her who had been with her that night and who could remember the whole thing clearly.

Her eyes met Catherine's above Beth's distant gaze. Their shared guilt locked and mingled above Beth's head.

'Mother told you to stop it or you'd both be sorry.'

Beth was right. Alex had barely touched the plates with the tea towel and had simply put them back in the cupboard. Catherine had noticed and was trying to chase her back into the kitchen to do the job properly.

Alex remembered hearing the warning and had idly wondered what their mother was going to do. Would she beat them both?

'Alex hid behind the sofa, in the gap that Catherine couldn't reach. Catherine stretched her arm trying to grab hold. Alex was taunting Catherine and Catherine was trying hard to stay stern.'

Beth swallowed but didn't blink as she continued.

'Mother was watching them both. Her face was hard and cold. She told Alex she had five seconds to get out or she would regret it for the rest of her life.'

The smile dropped from her face. 'Catherine stood aside but Alex didn't come out.'

Alex closed her eyes.

'Mother counted to five and Alex still hadn't come out.'

Alex tried to hold back the emotion but it was useless. 'I was stuck,' she whispered through the tears.

A glance at Catherine showed her wiping her cheek with her free hand.

Beth let go of Catherine's hand and moved towards the fire. 'Mother asked me to pass her the poker. I didn't understand because the fire didn't need prodding.'

Beth dazedly walked to the long-dead fireplace and retrieved the smoke-blackened poker. She examined it closely.

'As I passed it to her she pushed me into the fire.'

Alex heard a soft whimper of pain from Catherine, but she was more interested in the expression on Beth's face. Her unblinking eyes were locked on the poker with a child's inquisitiveness, as though seeing it for the first time.

'At first I didn't feel the pain. My instincts focused on trying to get out, but she held me down, amongst the flames, with this.'

Silence filled the room. Alex tore her gaze away from Catherine and stood. She took two steps and eased the poker from the grip of her sister.

Beth seemed to wake from a dazed state as though Alex had woken her from sleepwalking. Her eyes were innocent, yet haunted.

'How could she do that, Alex?' Her voice was filled with pain and disbelief.

'Because she was evil,' Alex said.

Catherine approached them. They all stood awkwardly in the middle of the small living room.

'Because she had worked out that we all cared about each other more than we cared for ourselves. It was the ultimate punishment, born of a twisted mind.'

For a split second Alex thought Beth was going to argue. Old habits die hard, she realised. It would take a while for the mother in Beth's mind – the one that Beth had invented in her safe world, built of lies and deceitful self-protection – to transpose into one truthful image of the real mother they'd had.

'We're so sorry for causing you all this pain,' Catherine offered, taking Beth's hand. 'If only we hadn't been arguing or if—'

'Shh,' said Beth, placing a finger on Catherine's lips. 'It wasn't your fault. It was a lottery and it could have been any one of us.'

Beth reached for them both and Alex allowed herself to be drawn into the embrace. It was the least that she could do for Beth.

'Please don't blame yourselves. It really wasn't your fault. I don't and never will blame either of you.'

'That fucking bitch,' Alex exploded, extricating herself from the embrace. She had the overwhelming urge to lash out and hit something. She wanted to channel the cancerous hate inside her into her balled fist and smash it into the wall.

Poor, sweet Beth who had probably suffered more than both she and Catherine combined had managed to preserve a genuine warmth and generosity of spirit despite their mother's best efforts to beat it out of her.

Beth's purity of heart and good nature had survived the war zone of their childhood and for that Alex was grateful. Beth reached for her, warmth and compassion filling her eyes. 'Alex, my sweet little sister. You have to let go of the anger. Don't allow it to destroy you. You're better than that.' Beth clutched her hands tightly. 'You have so much to live for and to give to other people. There are good things to come out of this. I mean, look at you two, finally back together after all these years. Now that is something to be thankful for.'

Alex felt the tears burn at the back of her throat and Catherine looked away, astounded by their sister's total selflessness, Alex guessed. Peacemaker was the part she'd always played in their earlier years.

'I hated it when you two fought.'

'You always found a way to bring us back together,' Catherine observed, fighting her own tears.

Beth shrugged and smiled wearily. 'I hated it when you were cross with each other. Somehow the world didn't seem the same place. It always felt terribly important that you two were friends. You had to stick together.'

Alex looked at Catherine who offered an awkward half smile. Perhaps there was hope.

Beth pulled away, leaving the two of them side by side. 'Now, I insist we have some tea.'

Alex collapsed back into the chair, emotionally and physically exhausted.

Catherine stared at the closed lounge door. 'Alex…'

'I know,' Alex said, not needing the words to be spoken.

Throughout the whole exchange their sister had not shed a single tear.

CHAPTER 15

Catherine

Catherine pulled gently into the kerb about fifty yards from the bright lights of the Thai restaurant. Light snow carpeted the ground in a white lace blanket. But fine raindrops now interspersed with the flakes.

Catherine was disappointed. She could imagine the girls staring out of their bedroom with wonder and awe at the glistening conifer trees that lined the back garden. Their faces set in joy, their mouths forming wondrous 'O's in the middle of their delighted, excited faces. The magical event – or miracle, in their eyes – of snow two weeks before Christmas would send them to sleep with contented smiles on their faces.

Catherine forced her gaze away from the festive twinkling lights, illuminating the darkness of the closed shops. Tinsel hung haphazardly in every window. Figures of Santa, snowmen and reindeer assaulted her from every direction. She wondered if Tim had dressed the tree yet. It was a job they normally shared the weekend that had just passed. She ejected the pictures from her mind. They served only to remind her of the impersonal emptiness of her hotel room.

She checked her watch as she entered the restaurant. She was ten minutes early and hoped that was long enough to gather her thoughts for what she was about to do.

She was surprised to see Tim already seated. She was early but he was even more so. All thoughts of what she needed to say to him fled from her mind as he turned and smiled at her nervously. Every muscle and tendon in her body reacted to the look in his eyes and it took every ounce of effort she had not to launch herself across the tables and diners that separated them. She dropped her gaze to the floor. She had to stay strong. He didn't know the whole story yet.

He stood as she approached and kissed her lips gently. 'You look beautiful.'

Catherine smiled her thanks as she sat, but she doubted his words. A thirteen-hour day at the office being trampled by a team of people with nothing but problems did not make for a serene, attractive appearance, no matter how many times she re-applied the wonder that was Max Factor.

'How is work?' he asked, safely.

'A bit like being bludgeoned by a herd of bison on a daily basis.'

'That good?' he asked, raising one eyebrow.

Catherine chuckled and began to relax. Why had her nerves been taut and strung all day? This was Tim. Her Tim. Because you don't know how he's going to react, said a voice inside her.

'How are the girls?' she asked, eagerly. Although she spoke to Tim daily she hadn't seen the girls since she'd left the house almost a month earlier. She also wanted to steer Tim away from the subject of her work. With what she had to tell him she couldn't bear the thought of seeing any hint of judgement creep into his eyes when he realised that her work had become the personal battleground on which she fought every day.

'They're wonderful,' he replied. The old familiar light returned to his eyes. 'They both made Christmas cards at school. Lucy's was beautiful. She'd worked so hard on it. The letters were perfectly formed of silver glitter. There was painted holly in each corner. Inside it said, "To Mummy and Daddy, I just want you both for Christmas.'"

Catherine felt a lump in her throat. She felt a rush of longing for her serious, studious older child.

'And Jess's card?'

'The words "Merry Xmas" scrawled in red pen and the words "Whatever Lucy said" written in the middle.'

Catherine laughed out loud. It was obvious that they hadn't changed too much.

'I'm not pressuring you, sweetheart. I understand that you have to do what is right for you, but it's important you know that the girls miss you and want you to come home. That's not emotional blackmail. It's to make you understand that whatever you feel you've done wrong, whatever kind of mother you think you've been, our girls love you very much and miss you terribly.'

Catherine swallowed the emotion that was building up in her throat. 'If it's any consolation, this isn't easy for me, either.'

Tim shook his head and reached for her hand. 'That gives me no pleasure at all.'

Catherine knew that he spoke the truth.

'I've seen Alex and Beth,' she blurted out.

His eyes registered pleased surprise. He'd always encouraged her to have more contact with her family, but that was without knowing the history they shared. Although he knew her childhood had been rough, she had placed herself like a barrier between him and the memories to protect them both. She hadn't wanted the filth of that time to infect him. She'd been happier to have him completely distanced, sterile and safe from even knowing about it. But Emily had convinced her otherwise.

'Tell me about them,' he said, after the waiter had taken their order. By asking that, Catherine knew that Tim was attempting to delay the purpose of their meeting. She had given him no indication. She decided to enjoy his company before the painful work began.

Through their entire meal she talked of Beth and Alex, mainly Alex. Of her descent into alcoholism, of the terrible beatings.

'She's had it rough,' Catherine said, as she pushed away the plate of half-eaten curry. 'Yet some part of her wants to survive. There's a will of steel buried somewhere deep inside her that even she isn't properly aware of. She's so spirited. She's fiery and angry and full of emotion but she's passionate.'

Tim smiled. 'Remind you of anyone?'

A picture of Jess forged into her mind as though transferred by her husband. Catherine smiled. There were definite similarities.

An expectant silence fell between them. It was time and Catherine knew that it could be delayed no longer. She could feel Emily watching over her shoulder.

Coffee was placed before them and Catherine took a deep breath. 'Tim, you know that I asked you to meet me tonight because I have something important to tell you.'

She paused and saw the fear in his eyes. He battled for a moment with his impulse to postpone or avoid whatever was about to come, but then resigned himself to hearing her out.

She reached across and touched his hand. 'I deliberately chose a public place because I need you to sit and listen to what I have to say and let me finish. It's going to be hard for you but please do as I ask.' Her eyes implored him to respect her wishes. She could see the growing fear in his eyes and was quick to reassure him that it wasn't what he was probably thinking. 'I'm only able to do this, my darling, because I love you with all of my heart and trust you with my life.'

The terror left his eyes and only concern and tenderness remained.

'I've never really told you much about my, our, childhood because I didn't want you infected by even the knowledge of my memories. It's not that I wanted to shut you out but more that I wanted to keep it out. I didn't want it to follow me into this part of my life.' She rolled her eyes. 'I'm beginning, with help, to realise that I can't treat my past like a room that I've walked through and closed the door. It's an impossible task. Somehow, those years have followed me and the events still haunt me now.

'I can't explain what was wrong with my mother except to say that she was just plain evil. She was never very loving, but when our father walked out she simply became unfeeling and mean. I can't detail every beating that I had or what they were for. Some I can remember better than others and some are just a blur of blood and pain.'

'Sweetheart…' Tim said, rising to hold her.

Catherine held up her hands. 'Please, don't, Tim.' She paused to get her thoughts in order. 'I can't even begin to explain how many different hells the three of us went through. Fear and anxiety lived in our stomachs from the moment we woke up to the moment we fell asleep. In our innocence we initially tried to adapt our behaviour to avoid the beatings. Kids are smart. If you get beaten for not making the bed properly you'll make sure you do it right the next time.

'And so it went. All three of us turned into good little robots – washed-out, scared versions of real children. We tiptoed around the house trying to do everything right to avoid the inevitable, but you see that was the trouble: however we acted, the beatings were inevitable.' She heard a rueful laugh and realised it was her own. 'I remember one time I was sent to the corner shop to get a tin of peas. When I came back I got a good hiding because once I'd left the house she'd changed her mind to carrots and I hadn't had the sense to know that.

'I think I was ten when I realised that day that no matter how hard I tried it didn't make any difference. I kept the knowledge to myself. It was my little secret. I thought that I could still protect the others, especially Alex. I tried to make sure that she did everything right, just in case, but of course, she had other ideas.'

'Were you close?'

Catherine nodded. 'You can't live through that without forming barriers and we did it for each other. We took care of each other and grew closer every day. I loved my sisters very much and would have killed for either of them.

'I think we all sensed that the cruelty was getting worse. The frequency and reasons were changing. The violence began to erupt for imagined slights. Mother often thought we were making comments behind her back. Alex got a milk bottle smashed over her head for that. I once got a broken finger for apparently looking at Mother sideways when I entered the room. I was twelve years old.'

Horror was etched on Tim's face. He looked older, haggard. Catherine knew he was reliving the memories with her, but she didn't want that. She didn't wish for anyone else to experience what she and her sisters had gone through.

'When I was fourteen,' she continued, casting her eyes towards the table, 'our mother deliberately pushed Beth into an open fire and held her down with an iron poker because Alex and I were arguing.' Throughout the story so far she had managed to remain unemotional and focus on replaying the events as distant memories. Now she felt her voice begin to tremble, but she fought to hold on to her control. 'I can still hear her screams now,' she said, shaking her head, trying to erase the memory of the sound from her mind. The emotion began to ball in her throat but she had to finish.

Tim's gaze was riveted on her face but the colour had drained from his cheeks.

'That night my mother placed me in care and told the authorities that I had hurt Beth.'

'And they believed her?'

'Of course. She was a very convincing liar. Back then child abuse was something that happened within the home. It was a shame, but no one really got involved,' she said bitterly. 'Neighbours had enough problems of their own and teachers weren't equipped to deal with it even if they spotted the signs. So, yes, they believed her.'

Catherine took a deep breath in a vain attempt to compose herself, but she sensed it was useless. The tears were poised in her throat and going nowhere. 'That night I was ripped away from my sisters. I felt lonely, abandoned and frightened.'

'And guilty.'

Catherine nodded. 'I couldn't protect them,' she said, and the tears overflowed from her eyes with the admission of that one simple truth.

'It wasn't your fault.'

Catherine reached for a tissue and wiped away the hot, bitter tears that were quickly replaced with new ones. She shrugged. 'It doesn't matter whose fault it was. I could no longer take care of them. I worried about Alex and all the little things she did without thinking and that I had managed to cover up before Mother noticed. I worried about who was watching them through the night in case Mother got up and imagined some slight or mistake they'd made while they'd been sleeping. I was sick with fear about what would happen to them without me.'

The tears rolled from her eyes as though being torn from a bleeding heart.

'Sweetheart, what can I do to…?'

'Let me finish. My mother used my own fears against me to keep me from seeing them. She told me that if I stayed away she would treat them better, but if I contacted them it would seal their fate.' She shook her head, angrily. 'And I believed her.'

'Catherine, you were fourteen years of age going on thirty. How could you have controlled these events?'

'I don't know, but I just could.'

Catherine could hear her own petulant voice. She reined in her emotions. She had to make him understand something that she was only just coming to terms with herself.

'For years my mother told me that I would be nothing and that I would never have anyone. She said I was a whore and a slut and good for nothing. She told me I was stupid and that no one would ever want me.'

A muscle in Tim's cheek tightened and relaxed like a pulse.

'Every night I was in that home I lay awake until the early hours devising ways in which to wreak vengeance on my mother. I planned and plotted and fantasised about violently hurting her and reclaiming my sisters, which in my reasonable mind I knew was impossible, but it got me through. After a while my thinking changed. I remembered all the things that she'd ever said to me and decided that the best revenge I could ever get was to make sure I didn't become everything she said I would. Once the idea occurred to me I knew it was right. It gave me a focus and that became the only thing I could think about. It drove me through school, college and two jobs to pay for university. It drove me to you.'

He looked confused. 'Am I part of your revenge?'

She shook her head. 'You're part of the vision that I aimed towards. You're part of what I aspired to. I had this big picture in my mind of a great job, a nice house, a good husband and a couple of children. Two girls,' she added, wryly. 'To achieve the whole package was my sole aim. It was my proof that I was never what she said I was.'

'You were never that,' Tim said, meaningfully.

She saw the pain of what she'd shared reflected in his eyes, yet his love for her shone through.

Catherine became aware that the restaurant had emptied around them. Three waiters stood at the front desk.

'I think you'd better signal for the bill before we get chucked out.'

Tim paid the bill and walked her outside. The cold night air bit into the bare skin of her cheeks.

'Will you please come home so that I can take care of you properly?' Tim asked as they stood beside her car.

Regretfully Catherine shook her head. The offer was tempting but she wasn't ready. She was learning new things about herself every day but there was still so much to understand.

'I can't. It's not the right time. I still have questions.' Although Tim didn't probe what these questions were, she guessed that he knew it was to do with the girls. She didn't tell him that if she couldn't resolve those issues inside herself she might never be coming home. It was a promise she'd made to herself the night she'd left her family behind. She either returned to them whole or not at all.

Tim pulled her into his arms and she let him. He stroked her hair gently. 'You went through so much, my love. You must have been so brave yet frightened. I want to help you through it. I want to help you heal.'

Tears pricked at her eyes. She didn't doubt the sincerity of his words and his willingness to help her every step of the way. She had yet to peel back a few more layers and find out if what was left was enough for him and their children. And that was something she had to discover for herself.

She returned his embrace and clung to him for as long as she dared allow herself. 'Maybe soon, my love, maybe soon.'

She extricated herself from his arms and slid into the car without meeting his eyes. She pulled away from the kerb and sensed rather than saw his solitary figure staring after her, his hair turning white with snow.

* * *

'I'm not going,' Alex bellowed down the phone at her.

'It's your first time. It's okay to be scared of—'

'I'm not fucking scared. I just don't want to be in a room full of losers who can't function without a drink.'

Catherine rolled her eyes. A smile tugged at her mouth. 'What have you got to lose by just going for one night?'

'My freedom if I just happen to throw a few punches at the bunch of self-absorbed idiots who are weak-willed and pathetic. I'm not like them.'

Catherine wondered just how long it would be until Alex admitted to herself and other people that she had a problem. The slight trembling that had been present in her voice since her last drink was more pronounced over the telephone.

'We've been through this a hundred times and you agreed to give it a try.'

'I never promised.'

Catherine wondered if Alex realised that those three words had passed between them countless times as children. Just about every time that Catherine reminded her youngest sister that she hadn't done something like make her bed or iron her school clothes.

'Look,' Catherine said, checking her watch. 'I'll pick you up at six thirty and take you there.' It was more to make sure that she actually went. This was the third dry run they'd had.

'But you won't be there with me, will you?'

Catherine heard the vulnerability in Alex's voice. Her defences were still so solid that she wouldn't admit to the fear of facing her illness.

She planned to duck out of the office and take Alex to the AA meeting and then return to work to finish off the monthly budget sheet. Mr Leigh had requested it by nine the next morning but if she got in around six she should manage to get it done.

'I'll be there, Alex.'

'How?'

'I'll drop you off and then wait in the car. Although I can't be right by your side, at least you'll know I'm not far away and that I'll be waiting for you to come out.'

'Well, if you really want to be that sad—'

'I'll see you later,' Catherine said, replacing the receiver.

Immediately her phone buzzed. 'Joyce Patterson has been holding for you,' said Becky, her new PA.

'Didn't I say not to disturb me?'

'But she insisted.'

'Do you work for her or for me?' Catherine snapped. This girl had been with her for over a week and still couldn't take simple directions. 'Tell her I'll call her back.'

Joyce was still chasing the contract for the make-up on the shoot due to take place in two days' time. The woman had found out the hard way not to call Catherine's bluff. Within two hours of their last phone call she'd lined up two make-up artists ready to sign a watertight contract. She had one signed and the other on standby. She wouldn't make the same mistake twice.

She turned her attention to the mound of paperwork that represented the media contracts. The legal department had forwarded them to her this morning after two weeks of chasing phone calls and emails. They needed to be authorised and returned to them tomorrow morning.

'Hey boss,' Lisa said, popping her head around the door.

Catherine could tell by her tone that something was wrong. 'Is she crying again?'

Lisa seated herself in one of the chairs opposite. 'Not yet but she's awfully close.'

Catherine put her pencil down and fixed her attention on her former assistant. 'I can't help it if she gets simple instructions wrong. I don't have the time to pander to her. We're all busy and stressed and I don't like repeating myself.'

'I know,' Lisa said, holding up her hands. 'But she really is trying to get it right. She's just frightened of you.'

'She's what?' Catherine asked, genuinely surprised.

'You've made it clear from day one that you don't like her.'

'It's not my fault that she's incapable of doing the job. She's slow and deliberate. She needs everything checked and double-checked and she puts calls through when I ask her not to.'

'And she's not me,' Lisa said, smiling.

Catherine chuckled, honest enough to admit that Lisa wasn't too far off the mark. 'You can say that again.'

'She's been here for little more than a week and she does things slowly because she doesn't want to get things wrong and she doesn't want you to shout at her. She's intimidated by you.'

'Well I can't help that,' Catherine said, dismissively.

Lisa got the point and stood to leave. 'Please just give her a chance. I was pretty awful for my first couple of weeks but you gave me the benefit of the doubt.'

Lisa left the office but her words lingered. The poor girl was completely nervous around her, which probably didn't help with her current performance. Becky did try Catherine's patience but that was no reason to bark at her every time she did something wrong.

'Damn it,' Catherine said to herself as she rose from the desk. Now Lisa had her feeling all guilty and responsible.

She opened the door to the outer office which housed her assistant and saw straight away that her eyes were red and puffy.

'Umm… Becky, that spreadsheet with the preliminary costings was very good. If I revise the figures, could you update it for me?'

The girl's face shone with relief and pride and Catherine felt even more guilty. She had been working so hard recently that she'd been blind to just how miserable the poor girl was.

'Look, I'm sorry for being snappy,' she said, deciding to go for an all-out apology. 'I'm not always this bad to work with. We're all just really busy and I need you to do what I ask straight away, okay?' She flashed a smile for good measure and saw the girl instantly relax.

'Mr Leigh called but I told him you were not to be disturbed.'

The smile froze on her face and she nodded stupidly before retreating back to her own office. Anger rose inside her, but she had to admit that for once the girl had followed her instructions to the letter. How was she to know that 'not for anyone' excluded the owner of the business?

She punched his number into her phone as soon as she reached her desk.

'Aah, Catherine. So busy that you can't speak to me?'

'Just a misunderstanding,' she hedged. 'Any problems?' she asked, wondering why he needed to speak to her.

'I'm meeting later with four potential new investors. They've expressed an interest in seeing the Finesse promotion.'

I bet they have, Catherine thought. This single promotion was about to launch a small advertising company into the big time and it looked like the gravy train was powering up to leave the station.

'It's not quite ready yet. There's still some artwork to be finished and the—'

'I'm more than happy to show them your original storyboard, providing you present it. Your team is talented and capable but none of them have your flair and passion for presenting an idea.'

A few months ago Catherine would have been flattered by his words but right now she was too exhausted to care. Her head had been buried in contracts and spreadsheets and office politics for so long that she wondered if she was capable of producing any excitement for the project at all.

'Of course, Mr Leigh, when is the meeting?' she asked, reaching for her diary.

'This evening at seven. We'll have a brief meeting beforehand to align our strategy.'

Catherine's hand hovered above the A4 diary page. 'I'm sorry, I have plans.'

'No problem, dear,' he said, affably. 'You have a couple of hours to cancel them and—'

'I'm afraid I can't do that.'

Shards of silence thundered through the telephone lines. When his voice came it was low and disbelieving. 'Catherine, there is no question that you will cancel your arrangements for this evening. This is an important part of your job and a responsibility that I will not allow you to take lightly. When you accepted this promotion it was on the understanding that occasionally you might have to put yourself out.'

Catherine's hand gripped the receiver so hard that it shook against her ear.

'And I think I've done that,' she replied, through gritted teeth.

During the last six months her life had been turned upside down. She had separated from her husband, her mother had died and her sisters had come back into her life and needed her. For every hour that her life had interfered with her work she had paid it back in triple through guilt and responsibility. She had worked fifteen-hour days and most weekends to keep the project on schedule. She had lived and breathed the campaign since the day she'd accepted the job.

She had put every creative instinct on ice to become the intimidating bore that everyone hated, spending each day chasing paper and money. Her creative brain had been trampled underfoot and she could no longer string a coherent sentence together. She'd been surviving on autopilot for weeks, afraid to give way to the fatigue that riddled her body – and Mr Leigh felt that occasionally she should put herself out for her work?

Catherine thought about her sister waiting on the pavement at six thirty, ready to take a brave and decisive step into the unknown. Alex had somehow found the courage to start moving forward, away from the memories that tied her to the past.

She had made a massive commitment, possibly without realising it, and in allowing Catherine to be a part of it she was opening herself up once more to having faith and trust in her sister again. And if Catherine didn't turn up it would seem to Alex that she had been abandoned all over again.

Catherine knew it was time to decide. Was she there for her sister or not?

CHAPTER 16

Alex

Alex hopped from one foot to the other, giving each sole equal time against the recently formed ice on the ground. The snow had been falling intermittently all day and had now hardened against the freezing temperature. She rubbed her hands against each other and then bunched them up and pulled the sleeves of her fleece down to cover them.

She strained to see the clock, barely lit in the newsagent's darkened window. She could just make out that both hands were reaching towards the seven. Catherine was late. She should have known. Catherine had probably decided to stand her up and leave her to face it alone. She tried to hang on to the anger that felt so familiar it warmed her, but a voice, a voice that sounded like Beth, told her not to be so stupid, that Catherine was not going to let her down again.

She backed into a doorway as an icy wind surged past her whole body. The fleece was little protection and her bare face became numbed against the icy breath. As the time ticked by she began thinking of reasons not to go to the meeting. Not least because all she wanted to do was buy a bottle of vodka and curl up in bed.

The worst thing she had discovered during her period of sobriety was the clarity. Thoughts, emotions and memories charged into her mind and they were so clear. There was no alcohol to blur the edges or obscure them completely, however temporarily.

For years she had hidden from the memories of her past. They had lurked there somewhere in a box covered with dust in the back of the attic space of her mind. Occasionally her mind's eye had happened upon the dusty cardboard container but she had always managed to avert its gaze somehow with the distractions of drink, Jay, Nikki. But as her other crutches had fallen away she had been left with only one mind-numbing, pain-releasing friend. And she had made the most of their time together.

Intertwined with her memories of the past were the more recent images of the night she'd been beaten. The pictures invoked feelings of pain, despair, loneliness and disgust. These were the memories that she wished to dissolve with alcohol. Not only because they were the most recent but because they were symbolic of the way she had been feeling for as long as she could remember.

A silver BMW pulled up and Alex was relieved to see Catherine beckoning to her. Soul-searching was definitely better done in small quantities, preferably with a drink of something in your hand, Alex decided.

'Took your time, didn't you?'

'Why the hell haven't you got a coat yet?' Catherine said, surveying Alex's fleece jumper.

'I'll get one when I can afford one.'

'For Christ's sake, let me give you the money—'

'I said when *I* can afford one.'

'Damn your blasted independence.'

'Yeah, it's nice to see you too.'

'Buckle up,' Catherine instructed as she pulled away from the kerb.

Alex stole a quick look at her sister's profile in the darkness. Her face looked pinched and tight as though her cheekbones were bursting out of her skin.

'Fucking idiot,' Catherine cried out as she was forced to brake hard at a set of traffic lights.

'You had plenty of time to stop.' Alex had seen the car in front gently braking to a stop behind a line of traffic. 'Have you spoken to Beth today?'

'No. We spoke yesterday.'

'And?'

'And what?'

'For Christ's sake, stop the car and let me walk.'

'What?' Catherine looked genuinely perplexed.

'If you hadn't noticed, I'm trying to have a bloody conversation with you but all I'm getting back are one-word robotic answers. If you don't want to be here, let me out of the car and I can do this on my own. I don't need you, you know.'

'I know, Alex, and I'm sorry. Surprisingly she sounded okay. She's done a spring clean of the house and plans to get some decorations and a tree over the next few days.'

Alex shuddered. She hated to think of her sister still living in that house. 'I wish she'd just sell that place and move on.'

'I broached the subject with her again but she completely evaded it. She said that the house means too much to her to leave.'

'Is she really okay?' Alex asked. A small part of her ached for the life that Beth had lived. Her own had been no bed of roses but at least she had escaped.

'It's hard to tell. Since that night she's pretty much refused to speak about our mother and the memories she now has. I've tried a few times but there's always an urgent task that needs her attention. I've gently advised her to try talking to someone but she simply doesn't see why. All she says is that the past is gone and it's only the future that matters.'

'It just doesn't feel right. Maybe there's more we should be doing.'

'There's no more that we can do. We have to trust in her way of handling it. If we push too hard it might be the worst thing for her.'

Alex knew that Catherine was right. Neither of them were therapists or counsellors and all they could do was be there if Beth needed them. But somehow Alex doubted that that would ever happen. Beth had never needed anyone. She had always kept her own pain bottled up inside.

'So, you're going to sit out here and wait for me?' Alex asked, as they turned into the street. She wanted to be sure that she'd understood Catherine correctly.

Her sister nodded.

'Don't you need to get back to your high-flying career?'

Catherine snorted. 'No, that's really no longer a problem.'

Alex detected a trace of fatigue in Catherine's voice. 'Oh well, suit yourself.'

Catherine parked the car. 'Wait a minute,' she said, as she turned off the ignition. 'I'm risking life, limb and a thoroughly abusive ear-bashing, but I want you to know that I'm proud of you. What you're about to do is far from easy but I've got faith in you to see it through.'

Alex stared down at her hands in her lap. A hundred vicious retorts sprang to her lips and just waited to be bounced into the space that separated them, but none did. She simply undid her seatbelt and said nothing.

As she got out of the car Alex caught a glimpse of a cardboard box and its contents spilling out on to the back seat. There were files and a couple of photographs. Alex instantly knew that

Catherine had left her job and had the unmistakable sense that it somehow had something to do with her. She made a mental note to ask her about it later.

She approached the blue door to the side of the Chinese take-away and hesitated. Perhaps she could escape under the cloak of darkness? But as she turned she saw Catherine's watchful eyes gazing at her through the driver's side window.

Beyond the blue door were bare wooden steps that led up and out of a mauve-coloured hallway. The sound of her boots echoed around the building. At the top of the stairs one door was marked 'Keep out' and the other was slightly ajar. Alex took her chances and pushed open the one to her right.

She quickly counted about eight people standing around. Some in pairs and a couple standing one their own and looking as uncomfortable as she felt. Was it their first night also?

A woman clad in Marks & Spencer clothes approached her with a welcoming smile. 'Hello, I'm Eleanor and we're about to start.'

Alex nodded as people began to take their seats. She wondered if there was any sort of hierarchy denoting where one sat at these things.

While Eleanor gave a quick chat on the format of the meeting, Alex did a quick appraisal and tried to fit these people into the boxes she perceived as their lives. She always made up stories about people's lives and invariably they were better than her own.

'So, I'll start. My name is Eleanor and I've been sober for three years and two months.' Applause rippled around the group. Alex sighed inside. This was turning out to be like every B-movie that she'd ever seen. She had a strong instinct to launch herself from the chair and aim for the doorway before anyone could stop her. But then she thought of Catherine, sitting in the car, waiting for her, and she knew she couldn't.

All too soon it was her turn. 'My name's Alex and I'm gonna be sober for the next hour or so.'

Her attempt at humour was met with blank stares and a couple of disapproving glances. She quickly realised that this was no place for humour. She cast her eyes down to avoid the chastisement of the group. I'll just get through this meeting, she promised herself, so that I'll have something to tell Catherine, and then never darken this doorstep again.

As she gently clapped for other people, she wondered again what she was doing in this soulless room that held no clues as to what it did for a day job. She wasn't like these people. She could stop drinking whenever she wanted. It had never caused her a problem and if it ever did she could handle it on her own. She could handle it.

Eleanor stated that they would recite and discuss the twelve steps. Alex had no idea what she was talking about so remained silent, willing away the minutes until she was free of these people.

'Step one: We admitted we were powerless over alcohol, that our lives had become unmanageable.'

Alex heard the words and discarded them until a vision of herself lying bleeding in an alleyway returned to haunt her. She pushed away the feelings that accompanied the memory and tried to view the event objectively. That night she had been powerless and her life had definitely become unmanageable. She remembered the sensation of her swollen, painful cheek resting against the cold, wet tarmac, unable to speak. Unable to move. The severity of the beating had paralysed her and she had prayed for help to come, but if she'd had to put a name to that help she would have been found wanting.

'Step four: We made a searching and fearless moral inventory of ourselves.'

During the long repetitive hours in the hospital bed, the events of Alex's life had passed through her mind while she tried to make sense of what had happened. In her forced state of sobriety she had been forced to question the direction of her life. What had gone so wrong to lead her to that point? What sort of person had she become to find herself in that situation? Was it a punishment for the harm she had done to all the people around her?

'Step eight: We made a list of all persons we had harmed, and became willing to make amends to them all.'

The image of Nikki flew into her mind. Alex was honest enough to know that Nikki had been her one true chance at a better life, but in her heart she knew she had never deserved it. She had treated Nikki badly and had taken her for granted and then when she could push her no further, she had simply walked out. She thought of Jay and the friendship they'd shared. They had been so close until the day that he had needed her and she hadn't even realised it.

Her mind began to swim in torment. She sat up straight and began to listen a little closer.

* * *

Alex stared into her cup of black coffee as she stirred it distractedly. She didn't have the will to raise her eyes and meet Catherine's gaze.

'The spoon's getting dizzy,' Catherine said, with a smile in her voice.

Alex put it down, wishing that Catherine hadn't bothered waiting for her. She would have preferred to be on her own. She needed to absorb all that she'd heard in the poky dismal room across the street and the feelings that now raged within. A lot of what she'd heard had made sense. A little too much sense.

'Jesus, I really am an alcoholic,' she said, brokenly.

Catherine took her hand, and for once Alex made no attempt to pull away. 'I know, sweetheart.'

'But how did this happen? When did I lose control?' Alex raked her free hand through her hair. The truth was emblazoned on her mind's eye in aqua neon lettering. 'At what point did I cross the line?'

'At the point where your life became too difficult to deal with alone.'

'But my life was fine until that bitch fucking died.'

'No, it wasn't. You've become everything our mother said you would be.'

Alex snatched her hand away, stung. 'Unlike you, Miss High and Bloody Mighty. You who has everything. I'm so very sorry I disappointed you and ended up like this.'

Catherine grabbed her hand again. Her eyes blazed into Alex. 'You could never disappoint me. You're my sister and I love you with all of my heart. I know you don't believe that, but I'm not going anywhere, so eventually you'll have no choice but to believe me. I'm patient and I understand how hurt you are but I wasn't making a judgement.'

Alex's anger dispersed as quickly as it had exploded. 'But how did we turn out so different?'

'We didn't. The only things that separate us are material. Yes, I got the great family, nice house and good job. What have I got to show for it now? I'm separated from my family and home and I've walked out on my job. In truth, you had more sense than me.'

Alex was intrigued by her sister's admission. 'How so?'

'Because I've spent the last fifteen years forming my life around a picture that I painted all those years ago. It was built on determination and the need to prove someone wrong. Everything I've done has come from that single motivation. I've lived my life with Mother on my shoulder. Every decision and choice that I've made came from that one promise I made.'

'But at least you have something in your life,' said Alex, feeling lonelier than she'd ever felt.

'There have been times in your life that you could have been happy, Alex. You don't say much about her but I think you loved Nikki. You had the chance.'

'And I threw it away,' she said, bitterly. Not one day had passed when she hadn't regretted her treatment of Nikki.

'Because you didn't think you deserved to be happy, so it became a self-fulfilling prophecy. You turned into what our mother expected of you because you don't have enough self-worth to believe that you're entitled to anything more.'

'Said Doctor Catherine, shrink to the people.'

Catherine chuckled. 'Don't knock it until you've tried it. But be honest with me, Alex. How was your life when you were with Nikki?'

Alex paused to find the right words. 'Peaceful, loving, comfortable, exciting…'

'And what did you do once that happened?'

Alex grew uncomfortable with Catherine's probing but she felt powerless to stop talking. She hadn't shared any of these feelings with anyone. 'I drew back. I started drinking, and other things.' There were some things that she didn't wish to share with her sister.

'You pushed her away?'

Alex nodded, realising that she had in fact done everything she could to push Nikki away and one day it had simply worked.

'You did so before anyone else could. Don't you see? Always in the back of our minds our mother has been there in one form or another. In my mind she's been goading me into everything she said I could never have, but with you she's been there threatening to take it away. Once you found a good life with Nikki some part of you became scared that it was about to be snatched away, so you took control yourself.'

Alex sat back. Catherine's words made sense but she had never consciously decided to push Nikki away. She had simply slid into a pattern of behaviour that seemed to fit at the time.

'How could I have been so stupid? I let the best thing in my life get away.'

'Is there no hope that the two of you could—?'

'No,' Alex said, cutting off the thought in Catherine's head. 'She has someone else and she deserves better than me.'

'Don't say that,' Catherine thundered. Alex was transported back to when they were children and Catherine would shout at her for not doing something quickly enough. Her words had often been harsh, but even then Alex had known that it was for her own good and that Catherine was only trying to protect her.

'But she does.'

'Don't put yourself down. You have lots to give and you're only going to get better. You're gutsy and determined and loyal and trustworthy.'

'I'm not a fucking puppy.'

'I can see your good points, so why can't you?'

'Her new girlfriend won't hurt her the way I did.'

'What exactly did you do, Alex?'

Alex shook her head. She was too repulsed by her own actions to utter them aloud, especially to her sister. For a reason that Alex couldn't fathom, Catherine's opinion meant something to her. She wasn't sure why but it just did.

Alex drained her coffee and stood. 'Will you give me a lift to the other side of town? There's something that I have to do.'

Catherine reached for her coat. 'Of course.'

They remained silent during the fifteen-minute drive, each lost in their own thoughts.

'Here, just stop over there,' Alex said, as they turned off the main high street.

'Will you be okay?'

'Yes. I've just about got enough for the bus ride back.'

Catherine fished in her purse. 'Here, take this and get a taxi. For me.'

Alex battled internally but decided to accept Catherine's offer. She opened the door to get out of the car but before she did impulsively leaned over and kissed her sister on the cheek. 'Thank you,' she whispered, as she scrambled out of the car. No further words were necessary.

The quiet familiarity of the street ahead almost forced the breath from her body. It was one of the best kept secrets in the area. A road that led to the back entrance of a furniture warehouse kept the traffic at a minimum. On each side of the road were tidy Victorian semis with neat hedges and Cotswold-stone walls. It was a gentle street filled with couples and young families. And it had once been her home.

As she approached the racing-green door, her eyes raised to the first-floor window. A vague shadow passed by the curtained glass. Alex instantly recognised the figure and felt a rush of fear in her stomach. She turned to walk away, briefly intending to use the money in her pocket for a bottle of something that would ease her escape from the terrorism of the feelings that now held her under siege. She took two steps and then turned again. She had to do this while she had the courage.

She pressed lightly on the button under which a single name stood where there had once been two. She knew that if pressed too hard the button refused to reset, sounding a continuous buzzing sound in the room above.

Nikki's gentle voice sounded questioning over the intercom.

'It's Alex,' she said, simply.

Alex felt Nikki's hesitation and understood it. She didn't need a drunken idiot making a fool of herself at this time of night.

'I'm not drunk and I don't want anything from you. We can talk down here if you'll come down.'

Alex heard the buzzing of the door and gratefully stepped inside. As she mounted the steps Alex heard the distant muffling of the television. Nikki had opened the door for her as she had always done when they were together.

Alex cautiously entered the flat and looked around. Her eyes rested on Nikki, who stood in the kitchen. Alex caught her breath. She wore cropped jeans and a vest T-shirt despite the temperature outside. Nikki was always warm. Alex thought she had never looked lovelier.

'I'm sorry to disturb you,' Alex said, casting a furtive glance around the room.

'I'm alone.'

Alex was not prepared for how relieved she was to hear those words. She accepted that Nikki had moved on with her life, but she didn't particularly wish to meet the lucky lady.

'Coffee, tea, anything?'

Alex knew what the anything meant and she shook her head, refusing all three options. This wasn't a social call. It was a necessity. Alex understood that now.

'Sit,' Nikki instructed, pointing to the sofa.

Sarah McLachlan's haunting voice sounded from the stereo.

Alex did as she was told and, after tidying an A3 sketching pad and watercolour pencils into a pile, Nikki took the sofa opposite. It was the stance they had often taken for a serious talk. Alex eyed the art equipment fondly. Many nights they had been content for Nikki to sketch out pictures in the lounge while Alex tapped away at the computer in the spare room. Those nights had been idyllic and Alex missed them more than she cared to admit.

'I've come to apologise,' Alex stated.

'Look, if this is about the night you got drunk and stayed here you have nothing to apologise for.'

'Not for that, although I am sorry that you got lumbered with me that night, but this is something else. I'm sorry for the things that I did.'

Alex saw the pain that came into Nikki's eyes and felt the sickness rise in her own stomach. They had reached the point where they could exist as acquaintances, even as tentative friends, providing that they pretended their past had happened to other people in another time.

'Which particular part?'

Alex realised that this was not going to be a Girl Scout picnic but she owed Nikki the truth, or the best truth that she had to give. She had to relive the pain from the beginning so that Nikki would understand what she had meant to her.

'I couldn't believe my luck when we first met. I used to pinch myself after our evenings together, unable to comprehend that you wanted to spend time with me. Before you there was only sex with strangers. My longest relationship was approximately three hours, and that was only if I couldn't get rid of them quicker, but you were different. At first I thought it was some kind of bet or a cruel joke but then I came to trust you and eventually fell in love. It was a strange sensation for me because it was something that I'd never felt before.

'I was frightened and exhilarated all at the same time. I moved in here and somehow all the bad things went away for a while. The loneliness that I rarely admitted to seemed a thing of the past. You made me feel like someone special and I revelled in the feelings. I began to trust your love for me and eased into the idyllic life that we created. For the first time in my life I was truly happy.'

'So, what went wrong?'

'It was all too easy. My mind began to play tricks on me and little voices started telling me that the axe was about to fall. I managed to ignore the voices for a while but they grew louder. I became convinced that it was only a matter of time before you realised how worthless I was. Once the thoughts took hold I couldn't get rid of them. They followed me and mocked me every waking minute. If you stayed late at work it was because you were seeing someone else. If you suggested going out for a drink it was because you were bored with me and wanted to go looking for someone new. Everything you did was because you had finally woken up and realised that I was a useless sack of shit.'

'How could you even think that I felt that way?'

Alex held up her hands to command silence. 'It's not your sympathy I'm after, Nic. I'm way past that. I just need you to understand what happened and why it all went so horribly wrong. I became suspicious of everything. If you suggested that I go into the room and write it was because you wanted to get rid of me. I felt that you were bored with my company and wanted me out of the way. There was nothing that you could do or say that I didn't manage to find an ulterior motive for, however tenuous.

'I started to do things to test you. I'd deliberately want to make love on nights that you were physically exhausted so that I could confirm to myself that you no longer found me attractive. I would intentionally invite an attractive woman over to our table at the bar so that I could see how you acted. It didn't matter if you showed no interest because then I just convinced myself that you were a good actress and were burying your attraction. There was no way that you could win. I began to put undue pressure on you to see how much you could take before giving up.'

'I didn't pass that test too well then, did I?'

'You put up with me for longer than anyone else would have done but you couldn't win. There was always going to be a breaking point and I wouldn't have been satisfied until I found it. I was like a child who needs to test the unconditional love of their parents, but I wouldn't have rested until you finally threw me out. Every torture would have been more cruel and imaginative until I got the result that my head was telling me was a foregone conclusion.

'Please understand, Nikki, that the outcome of our relationship was beyond your control. It was always down to me and there was nothing you could have done to stop it.'

'When did you start being unfaithful?'

The sickness rose in Alex's stomach and she feared that the recent coffee was travelling upwards.

'The day after your twenty-fourth birthday. I deliberately stayed out all day and all night and returned drunk with no card or present to see how you would react.' Alex shook her head. 'You kissed me on the forehead and told me not to worry about it.'

'I remember it almost broke my heart.'

'The affairs started the next evening. I deliberately left phone numbers in my pockets.'

'I know. I found most of them.'

Alex's face coloured with the shame of her actions. 'But why didn't you say anything?'

'Truthfully, because I didn't want to lose you. I knew you were punishing me for something but I didn't know what it was, and every time I tried to talk to you, you became so angry and hostile that I just hoped it would pass. I knew that we'd been happy once and I prayed that you would return to the person you'd been before and that we would be happy again. Sounds weak, doesn't it?'

Alex shook her head, aching for the person that Nikki was and the pain that she had put her through. 'And because you didn't say anything I thought you knew and didn't care. Again, I turned everything around to suit the preconceived ideas in my own mind.'

'Is that why you brought that girl back?'

Alex nodded and the old self-loathing returned to devour her soul. Her body suddenly craved a drink to escape the feelings that were like thick black tar on her heart.

'And you knew that I'd come home and catch you in our bed?'

'Yes,' Alex admitted, weakly. 'I knew there would be no way that we could get back from that. I knew that my doing such a vile, unforgivable thing would push you over the edge and the voices in my mind would finally be satisfied.'

Nikki sat back into the sofa. Her eyes were busily darting around the room, meaning that she was processing the information.

'Did you hate me that much?'

'I didn't hate you at all. Even then I still loved you, but in my mind the destruction of our relationship was inevitable. It was destined to fail.'

'Why now, Alex? Why are you telling me all this now?'

Alex thought very carefully about her next words and knew that after this there would be no going back. With her next sentence she was committing herself to brutal honesty and awareness of her own failings. 'Because I'm an alcoholic who has caused a lot of pain and I have to try and put things right.'

Alex saw the surprise on Nikki's face. 'Yes, I've finally admitted it and I'm trying to take it seriously. I have a problem and I have to deal with it. I haven't come here tonight to ask for your forgiveness. I'm starting to realise that I have no control over the actions of other people. I accept how much pain and heartache I've caused. I know that we can never go back, but I'd seriously like you in my corner as a very good friend.

'I want nothing from you but it's important to me that you know how much I loved you and that my time here was the happiest time of my life. I don't expect to go back, and believe me when I say that I love you enough to want the best for you and I hope that you've found it.'

The words almost stuck in her throat. The thought of Nikki with anyone else caused her physical pain similar to that she'd felt the night she'd been beaten to within an inch of her life. But in her heart she meant what she said, which surprised no one more than her. Nikki did deserve the best of everything life had to offer and Alex knew that that could never include her.

'My biggest regret is that I didn't have the sense to realise that I was trying to lose the most precious thing I'd ever had. It's a mistake that's mine to live with.'

'But why, Alex?' Nikki asked, her eyes gleaming and pained. 'Why did you have to push me away?'

There it was. The question that she'd avoided answering for years. The crux of everything that had gone bad between them. Did she have the courage to share her deepest, darkest fears with the only woman she had ever loved? A woman who was now lost to her but who deserved to know the truth. Did she have the strength to relive it or would she come out the other side more damaged than she was now? Could she take that chance and risk inching closer to the edge of the cliff?

She took a deep breath. 'I think there are some things about my past that you deserve to know.'

CHAPTER 17

Catherine

Catherine stared again at the watercolours that furnished the doctor's wall.

'Are you really paying me to let you sit in a comfy chair for fifty minutes?' Emily asked.

'What?'

'You've sat and stared for the last ten minutes at items you've seen many times before. We've talked at length about your mother and you claim you have nothing left to say, yet here you are again. Why?'

'I don't know.'

'Yes you do, so be honest.'

'I really don't know. I've told you.'

'You've skirted around the issue throughout all our sessions and now the time has come. You can't avoid it any longer.'

'I don't know what you're talking about,' Catherine said, examining the length of her nails.

'Get the words out. Tell me what it is that you want to say.'

'Okay, I'm frightened that I don't love my children. Is that what you want to hear?'

Emily's face remained expressionless. 'Finally, we're starting to get somewhere.'

Catherine felt relief that the words that had been so close to her thoughts had finally been given a voice. The words themselves hadn't really formed in her head, but a feeling, an emotion, had been present for months. The feeling had represented a dark space within her, a part of herself that she had no wish to explore. And despite her best efforts, the feeling had remained.

'How do you feel?'

'Relieved and disgusted.'

'Why disgusted?'

'Didn't you hear what I just said?'

Emily nodded. 'I heard what you said but did *you* hear what you said?'

'Of course I heard,' Catherine snapped. Sometimes the whole point of therapy wore her down. Sometimes, just occasionally, she wanted an answer from someone else. She didn't want to dig and dissect her feelings. She just wanted them gone.

'So what did you actually say?' Emily asked, unruffled.

'I said that I don't love my children.' Catherine groaned at having to repeat herself. It was bad enough saying those words once. Mothers weren't supposed to feel that way about their children.

'No, Catherine, that's not what you said. Listen to the difference in the words. You said, "I'm frightened that I don't love my children." Do you see?'

'How is that so different? Surely it amounts to the fact that I'm a failure as a mother?'

'Only if you want to be, but we'll come on to that in a little while. The difference is the three words at the beginning of the sentence. To state "I don't love my children" is quite emphatic and without doubt. It is an irrevocable statement. That's not what you said. The first thing is that you said the word "frightened", which indicates that it is not an emotion that you wish for. The thought that you don't love your children scares you.

You also used the word "that". If you put those three words together before the statement it indicates both doubt and fear. Both are positive signs.'

Catherine felt the frustration grow. 'Why are you picking on the wording of the sentence instead of actually addressing the problem with me?'

Emily sighed. 'Your wording is important because you didn't give much thought to the sentence before it left your mouth, which often means that it is a true representation of your inner feelings. Had you taken longer to form the words before saying them we might not have got the whole truth.'

'But this is not just recent. It's not a feeling I've had for a few months. If I'm honest, I've never been close to either of my girls.'

'Aah, now you see, not being close to them is not the same as not loving them. Don't give your answer too much thought but just tell me how you felt when you first became pregnant.'

'Delirious,' Catherine said without thinking. She quickly realised it was true. She had known before the official test from the doctor that she was pregnant and she'd been euphoric when the test had confirmed it. She remembered sitting in a coffee shop two streets away from the home she had then shared with Tim, hugging the knowledge to herself for just a little while over a latte and a muffin. She had devised all sorts of elaborate ways in which she was going to tell Tim the news. But when she'd walked into the flat the words 'Tim, I'm pregnant' had exploded from her mouth.

'We were both thrilled. Each night we would lie in bed play-fighting over names. Tim teased me mercilessly about wanting the name Wilbur for a boy or a girl. When we found out it was twins our joy simply doubled. Many of our friends rolled their eyes but we didn't care. There were no disadvantages as far as we were concerned and we saw it only as a double blessing.'

'Were you scared?'

'No more than any other mother, I think. We did everything we were supposed to do. We attended all the classes and bought all the books. I remember the first night I felt a kick. It must have been Jess. I reached for the book and told Tim, "They're not supposed to be kicking yet", and he said, "Maybe they haven't read the same books as us." I've never forgotten that,' she said, growing sad. For a while she had relived the innocent excitement of all their dreams coming true. The anticipation of seeing the lives they had created.

'What went wrong?'

Catherine remembered the day the twins were born as clearly as if she had just been wheeled out of the delivery room. Two bundles of wool and flesh had been placed into her waiting arms and the excitement was suddenly replaced by darker emotions that she had never cared to examine.

'From the moment they were born I wished they belonged to someone else. I didn't want them. How sick does that sound?'

'Not sick at all. It's surprisingly common. Tell me more about how you felt at that time.'

'I didn't know them,' Catherine admitted, reliving the memory of the two similar faces before her. 'They were like tiny little strangers to me. Tim was enthralled from the second he set eyes on them and I couldn't understand why. I watched him with fascination and wondered why he felt this immediate affinity with these things in my arms. They meant nothing to me and all the feelings I'd had before their birth simply disappeared. You see, I'd loved them before they were born.'

'Well, no, actually you loved the idea of them before they were born, before they were real. Did you feel guilty about your feelings?'

'Of course I felt guilty. Everyone was cooing all over them and I felt numb inside. I couldn't understand what all the fuss was about. If I had thought Tim would agree I would have suggested that we give them away. There, now you know the truth and you can hate me as much as you like. It'll make little difference to the way I feel about myself,' she said, miserably.

'How did you cope?' Emily responded, without judgement.

'In what way?'

'Well you had all these people telling you what gorgeous, beautiful children you'd produced, and you didn't agree. I'm assuming that you didn't share your innermost feelings with a roomful of doting relatives, so how did you cope?'

'Umm… I just did. I think I watched Tim and copied his actions and hoped that I would look genuine. I prayed that no one would notice and I just hoped that the feelings would come in time.'

'But they didn't?'

Catherine shook her head, mortified that she had divulged so much of her darkness to Emily. She waited for the therapist to order her out of the room whilst refusing to see her any more.

'Did you never talk to anyone about how you felt?'

'How could I? It would have made me sound like a monster. I know how evil it must sound to you…'

'It sounds to me like post-natal depression.'

'What?' Catherine cried, her eyes and mouth forming circles within her face. She'd heard of the condition but hadn't applied it to her. 'I couldn't have had that.'

'Why not?'

'Because it was much worse than that. I read about it and in most cases it gets better within the first few months after the birth.'

'In most cases. Not all mothers with post-natal depression are carrying around your baggage. It's far more common than you think. Do you think every mother looks down at their new-born and experiences unbound joy from that moment on until eighteen years later?'

'Not at all.'

'Then why do you expect it of yourself? Why do you not allow yourself any negative emotions? It doesn't make you a monster, just human. Ask any mother if she has never felt a modicum of dislike for her child and if the answer is "Never", I'd call that mother a liar. It's just not realistic.'

'But it couldn't have been that,' Catherine said, pushing away what she felt was a simplistic view. 'The girls are six years old. Post-natal depression doesn't last that long.'

'It started as PND but you saw it as something else. What was the predominant thought in your mind while you went through these feelings alone?'

'Why don't I love my children?'

'To be accurate that sentence should have had the word "yet" tagged on the end. Over time that question became replaced by a statement. Whether it was a conscious thought or working away somewhere in your unconscious mind, you developed an answer to your own question. Do you know what it is?'

Realisation began to dawn on Catherine. The conscious thought had tried to come through many times but she'd always pushed away the words before they had a chance to become a whole statement, so abhorrent was the idea.

'Well, what was the answer?' Emily urged.

'Because I'm like my mother,' Catherine said before covering her mouth in horror. 'But I wouldn't let myself think that, not on the surface, anyway. I always pushed it away.'

'Never underestimate the power of the unconscious mind. It works away in the background without your knowledge, sometimes protecting you and other times not.'

Catherine felt shell-shocked by Emily's words. Dare she hope that anything Emily said was true? Any hope at all would give her something to cling to.

'But for years I've kept my distance from them. I've been unable to get close to either of them in any way at all.'

'What you've done is protect them.'

Catherine shook her head, vehemently. Emily was really asking her to take a leap of faith with that one. She couldn't see how her actions at any point could be perceived as protecting her girls.

'Imagine your subconscious mind working in the background and making you believe that you're like your mother. Avoidance was the only way. You were protecting them by keeping your distance so that you wouldn't hurt them, but it just made the problem worse. The more you distanced yourself from them to protect them from what you perceived as the evil gene inside you, the harder you made it for the feelings hatched at their birth to go away. Yet still something inside was maternally strong enough to protect them in the only way you knew how. Your doubts about your own abilities to be a mother were fed by the post-natal depression and you began to think that you were just like your own mother after all, that some abusive gene had been handed down. So, you see, what you did was to protect them by keeping away.'

'It's just not possible,' Catherine said, closing her eyes. The torment of the last six years could not be explained so easily.

'But I hit my child,' she admitted, miserably.

'And then you did the responsible thing of walking away until you could understand your reasons for doing it. It would have been easier to stay within your nice, safe life and pass it off as a solitary event until the next time it happened. Again, you protected them by leaving.'

'I'm scared of doing it again.'

'There is no cast-iron guarantee that something like this will never happen again. Even the most stable of mothers can lose their temper at some time or another, but smacking your child once is not reason enough to leave behind for ever the home and family you've created. At some stage you're going to have to take the risk.'

Catherine tried to absorb all that Emily had said. She wasn't sure if she dared believe it.

'Am I not supposed to be doing all this talking?' she asked with a wry smile.

'No, you're on my time now and I'm trying to offer you a gift for Christmas. As with all gifts, it's up to you how you choose to use it.'

* * *

Those words reverberated around Catherine's head during the phone call to Tim and the drive to the restaurant.

She was the first to arrive and sat nervously, folding and unfolding her napkin. There were two false alarms with the door but on the third her breath caught in her chest. Tim ushered the girls into the restaurant and suddenly Catherine's eyes became hungry for a look at them. Immediately she noticed that they'd grown, and a wave of sadness rode over her. She had missed what looked like precious inches but could only have been millimetres.

They paused at the door to remove jackets, hats and scarves, unaware of her unwavering eye. Tim took their outer garments while maintaining a low and steady conversation with them both, capturing their full attention. How did he do that? she wondered. How did it all come so naturally to him? It hit her that the three of them were a family and she was the outsider. Suddenly she wanted to run back to the sterile safety of the hotel room and regret her inability to succeed like a failed diet. I'll try again tomorrow.

Emily's words came back to haunt her. Was she so quick to reject the gift that she'd been offered?

She physically forced her body to remain where it was. Tim spotted her and gave a little wave as he guided the girls towards her.

Jess was dressed in her clothes of choice, a T-shirt and trousers. Her only concession to girlhood was the row of sequins that bordered her front pocket. Lucy was a vision in pink with a Barbie handbag to match.

As they reached the table Tim leaned down and kissed her on the cheek. There followed a moment of awkwardness as Catherine came face to face with her children. She sensed their confusion matched her own as the correct form of greeting was established. Take it slowly, Catherine advised herself.

'Your hair has grown,' she said, reaching out to touch Lucy's fine, silken locks. Her daughter did not recoil as she had expected. She simply stood still, unsure what to do next. 'And you,' she said, turning to Jess. 'Your eyes sparkle like those sequins there.'

Both girls just stood and looked at her. Catherine looked to Tim for guidance. He assisted the girls into their chairs and pushed their legs beneath the table.

A waiter approached immediately and laid down menus for them all, although Catherine was sure that she detected a slight sniff when he glanced at the girls. Her sudden appraisal of the recently opened Malaysian restaurant told her that Lucy and Jess were the only children in the building.

Tim ordered soft drinks for the children and a bottle of wine while she busied herself perusing the menu. Her throat had dried and tightened. She felt panicky and had no idea what to say to the girls.

'Shall we order straight away?' she asked, hoping the choice would give them something to talk about.

Tim seemed surprised by her speed. Normally, when dining out, she preferred to savour the menu over a half glass of wine and leisurely make her choice, but tonight wasn't like any normal night.

'I think I'll go for Loh Bak,' she said, brightly. She had tried the pork and prawn rolls elsewhere and hoped that these would live up to her memory.

Tim took a little more time and Catherine took the opportunity to appraise him. He looked tired and a little pale. Although he'd been keeping her up to date with all the presents he was buying for the girls, the task of single parenthood as Christmas approached must be taking its toll on him. Yet, she realised, not once had he complained. Instinctively, she reached across the table and squeezed his hand.

Without words she hoped that the love and respect she felt for him was reflected in her gaze. She hoped it was true that eyes were the reflection of the soul because if so he would be left in no doubt as to the way she felt about him.

'I'll go for Sambal Sotong.'

Catherine pulled a face. 'Squid?'

He laughed at her expression. 'Live dangerously.'

She shook her head. 'Jess?'

'Can I have a hamburger, please?'

Tim leaned over towards her. 'They don't do hamburgers here, sweetheart. Let's have a look at the menu together.'

Catherine was amazed at the ease with which he communicated with the children and not for the first time felt a little envious. She wished it came as naturally to her.

'Lucy, have you chosen?' she asked, aware that her eldest was sitting silently.

Lucy pointed at the first item on the menu. Cili Udang.

'That's chilli prawns. Are you sure that's what you want?'

Lucy first nodded and then shook her head and Catherine sensed that she was just ordering the first thing she saw so that she was no trouble.

Catherine leaned over the menu. 'Shall we choose something together that you might like a bit more?'

Lucy nodded and looked up at her with absolute trust in her eyes. How can you do that? Catherine wondered silently, looking into the innocent eyes. Her gaze travelled to Lucy's cheek and without thinking she reached out and touched the soft, warm skin where her hand had struck two and a half months ago. Contempt shrouded her and she wondered how long it would be before the invisible handprint would fade from her daughter's face.

'Are you okay?' Tim asked.

Catherine nodded, pulling herself together.

'We've decided on Satay Ayam over here.'

Catherine turned to Lucy, whose gaze hadn't altered. So lovely, so trusting. 'That's chicken pieces on a stick. You have to pull them off, like this,' Catherine said, demonstrating.

Lucy again nodded.

The waiter approached and Tim recited their order. As the waiter moved away he left an uneasy silence at the table.

'How are Beth and Alex?' Tim asked.

Catherine relaxed slightly. Something that she could talk about. 'I'm still a little worried about Beth. She seems to act as though nothing has happened. I'm concerned that the memories have been buried again. I talk to her almost every day and try to prompt her to talk about things but she always manages to swing the conversation away. I don't know if I'm doing the right thing by trying to push her.'

'You're not an expert, love. Has she spoken to anyone, a professional I mean?'

'She evades the subject every time I try to mention it. As long as I talk to her about normal everyday things she's quite content and animated, but as soon as I broach any difficult subjects she just clams up and gets off the phone as quickly as possible. Even Alex is calling her every few days to see if she can get anywhere.'

'And how is Alex?'

Catherine told him all about the meeting at AA and the difference it seemed to have made to her sister. She told him about their daily conversations that were now sometimes being initiated by Alex. She was in the process of recounting their earlier conversation when their food was delivered to the table.

The mixture of aromas immediately assaulted her senses. The smell of coriander from her own dish mingled with the ginger from the chicken dish. Lucy and Jess surveyed their own plates but said nothing.

Suddenly, like a bolt from the sky, Catherine realised that throughout her conversation with Tim the girls had remained silent and unmoving. She watched as they communicated silently across the table as only twins can and made a pact with each other. Catherine was surprised that she could tell what had transpired between them. Neither of them liked the look of what they'd been served but had mutually agreed to silently eat it anyway.

The horror of the situation crept up on her. Her children were behaving like two painted dolls. She was reminded of the three wise monkeys and instead of seeing her daughters sitting either side of her she suddenly saw the automatons that they were trying to be.

She glanced around at the stillness of the restaurant. Couples were engaging in intimate conversations. The lighting was low and romantic. Malaysian music played in the background but did nothing to soften the staid, upright atmosphere of the surroundings. It was a first-date venue, ideal for talking softly and getting to know each other. It was not suitable for a family meal.

Catherine dropped her fork, caring little for the noise she made. 'Tim, what the hell are we doing here?'

'Huh?'

'Hurry and pay the bill,' she instructed, breathlessly. There was no way she was going to be able to get to know her daughters in a place like this.

Tim left the table and approached the maître d'. Catherine could tell that Tim was having to explain that there was nothing wrong with the food. She didn't care.

She took a deep breath and removed her safety rope. Would she fall? She leaned down conspiratorially. 'Come here,' she said to the girls who looked at each other before lowering their heads. 'On the way here I saw an ice rink with a couple of rides and some stalls. Would you like to go?'

'Can I have a burger?' Jess asked, wide-eyed.

At that moment Catherine felt a rush of love that had previously been alien to her. She had the strong urge to gather Jess up in her arms and thank her for not being the robot she seemed to be.

'Of course you can.'

'And candyfloss?' Lucy asked, quietly.

'As much as you like.'

'What's going on here?' Tim asked, with a strange look in his eyes.

'I'd like to go ice skating and the girls have agreed to come along and make sure I'm safe.'

Tim laughed at her expression. 'Let's go.'

Catherine followed them out of the restaurant and floundered for a second. On one hand she felt alive and strangely carefree but on the other she felt frightened, terrified that she couldn't do this, that she would never love them as a mother should. Getting to know her daughters was too huge an obstacle to overcome.

Tim handed her Lucy's coat and woollens as he turned to Jess. She knelt down to Lucy's level and froze, not knowing what to do. Suddenly her old fears came back to haunt her and she remembered how she had felt about the children when they were born. Doubt rendered her immobile.

'I can do it, Mummy,' Lucy said, taking her breath away.

Catherine lifted her head and met the questioning eyes of her daughter. 'How about we do it together?'

Lucy nodded and squirmed into the coat. Catherine pulled up the hood and double-looped the scarf around her neck.

Feeling a little more comfortable, Catherine glanced at the progress of Tim and Jess. 'I think we're going to win,' she said, smiling at Lucy.

Lucy quickly pulled on the mittens and declared herself the winner.

'Unfair,' Tim cried. 'We didn't even know that we were racing.'

As they left the stifling cocoon of the atmosphere Jess glanced over but said nothing. Even beneath the street lamp Catherine could read the suspicion in her eyes. It occurred to Catherine that she had always known it was going to be harder with Jess. Although she'd never been close to either of them the silences between her and Lucy had always been a little easier, less fraught with the accusations of her shortcomings as a mother.

Tim opened the driver's door.

'Let's walk. It's only a few streets away,' Catherine said. Although the night was cold, it was clear and crisp and the pavements were empty.

The girls fell into step together in front and Catherine automatically linked her arm through Tim's.

'How is everything at the house?' Despite her absence from their home she often went to sleep thinking of the green Christmas tree with frosted branches that sparkled beneath the fairy lights. She imagined the tinsel above the fireplace and the two woollen stockings hanging either side of the fire. She wondered if Tim had attached the card holders to the door. It was a job that had become ritualistic for her to remind him to do.

'Bare.'

She pulled her arm from inside its comfortable resting place. 'Tim, you have to decorate the house. Just because I'm not there it's not fair on the girls…'

'They won't let me.'

'Don't be silly. They love to decorate the tree.'

'They've always done it with you. They won't let me get the tree until you're home to do it with them. Lucy went into a sulk when I tried and Jess threatened to burn the thing down. And knowing Jess as we do, I felt I had to take that little threat seriously.'

Catherine replaced her arm against Tim's, her palm wrapped around his forearm. How could her girls feel like that after all that she'd put them through, after her distance for the whole of their lives? How could they feel that way?

'You didn't think they'd notice that you'd gone, did you?'

Catherine shook her head. 'It really was the right thing to do. I did it for their sake.'

'And now?' Tim asked, hopefully.

'I'm working on it, sweetheart. I really am.'

Lucy and Jess turned the corner two seconds before Catherine and Tim, who almost walked into the back of them. They had come face to face with a big wheel, a skating rink and a few brightly lit stalls. It was as though the sight of the amusements flicked a switch in both her daughters. The air was filled with animated chatter of 'Can I…?', 'Will you…?', 'Does it…?'

Catherine laughed at their sudden animation. It was as though someone had suddenly cut away the strings that had bound them.

'I want a hamburger,' Jess cried.

'I want one of those,' Lucy said, pointing to a wooden hut selling frankfurters.

Catherine realised it was a festive German market that encircled the perimeter of the ice rink.

'I am feeding them, honest. It's just a little past their supper time.' Tim said.

'I can understand how they feel. The smell is delicious.'

They headed over to the food stands and bought an assortment of food which they ate as they perused the stalls. Christmas had never meant a lot to Catherine but on this night, viewing hand-crafted candle holders and her daughters' wonder, she began to feel the festive spirit within her. Gentle carols wafted from speakers around the rink. A glass of sweet mulled wine with added rum and orange brought a warm flush to her cheeks.

'I want some chestnuts,' Jess cried, as they passed another vendor.

'No, Jess, you've had quite enough,' Tim said, firmly.

'I want chestnuts,' she screamed, upping the verbal ante.

'I said no. You've eaten very late as it is and I don't want you up with stomach ache all night.'

'I want—'

'Oh Jess, shut up,' Lucy said.

Catherine felt all the warning signs of a major tantrum from Jess. Her back began to straighten and tension entered her shoulder muscles. This was her cue to turn and run. She had never been able to deal with Jess's tantrums. The whole night had been too good to be true. She walked on a few steps. Tim always knew how to handle these situations and it was better if she didn't get involved.

'Shut up yourself,' Jess screamed in Lucy's face.

Catherine hunched slightly as protection against the shrill voice that had the power to wind her up like a clockwork toy.

'You always want what you can't have. You're spoilt.'

At Lucy's words Catherine turned, ready to intervene but not sure how. Her militant methods had failed miserably in the past. As she looked at her daughters in a face-off she waited for the familiar feelings of despair mixed with anger mixed with impatience mixed with rage. None came.

Instead she found it amazing how Jess's eyes flashed a different colour when she was angry and how, despite her aggressive posture, Lucy refused to back down. Catherine had never noticed these things before. She stood and watched them for a moment longer, eager to find out more about her children. The shouting of her youngest daughter went over her head as she observed the total passion and conviction that accompanied every word. By contrast Lucy remained as cool as a cucumber and didn't rise or react to any of Jess's insults. Her face remained a mask of control. Catherine was mesmerised by these qualities in her children.

Tim sighed beside her and suddenly the fatigue she'd seen in his face earlier returned and doubled. Her heart ached for the position she'd put him in, but she would never regret her decision to leave. It had been right for them.

Without realising what she was doing Catherine moved forward and placed herself between her two girls, facing Jess. She lowered herself to her haunches so that her face was almost at equal level to Jess's. Confusion reigned in the eyes of her youngest daughter and Catherine saw her body prepare itself for incoming rage.

'Jess, you've had enough to eat. You can't be hungry,' she said, reasonably.

Jess frowned and opened her mouth to argue, despite the suspicion in her eyes.

'I don't think you're going to be able to ice skate if you have any more food. I think you'll be ill. Do you want to ice skate?'

Jess nodded, her gaze fixed on Catherine's face, mesmerised by the gentle tone of her words.

'Let's go, then,' Catherine said, simply.

Jess began walking in front and then hesitated as though she wasn't sure what had just happened. Despite her confusion, she followed Lucy to the edge of the rink.

'Nicely done,' Tim said, wrapping an arm around her shoulders.

'Not sure how many times that'll actually work,' Catherine admitted. 'Although I did just learn something. I realised that although I can't control Jess's actions I can control my own and if I don't rise to her anger it leaves her no place to go.'

'Psychology of Parent, Child, Adult.'

Catherine nodded and smiled to herself as though she'd just developed a tar-free cigarette.

The girls were on the ice within minutes and took to it like prize-winning skaters. Catherine was not so sure. Once ice-borne her legs seemed intent on going in opposite directions and her arms flailed uselessly in thin air. For safety she began to stagger forward to stop herself from falling down but she realised too late that attempting to walk across the ice on blades was futile. She landed with a thud.

Within seconds Tim was beside her and helping her to her feet.

'Hang on to me, for what that's worth, and after a few trips round to show willing we'll bow out and leave the kids to it.'

Catherine gratefully held on to Tim and although they increased their speed from humiliatingly awful to embarrassingly medium, they made little headway on the small graceful figures of the girls who skated hand in hand.

'Okay, that's enough for me,' Catherine said, making a leap from the ice to solid ground. She sat down and took the tight skates off immediately. Tim did the same and exchanged the boots for their shoes.

'How do they do it?' Tim asked, shaking his head.

Catherine followed his gaze as the girls circled in front of them. Catherine was thrilled to see Lucy's face alive with the pleasure of the experience. Her oldest child had always been far too serious and studious. It was a relief to see innocent, child-like joy in her serious eyes. For once she didn't look like an adult in a small body. She looked how she should look, like a child.

'I've quit my job,' Catherine blurted out as the girls reached the far side of the rink.

'What... why ... I mean... Christ.'

Catherine laughed, understanding his shock. A few months ago her work had been the most important thing in her life and they had both known it. It had been her reason for getting up each morning. The point that she had to prove. The summit that she had to climb.

'I wasn't happy,' she said, simply.

He turned on the bench to face her so that she had no alternative but to look into his eyes. 'And you think I'm going to be satisfied with that answer?'

Catherine had known that he wouldn't be and besides, he deserved so much more.

Keeping one eye on the girls, she told him about how her work had developed over the past few months. She told him about the early mornings and late nights and the fitful sleep she'd had most nights having never felt she'd done enough. She told him that the job had been awful and drained away her creativity and that quite honestly she'd hated every minute of it.

'Go on, you're entitled. Say it.'

'What, that I'm pleased? I won't lie. I am pleased but not for the reasons that you think. I don't want to gloat as though it's some kind of victory. If it's made you miserable then it's no triumph to me. I'm only pleased that you're no longer doing a job that you hate. It's too political for you. You love to have ideas. You long for the limbo time just before sleep so that your best concepts can flourish. You live to create new visions, thoughts. Budget sheets and board meetings are not where you are at your best.'

She shrugged. 'I'm not sure what I'm going to do now.'

'Of course you are. You'll do what you should have done years ago and work for yourself.'

'But—'

Tim held up his hand. 'There is no pressure in what I'm going to say. When you come back to us – and I say when instead of if, because I know that we are strong enough to weather this – you should start your own business. Why let others feed off your creativity? You were always the one with the brilliant ideas. Start small, work from home and do what you love to do. Don't get bogged down in the competitive rat race of reaching every goal out there. Simply enjoy what you do.'

Catherine thought carefully about his words. She had urged him many times to go for promotion, but he refused every time. Tim enjoyed being a teacher. He revelled in opening up new minds to fresh possibilities. He thrived on seeing new information sink into impressionable brains. He enjoyed his work.

She leaned across and kissed his soft lips. 'I love you.'

'I love you too.'

They fell into an easy silence as the girls continued skating around the rink. Tim chuckled as Jess fell clumsily and almost catapulted back up to show that the fall hadn't hurt her. Within minutes she fell again.

'I think they're getting tired now,' Tim said. He signalled for them to return to the edge just as a group of teenagers hit the ice.

'You did brilliantly,' Catherine said as their red, glowing faces reached her. The words had come a little easier and she'd meant them

'I want to go on that,' Jess said, pointing to the big wheel. Lucy looked up in wonder, but when her gaze returned to ground level her eyes were filled with excitement.

Catherine's stomach turned and her eyes beseeched Tim.

'Come on, you've been so brave tonight, one more challenge won't hurt you,' Tim said, with a twinkle in his eye. His statement left her in no doubt that he understood just how hard she was trying.

'I can't, I'm terrified,' she protested, even as she felt herself being gently nudged toward the terrifying object.

'You'll love the view.'

'I've seen the inside of my eyelids plenty of times, thanks.'

They hopped into the car. Tim and Lucy settled on one side and Catherine and Jess sat opposite. Catherine listened as Tim explained to the girls exactly what they were going to see as the car crested the top of the wheel. She focused on his words but gave a little start as the car started to move in an anti-clockwise direction. She stared into the blackness ahead, too frightened to look down and see how high they were climbing. Tim gave her a reassuring look but she could barely tear her eyes away from a safe view in front of her.

Her nerves felt the continued rise and her legs began to shake and weaken as her body moved further away from the safety of hard, solid ground. The car stopped at the highest point of the wheel and Catherine was sure she was going to suffocate. Her breathing became laboured in her chest as she focused all her energy on the emergency button. Her mouth opened to tell Tim to push it before she stopped breathing, but then she felt something. She looked down into her lap to see a small hand burrowing inside her own trembling fingers.

'It's okay, Mummy,' Jess said, squeezing tightly. 'We'll be fine.'

A feeling that Catherine had never felt before flooded over her with the force of a tsunami. It washed away the terror that wracked her body and every ounce of fear she had about her love for her girls. The emotion raging inside her defied belief. It exploded from her heart and reached out to every corner, every extremity, like an erupted volcano. Every instinct in her body wanted to pull these beautiful, special, gifted girls to her and hold them tightly and never let them go.

Tears gathered in her eyes and began to spill over onto her cheeks. Tim frowned but she smiled through the tears, assuring him that she was okay.

'Jess, I think you're right and if Lucy would come and protect me on the other side I think I'd feel a whole lot better.'

Lucy scrambled across the car and Catherine raised both arms so that the girls could snuggle against her. The sensation of their small bodies against her own was alien but well overdue. Her arms around them felt that they were doing what they had been designed to do.

She sat, flanked by her beautiful daughters, relishing the feel of them against her, holding her husband's disbelieving gaze. It wouldn't be long until she was free from the ride, but for now she was okay because she knew that once it finished she would be going home.

She didn't want to be away from her girls for another minute.

CHAPTER 18

Alex

'It's okay for you,' Alex said, twirling the phone cord in between her fingers. Her daily phone call with Catherine was about ten minutes in. 'I mean you've had plenty of practice in apologising. You could even give training on the art form. You've had plenty to apologise for.'

Catherine's throaty laugh confirmed to her that her sister had taken the comment in good humour, just as she'd intended. 'Just tell him the truth and be genuine.'

'Jeez, I'm fucked on both counts.' Alex was only half joking.

'With your charm and magnetism you can't lose. You couldn't possibly fail to win him over. It's in the bag.'

'Okay, sis, what exactly are you after? I have no money, no car, no jewellery except for the bar that's gone septic in my belly button, so what do you want?'

Catherine covered the phone but Alex still heard her telling Jess that there were no fizzy drinks before bedtime. Alex recognised the tone from her own childhood. She could imagine the firm set of Catherine's mouth. You're on to a loser, kid, she thought, knowing from her own experience that Catherine would not relent.

'Trust me, Alex, once Jay sees how hard you're trying he'll forgive you for being the selfish, brittle, loud-mouthed bitch that we all know and love.'

'Thanks.'

'Oh bugger, gotta go. Jess has scaled the breakfast bar to get the Coke.'

Alex replaced the receiver laughing to herself. She had a feeling she was going to like that child. She could imagine the hours they might spend together dreaming up new cruel and unusual punishments for Catherine. It was strange to realise that she might actually enjoy the thought of spending some time with her nieces. Her only memory of them had been the day at her mother's house when Catherine had struck the wrong child.

Alex still remembered the dense sickness that had overwhelmed her upon witnessing her sister inflict their mother's sick, sadistic practice of punishing the wrong child. Even before the smack had reverberated around their past, Alex had been struck by the two little girls and not for good reasons.

The oldest, fair child had seemed too old, too responsible. Her eyes had always been watching Jess whatever she'd been doing, part of her attention focused on her younger sister, always in a state of alert, ready to diffuse any situation that the more spirited child might inflict, as though trying to protect her from anger. Christ, how history repeats itself, she thought, wondering if Catherine saw how clearly her own children reflected themselves years ago. Did Catherine have any idea how much she had in common with Lucy?

The younger child had intrigued her. Slightly smaller than her sister, she was a ball of pent-up anger reflected in every single movement of her animated body. She didn't place anything. Everything was slammed down or thrown. Her legs didn't move slowly; every step was a purposeful stride that had a reason, to take her to wherever she wanted to go, but it was the eyes that had caught Alex. The deep chocolate brown left almost no whites to tone down the rage that sparkled within.

Alex found herself hoping that Catherine had returned to her family in time to save it. A couple more years of their behaviour going unchecked and the twins would be set for life, irreparably moulded like a model from the kiln. She hoped Catherine could mend the cracks before her children fell through them.

Alex was thrilled for her sister and although she had only spoken to her once since the reunion she could hear something different in the voice on the other end of the phone. Her tones undulated more as though her vocal chords had been liberated. The intonation in her voice had warmed and an element of the secret joy never seemed to be far from the back of her throat.

For her own part, for the time being Alex had to be satisfied with mending her own life. She viewed it as an old rusted bucket full of holes that she was trying to fill with paper tissues. Catherine's voice floated into her mind like a gentle, reassuring mist. 'But at least you've found the paper tissues,' the voice said.

She wondered how many paper tissues she might need in about half an hour – boxes of the stuff, she suspected – but one thing she'd learned in her last meeting was that she had to try.

Arthur, a GP in his late fifties, had informed the group that his relationship with his twenty-two-year-old son had been non-existent for four years. He recounted the physical and psychological abuse that he'd put his son through over a period of fifteen years. He had finally worked through the guilt and regret and found the courage to make contact. Despite her affinity for the son and all that he must have suffered, Alex had been surprised at the depth of torture this man lived through daily, and not for one moment as he laid himself bare before them had she doubted the sincerity of his regret. Surprisingly, she had found herself hoping for a happy ending.

Unfortunately, his son had stated that although he was pleased his father was getting help for his problem he did not feel ready to re-establish a relationship.

'Don't you feel rejected?' Alex had asked.

'Absolutely, but I'll keep trying anyway. He has every right to his anger but if I keep trying then I live in hope that one day he'll relent.'

That night Alex had lain awake working up the courage to call Jay. She desperately wanted him to know that she was deeply sorry for hurting him. On the other hand she was terrified of the rejection she would be facing if he refused to see her. Before she made the phone call she wondered if she was strong enough to survive the rejection or would it send her to the nearest bar?

'Well, I'll know in about ten minutes,' she mumbled to herself as she entered the kitchen.

The familiar knock at the door sounded all too quickly. A rush of panic tore through her. She wasn't ready. She hadn't rehearsed her words enough to get in as much as she wanted to say before he simply turned around and walked back out the door.

She froze in the kitchen as the door sounded again, louder. A vision of Catherine came into her mind. As did the knowledge that her sister would call to check on her progress. Damn you, Alex cursed, as she moved slowly towards the door. She was incapable of admitting to her sister that she had failed at anything.

She opened the door and for a moment their eyes locked and suddenly Alex didn't know what to say. She didn't have to wait for long before Jay elaborately threw his free arm around her and hugged her closely. His other hand held a chocolate cheesecake from the patisserie on the corner. Her favourite. She returned the embrace, gratefully.

'Fuck, darling, I love what you've done with the place,' he said, moving past her into the flat.

'I tidied up.'

He nodded approvingly and handed her the dessert. 'Pop it in the fridge, and it will be perfectly chilled after the abomination that is your cooking.'

Alex chuckled. Her inability to so much as boil an egg had always been a source of amusement to him.

'Coffee?' she asked, eager to be focused on doing something. He was acting as though nothing had ever happened between them.

He shook his head and produced a handful of teabags from his pocket. 'I'll have one of these, sweetie. They're camomile and better for the skin than all that caffeine. Try one; you need it.'

'Cheers, mate,' she said, putting instant granules into her own cup. Her skin was the least of her problems. In the absence of alcohol, caffeine seemed the least price to pay.

'It really does look bigger,' Jay said, as he perched at the breakfast bar that was nothing more than a counter top separating the tiny kitchen from the rest of the room. It had become the place they always sat and chatted.

'It's surprising how much floor there was beneath the beer cans and bottles,' she said, edging the subject towards the reason for him being here.

'There's still not much of you here though, is there? Are you moving in some time soon?'

Alex cast her eyes over the bare magnolia walls and the uncluttered surfaces. Her mind never registered this as home. One day she would either move out completely or personalise it somehow, but not yet. It took all her time just to function somewhere near normal.

Alex poured the water into the cups and concentrated as a light brown caramel colour oozed from the tea bag. Jay was being his normal self. She realised that it would be quite easy to simply fall into step beside him and pretend that nothing had ever happened. There would be no awkward silences or scrambling around for words that would show how sincere she was. It could all simply go away. The colour continued swirling away from the teabag, filling the cup.

The teabag was becoming lost in the colour of its own making. It was destroying itself. That had been her, she realised.

'Listen, Jay, I asked you here tonight because—'

'Oh, you'll never guess who that tart Letitia is sleeping with this week.'

Normally, Alex would have loved to hear the community gossip, but she understood what Jay was trying to do and although it warmed her she couldn't allow him to do it.

'Jay, don't make this easy for me,' she said with a knowing smile. 'It's important that you listen.'

'But Nikki has told me how hard you're trying. You don't need to…'

'Even so, I have to do this for me.'

'Oh gawd,' he said, rolling his eyes, dramatically. 'It's always about you.'

Alex relaxed into his chuckle. It was something he'd said to her often.

'Before you say anything I have an apology of my own. I heard about the beating when I came back. I was away, otherwise I would have come to see you.'

'Away where?' she asked, seeing the twinkle in his eyes.

'A few days of sun, sex and shagging with Nicolas.'

'Nicolas?'

'Yes, darling, he returned to me with armfuls of guilt presents.' He inspected his nails. 'Of course, I had to take him back.'

He sobered. 'But seriously, I didn't know until you'd left the hospital and I really would have come to visit.'

'Despite the way I treated you?' It had occurred to Alex that she had hurt Jay so much that his absence from her bedside had signalled the end of their friendship for good.

'For goodness' sake, darling, I wouldn't have allowed a little tiff like that to come between me and my Florence Nightingale impression. Wouldn't I just be gorgeous in green scrubs?'

'Of course you would but back to what I need to say. Firstly, you're my oldest and dearest friend and I love you. And if you ever expect to hear that again, you should have recorded it.'

Jay bristled with embarrassment. Their friendship had never been sentimental. Statements like that were a given between them and had never been vocalised.

'Okay, on to the real juicy stuff. You tried to tell me where I was going wrong and I wouldn't listen. You were a good friend to me and I threw it back in your face. I'm not going to make excuses but I am learning that I'm not alone. No alcoholic will listen to their reasonable friends. I was bent on destruction and nothing was going to stop me.'

'This isn't necessary.'

'It is. I know you forgive me but I have to forgive myself. I lied to you and broke promises and was nowhere to be found when you needed a friend. If you put all that together I'm not sure how much harder I could have tried to destroy our friendship.'

Jay shook his head. 'Never gonna happen.'

Alex smiled gratefully. 'I'm glad to hear it because I need you in my life. I need your strength.'

Jay pulled a body-building pose. 'No problem there. As a kid I was borough weight-lifting champion – until I discovered Barbie, that is.'

Alex laughed and then sobered. 'I know my drinking caused you a lot of pain because of your father and although we've never talked that much about our pasts I hope that some time we will. It'll explain a few things for both of us.'

Alex could see the emotion in his eyes but she was almost done. 'Anyway, the main thing that I want to say is that I'm sorry. I fucked up and I know it and although I'm never gonna be the easiest person to know I'm always going to need you around. If that's okay with you.'

Jay stood and hugged her tightly. She felt a couple of gentle sobs wrack his body but when she pulled away he had almost recovered.

He wiped one eye with the back of his hand. 'Darling, I find the drama of you cooking far harder to stomach than your apology. For God's sake, let's order a takeaway, put Liza Minnelli in the video and get this night started.'

Alex was more than happy to oblige.

* * *

The day was heavy with a darkness that had never quite lifted. Alex trudged through the grey sludge left over from the earlier whiteness of the snowfall throughout the night. She avoided the deeper puddles, aware that her old trainers would be lucky to survive the immersion. Even defibrillator paddles wouldn't save them.

Christmas, she mused. A time for laughter, families, presents and love. She allowed herself a bit of hippo time and wallowed in the fact that she would have none.

With three days to go she anticipated a day similar to every other. In truth she just wanted it out of the way. The buzz of excitement and expectation around the shops during the last couple of shopping days served only to remind her that the Queen's speech would be toasted alone with a glass of something soft.

She ducked into an old bookshop, loath to go home to her empty flat, which bore no signs of the coming event. Through sober clarity the place had a lonely, unwelcome feeling of belonging to someone else, so she spent the least amount of time there that she could.

The shop was busier than she expected and she was quite surprised to see a few people queuing. Most people relied on the big chains and the internet but Alex had spent many hours in here poring over the old books.

She gravitated towards the art section and picked out a book of Old Masters. Nikki would love the book but Alex simply couldn't afford it.

Alex turned as she heard some commotion at the counter. The woman serving was in her early sixties and Alex vaguely recognised her from earlier visits. The queue hadn't shortened and the woman was becoming flustered. Other people waiting were showing signs of impatience through secret nods and rolling eyes to each other.

'For goodness' sake, love, I haven't got all day,' said a burly man wearing a large camel overcoat.

'I'm really sorry,' the woman said. Her face was flushed and filled with a growing panic. Alex edged closer, just in time to hear the man sigh dramatically.

'It just won't open,' she said, hitting buttons on the cash till. Alex recognised the contraption from the bar. It was a computerised system that often locked the till drawer if you didn't hit the right buttons in the correct order.

'If you want people's business you should at least know how to operate your own equipment,' the man said, playing to his audience. He was rewarded with nods and sighs of approval.

'I'm so sorry. I just…'

'May I?' Alex said, before she had chance to analyse her own feelings. All she knew was that she felt uncomfortable watching the old woman in so much distress. 'I've used one of those things before and I think I can get it open.'

The old woman looked at her gratefully and motioned her around the other side of the desk. Alex quickly saw that in panicking the woman had pressed every button she could find and in doing so had locked the drawer completely.

It took Alex a few seconds to cancel all transactions before putting the correct price in for the book the man was holding. The drawer pinged open and Alex felt like a hero as relief passed over the faces of everyone in the queue. Alex stepped back as the old woman took the man's money and bagged his book. His face was set in stern disgust at the wait he had been forced to endure.

Alex tried to keep her mouth shut but as he moved away from the counter without so much as a thank you, she shouted, 'Have a nice Christmas, sir, and I hope someone treats your mother the same way.' He turned to retort but Alex pushed herself forward and stared him down.

'Thank you, dear. Thank you so much.'

'No problem,' Alex said, sidling off while she continued serving the customers in line.

'Oh dear, I think it's stuck again.'

Alex moved back behind the counter and by silent agreement operated the till until the line was gone.

'I don't know what to say, dear. That was very nice of you. My son insisted that I install this contraption. He said it would be more efficient but I'm not so sure.'

Alex warmed to this woman immediately. Her face was pleasant and open and every expression was there for the world to see.

'They are quite good when you get used to them. Because they're linked to a computer it does all sorts of book-keeping for you and even lets you know when you're running short of stock.'

Alex could see that the woman had no idea what she was talking about.

She thought about returning home to her empty, soulless flat.

'Listen, how about I show you how to use it? I'll just show you the basics so that you'll be able to carry on taking people's money.'

The woman looked scared but inched closer to the frightening machine. Alex admired her willingness to learn.

'I'm Nancy, by the way, and you are?'

Alex introduced herself and began pointing to certain buttons. 'You have to press this one first to tell the till that you intend to start a transaction.'

Nancy nodded but Alex could see that she was terrified by the whole thing.

'Don't worry, you'll get it.'

'I'm quite a slow learner, dear. I won't blame my age. I've always been a slow learner so it might take me a while to get it. My son showed me once and then left me to it.'

'Here comes a customer now. I'll talk you through it.'

Three hours later Nancy had finally got the hang of enough of the bare essentials to be able to get her through. Alex remained patient and explained what to do every time someone came to buy a book. The shop was busier than Alex could have imagined and for some reason she was pleased.

'You've been an absolute treasure,' Nancy said, turning the sign on the door.

'No problem.' If she was honest she'd enjoyed every minute and the afternoon had sailed by.

'I think we deserve a nice cup of tea after all that work,' Nancy said, walking to the end of the shop. She seemed to take it for granted that Alex would follow, so she did. The kitchen was small and dark, having no window to the outside world. It was fitted simply with a couple of cupboards underneath the sink and a microwave against the wall. There was a folding card table with two deckchairs either side.

Within minutes they were both seated and Nancy regaled her with the story of the cash till being fitted. The absence of a wedding ring told Alex that the woman lived alone and this bookshop was her life. She guessed that the fitting of the cash till had been the biggest event in her life for some time.

'I really don't know what I would have done without you.'

Alex was embarrassed by Nancy's praise. She'd hardly done anything.

'Please let me pay you,' Nancy said, reaching for her purse.

'No, honestly, I've enjoyed it. It was a pleasure to help.'

'Please, dear, I'll feel awful if I don't.'

Alex thought about the book that she'd looked at for Nikki. It was hardly the cost of an afternoon's work but out of her price range all the same. Alex shyly asked Nancy if that would be okay.

'Of course dear, it's the least I can do.'

They walked out to the shop after finishing their cups of tea and Alex located the book.

'Can it really do all those things that you said?' Nancy asked, viewing the till as if it were an arch enemy.

Alex nodded. 'It's storing all the information so that you can use it to help the business. There's so much it can do to help you once you know how to use it.'

'Do you know how to use it?'

'Most of it.' In her more sober days she had often helped out in the office at the bar.

'How did you learn?'

'It was the same as the one I used at my last job.'

'Your last job?'

'I don't work there any more.'

'Jolly good,' Nancy said, clapping her hands together. She suddenly looked much younger. 'Would you like to come and work with me? I couldn't pay that much and it would only be maybe three days a week, although it may be more as I'd like to take some more time off, but I'm on my own you see.'

'Yes,' Alex answered to the question. Her only experience was in bar work and that was no longer an option. Anything would be welcome at the moment and Alex had a feeling that she could settle very easily into this place.

'Oh, that's wonderful, dear. I feel much better about that thing,' she said, pointing to the offending object, 'knowing you'll be here to help me. Come back in the morning and we'll sort the details then.'

Alex left the building feeling far lighter than when she'd walked in. She had a job. Somehow, on this dark day, she had done someone a favour and now she had a job. She trudged back to the flat not caring if the big puddles drowned her worn and tattered trainers. She had a job and she'd be able to afford new ones.

She opened the door to the flat to the sound of a ringing phone. It could only be Catherine and Alex couldn't wait to tell her the news.

'Alex, it's Nikki.'

Alex sat down, surprised to hear this voice.

'I think you need to come over.'

'Why?' Alex asked, hearing the grave tones in her ex-lover's voice.

'Because I've found something of yours and it's something you're going to need.'

Alex replaced the receiver and headed straight out of the door, clutching the book in her hands.

* * *

As the door to the flat opened Alex could smell the scent of fresh pine. Nikki always insisted on a real tree and delighted in picking the shed pine needles out of the rug in front of the fire.

Nikki ushered her in, without speaking, and Alex took a deep breath. The room was bathed in a warm comforting glow from the twinkling tree lights and altar candles spaced around the room. Nikki hated having more light than she needed and used the ceiling lights only if she was doing close work.

Alex stood in the middle of the room feeling awkward walking into this intimate atmosphere that was familiar to her because she had once shared it, yet alien because on this occasion it wasn't meant for her.

'I bought you this.' Alex handed her the book and then stepped back to her place in the middle of the room. A smile played on Nikki's lips as she realised the relevance of the book. She placed it on the coffee table.

'I'm sorry, I haven't…' Her words trailed off as Alex waved away her apology. She hadn't expected any kind of gift. After the way she'd treated Nikki she was lucky to be in the same room.

Nikki wrung her hands. She had never hid nervousness well. It was not a natural state of being for her. It occurred to Alex that she was expecting someone. The room had been staged for romance and intimacy and that arrangement did not include Alex. The stab of pain in her heart felt like a physical wound as she thought about another woman coming into this room that was warm and comfortable and intimate with ambiance made for tenderness.

'You said something about an item of mine.' The words were sharper than Alex had intended. She knew that Nikki's insensitive timing was an oversight, but it was crucifying her all the same.

'I have three questions before I show you what I found.' Nikki stood before the full-length window beside the tree. The reflection of the twinkling lights played around her hair.

Alex was happy to answer any questions as long as Nikki was quick. She had no wish to meet the woman in Nikki's life. Violence was not a part of the twelve-step programme and she could do without anyone else to apologise to.

'First question is, do you really fully understand that the things you did to me were wrong?'

Alex thought about the question. If Nikki wanted her to detail every shitty thing she'd done followed by the reasons it was so cruel, she could. There was so much she could say about the mistakes that she'd made but Nikki wasn't asking for another apology. She was asking for the truth.

'Yes.'

Nikki seemed satisfied.

'Why did you go into that room when you stayed here?'

Alex felt the shame burn her face. She felt like a child caught stealing sweets. 'I... umm... '

'The truth, Alex.'

'I wanted to see if you'd changed anything. I wondered if all the stuff would be gone, as though you'd deleted me from your life.'

Nikki's eyes bore into hers and Alex knew she could hold nothing back. Nikki's gaze was peeling back the remaining layers of secrecy. 'And for a moment I wanted to pretend that nothing had changed.'

Emotion rose up in her throat. For those few minutes that particular morning she had allowed herself to think that she was back in her cherished world, back in the only place she had ever felt safe and the best chance she'd ever have for escaping the future that had been laid down by fate or her mother.

A tear spilled over her cheek as the enormity of what she'd thrown away settled all around her. It lived in the furniture, the walls, the flickering candlelight, the very essence of the room, and of course, Nikki.

'Do you still love me?' Nikki asked, her hands wrung out and still.

'I've done things that I can never undo. I've hurt you so much.'

'I said, do you still love me?'

Alex nodded dumbly. Never had it been so painfully clear what she had lost. She loved this woman more than she had ever thought possible and she had thrown it away because she couldn't believe that she'd deserved it. That was her own problem to resolve. It should never have been Nikki's.

'Of course I still love you,' Alex breathed. Never more so. It was her time with Nikki that had allowed Alex to be herself. During the early months she had blossomed into someone that she could almost like, but that was before she'd done the damage.

Nikki took her hand gently, nervously, and Alex followed.

Nikki opened the door to the spare room. 'This is what I found.'

Alex viewed the desk and the computer that lit the room. A desk lamp – her desk lamp – arced over the edge of the desk and shone on to her old exercise books filled with notes and stories. A single shelf was filled with books ranging from ancient wisdom to psychology to quotations. Some she recognised and some were new.

Alex turned to Nikki who had not loosed her hand. 'But I don't understand.'

'I found something that I thought you might need, Alex. It's your life. Your life here with me.'

CHAPTER 19

Catherine

'Turn right. It's that green door on the left.'

Tim pulled up and parked easily.

Catherine viewed the house. With Tim beside her and the girls chattering she didn't feel quite so intimidated. Now, it was just a house.

'Can you manage those?' Catherine asked as the girls jumped out of the car, laden with festive bags full of gifts. She had made sure that the bags weren't too heavy and was rewarded with seeing four similar eyes roll upwards.

The door was answered before they had knocked and Beth stood before them clad in black jeans and a red roll-neck jumper. Catherine was a little disappointed that Beth felt the need to hide herself from family, but she said nothing.

Beth offered her hand to Tim. 'I've heard so much about you.'

Tim ignored the outstretched hand and pulled her into a warm embrace.

'Hello Aunty Beth,' the girls said, walking nonchalantly past the hugging couple, and Catherine had never been so proud of her family.

Tim let Beth go and Catherine saw the flush of pleasure on her sister's face. Catherine followed suit and hugged her warmly.

'Merry Christmas, Beth,' she whispered into her hair. As she let Beth go Catherine stared in awe at the new front room. Beth had transformed it.

The Anaglypta wallpaper had been covered with magnolia paint and a couple of attractive watercolour prints. The busy brown carpet had been replaced with beech laminate flooring and a huge mirror dominated the fireplace wall. The suite from the other room had been covered with cream throws, and festive candles littered the surfaces gracefully.

A five-foot lush green tree adorned the alcove to the right of the fireplace. Presents were stacked around the bucket in matching red paper, which contrasted beautifully with the array of silver decorations that sparkled from the tree.

'Wow, Beth, what a transformation,' she said, turning around to fully appreciate the style that had worked its magic on the room. 'It's fantastic. Are you going to take our advice and sell up?'

Beth's pleasure disappeared as she shook her head. 'No, I won't move from here.'

It was said with such finality that Catherine decided there were other days better suited to tackling that particular problem. She felt strongly about Beth's inability to move on with her life while remaining in this house. Beth would not discuss it.

'Thank you for inviting us,' Tim said, remembering manners for all of them.

'Not at all,' Beth said, taking their coats. 'I'm pleased that you're here.'

There really hadn't been any question when Catherine had received the phone call two days earlier and asked for just one decent Christmas together. Although they had already arranged to go to Tim's mother for lunch, he had happily delayed that visit until the early evening.

'That'll be Alex,' Beth said, as a thunderous knock startled them all.

Catherine turned expectantly, eager to meet Nikki. During their last couple of phone calls Alex had talked about Nikki so much Catherine felt as though she knew her already.

Beth hugged Alex, and Catherine could see that her younger sister tolerated the contact and even attempted to return it but there was still a long way to go. Nikki walked in almost shyly behind Alex and Catherine warmed to her on sight.

Her slightly hunched demeanour spoke of someone on the outside. As far as Catherine was concerned they were all on the outside and this situation was new to them all.

'Hi sis,' Alex said, nudging her in the ribs. Catherine understood that to be Alex's attempt at friendly sisterly contact, but it was not sufficient. She turned to Alex and forced her into a hug. Alex squirmed as though she was nine years old and being suffocated by an affectionate grandmother. Catherine laughed at her discomfort and whispered, 'She doesn't look gay.'

'Meaning that I do?' Alex said, affronted.

Catherine chuckled at the offence in her sister's eyes. Catherine turned and caught Beth's stare which she quickly tore away, but not before Catherine saw the satisfaction that lurked there. She briefly had the look of someone who had crossed a barrier and achieved some great feat. When Beth turned around the expression had been replaced by a look that darted all over the place, eager to collect coats and offer drinks.

Catherine traversed the short but busy space towards Nikki and introduced herself. The wariness began to dissolve from her eyes. Catherine gripped her hand tightly.

'Anyone who can put up with her has my love, respect and sympathy in equal measure.'

Nikki returned the squeeze of the hand. 'I can't argue with an obviously intelligent woman.'

'Oh, Alex, she's a keeper,' Catherine cried over her shoulder.

Catherine was relieved to see the tension fade from her eyes. There was something genuine about Nikki that she liked immediately. She sensed that the woman wore every expression openly.

'Please, sit down,' Beth said, graciously. The room was crowded with five adults and two children. Catherine wondered if they might have to play musical chairs to get a seat.

Nikki took the single chair by the window opposite the other single chair beside the Christmas tree into which Alex had flopped. Catherine and Tim eased down on to the three-seater sofa and, following some good-natured tussling between the girls, Lucy got the third seat and Jess sat on the floor in between her sister's feet.

Catherine hid the smile that started in her stomach. The balance of power between the two of them was shifting and Lucy occasionally got her own way, which was surprising, but even more so was the fact that Jess didn't have a tantrum every time she did. The dynamics were changing and they both seemed to accept it.

'Shall I take the presents out of the bags?' Jess asked, turning her face towards Catherine. Her eyes had already settled on the pile of presents beneath the tree. Catherine forgave her impatience. She would have felt the same if she had ever seen presents beneath a tree in this house.

'Take them out and place them over in that corner,' she said, pointing to the other alcove. 'So that no one trips over them.' Catherine was conscious of the limited space in the small room.

Beth returned with a tray holding seven small glasses of a milky yellow liquid. 'It's eggnog,' she said, lowering the tray for everyone to take a glass. 'There's no alcohol in it,' she offered to no one in particular, but the words found Alex's ears first.

'May I?' Beth asked Alex, indicating that she would like to sit in the chair nearest to the presents.

Alex removed her gangly legs from the chair and positioned herself on the floor in front of Nikki's legs.

Catherine sipped at the warm liquid and found it surprisingly tasty and creamy. A gentle heat coursed through her and she found herself contented and calm. From the kitchen she could hear the low hum of Christmas carols playing on the radio.

'Do you mind if I...?' Beth asked, indicating the pile of presents.

'Of course,' they all chorused.

As Beth leaned over the edge of the chair Catherine was struck by a distant memory. She had the vague recollection of the three of them in bed one Christmas Eve night. Despite their shared terrors they had still had the innocence to hope.

They had all crowded onto Catherine's bed, listening out for the sound of sleigh bells and, although they had all known that Santa didn't exist in their house, some flicker of hope ignited and shone every Christmas Eve.

They had lain there and shared their fantasies and agreed on one definitive version of heaven. They hoped that they would be woken gently by their mother to find stockings filled with fruit and nuts at the bottom of their beds. They had hoped that they would tear downstairs into a warm cosy room to find a pile of presents beneath a sparkling tree. They had hoped that their mother would sit beside the presents and hand them out one by one with an expectant air and a loving smile.

Catherine glanced across at Beth whose eyes were alive with anticipation and was in no doubt that she remembered too. It was clear to her that Beth was trying to act out the fantasy that they had all dreamed many years ago. She felt a rush of love for her sister's generous nature. All her life she had put other people before herself.

'This one is for Jess and this one is for Lucy.'

Catherine was relieved that they both had the manners to say thank you. She was beginning to realise that as a parent even the silliest things were a cause for concern. Her children's manners had never interested to her before, but now they were important. She wanted them to demonstrate the polite and loving children that she knew them to be.

Catherine leaned forward, feeling the eagerness of their shining expressions as though their excitement was her own. 'What is it?'

'Give them a chance, love,' Tim said, also leaning forward.

Unsurprisingly, Jess got into her package first and pulled out a Hello Kitty backpack. Catherine was thrilled.

'Cool, Aunty Beth, cool.'

Beth seemed to take the word cool for thank you as Lucy managed to gain access to her package. A set of Beatrix Potter books lit up her daughter's face.

'And this is for Tim.'

'You really shouldn't have,' Tim said, seriously. Good manners dictated that one did not buy presents for virtual strangers but, then again, he hadn't bargained on Beth.

Catherine watched with interest as he unwrapped a waterproof sports watch with all sorts of gadgets including a stopwatch. Catherine was shocked. She had told Beth that Tim had started swimming laps again; this gift would be invaluable. She was also a little dismayed that she hadn't thought of it.

Tim struggled to hide his embarrassment. 'Really, Beth, I can't accept this.'

'Don't be silly. You've been my brother-in-law for eight years. Call it a catch-up present.'

Tim looked to her for guidance. He was struggling with conscience and good manners but Catherine shook her head slightly, instructing him to accept. This was Beth's chance to act out their dream, their fantasy. It was important to her.

'Oh look, another two for the girls,' Beth said, excitedly, as though just discovering them for the first time. They all laughed and the atmosphere became one of fun and excitement. The girls eagerly ripped off the paper to find a pair of walkie-talkies.

'Nikki, I hope you like this,' Beth said, handing her what looked like a rather heavy-looking box. Nikki thanked her, genuinely surprised at Beth's thoughtfulness. She opened the wrapper to display a black box with a buckle fastener. When opened it revealed a treasure chest of art materials, linseed oil, turpentine, canvases, a palette and a selection of brushes and pencils.

'I don't know what to say,' Nikki said, shaking her head in amazement. She lifted the brushes with the reverence of a true artist.

'Jeez, thanks sis. Makes my gift look kinda crappy,' Alex moaned, good-naturedly. Catherine could see that she was touched by Beth's thoughtfulness.

'Oh look, last two for a couple of little girls.'

Catherine had had enough. 'Beth, this really is too much. I can't let you—'

'Catherine, shut up,' Beth said, firmly.

Catherine's mouth slammed shut whilst Alex burst out laughing. 'Christ, it's a miracle.'

Catherine offered her a withering look to which Alex bobbed out her tongue.

'Well, at least let us give you a gift,' Catherine said, regaining the use of her mouth.

'Let me do this my way, please.'

The girls opened their gifts at the same time and shared an intake of breath. Lying inside a velvet box on black velvet cushions were gold bracelets that differed only in the colour of the stones that were separated yet held together by gold knots the whole way round. Jess's bracelet was filled with tiny sapphires and Lucy's with emeralds.

'Tim, will you please speak to her?' Catherine begged. The bracelets looked very expensive and Catherine felt uncomfortable.

Tim shrugged. 'If she's anything like her sister she's hardly going to listen to me.'

Beth ignored them and turned to the girls, who were transfixed by the jewellery. 'They're not the same but they're similar. They're both precious and beautiful. I want you to look at these and remember that you're sisters, just like Mummy and Aunty Alex.'

'And Aunty Beth,' Alex finished.

Alex was next to receive a gift, which was the entire works of Charles Dickens.

'This isn't like the others,' Beth said, reaching for the last present underneath the tree. It was a large envelope that looked like a card. Catherine was intrigued. She opened the envelope and saw a beautifully crafted card with ribbon and glitter. She began to read the verse, which was so heartfelt that she knew that Beth had pored over the inscribed words for hours until she'd found the right ones. As the verse continued into the card she opened it up and something fell on to her lap but she continued to read. Beneath the printed verse, Beth's sure hand had written:

To my darling sister, Catherine, you were the angel of my dreams and the saviour of my day. You guarded me always.

* * *

Catherine's eyes glazed over, the words on the card blurring into obscurity like a windscreen with no wipers on a rainy day. She wiped at her eyes, and her gaze rested on the item that had fallen out of the card. Her eyes narrowed as she recognised the Christmas card given to her mother many years ago. She read the words in childish handwriting on the front of the card. She locked gazes with the snowman in the top right-hand corner, his nose obscured by a mark on the Sellotape.

'You kept it?' Catherine asked, shaking her head in disbelief.

Beth nodded and Catherine could see the emotion in her eyes. 'I remember the day you brought it home from school. You were so proud and full of hope that she would like it. You were devastated when she threw it in the bin. You cried for hours. Later that night I took it out of the bin and cleaned it up. It was so beautiful. I didn't give it back to you at the time because in anger you would have ripped it up.'

'I can't believe that you kept it,' Catherine said, handling it as though it were a precious scrap of papyrus bearing the earliest hieroglyphics.

'I kept it in the back of a book to protect it. I always knew it was there and always intended to give it back to you. When the bitterness was gone. Now it's time.'

Catherine struggled to hold back the tears. There was no better present that she could have received from her sister. It was like being handed back her life. She could look at the card now and feel no anger for her mother, only the joy she had taken in creating the object at school.

With the card clutched in her hand Catherine stepped across her daughters and hugged Beth tightly, imparting within that embrace exactly how much the gesture meant to her.

Within minutes gifts seemed to be travelling across the room from all directions and Catherine almost lost track of which present was from who, but the red Christmas card was never far from her grip.

Every gift was so thoughtfully chosen. Beth's heart had gone into these presents for every single one of them, even Tim and Nikki who she had never met before this day. Catherine was overwhelmed with a feeling of love and devotion for her sister.

Beth slipped silently from the room to tend to dinner. The girls were happily playing with their presents whilst Nikki and Alex were inspecting the contents of Nikki's art box. Tim was pressing buttons on his watch. Catherine followed her sister.

She passed through the inner room and noted the transformation there also. Beth had kept a similar colour scheme throughout the lower level of the house and the walls looked clean and fresh, giving the room an airy, cool feel. The room was dominated by a round dining table already laid with care and precision. Stylish silver crackers were meticulously set beside exquisitely folded napkins.

'How long did it take you to do all this?' Catherine asked, as she entered the kitchen. It too had been worked on, and without the encumbrance of an eating area had gained in space. The counter tops and cupboard fronts had all been replaced and a gleaming new cooker busily roasted and boiled like an orchestra, producing a cacophony of delicious smells.

'It's nothing. I just wanted my family here for one good Christmas.'

Catherine placed an arm around her sister's shoulders, feeling her bony frame beneath the chunky jumper. She opened her mouth but decided against it. Beth looked so content that Catherine didn't want to spoil it by nagging her.

'And there'll be many more like it. Seriously, though, Beth, this is wonderful. Everyone is really enjoying themselves and it's all thanks to you.'

Beth's face lit up with gratitude and then turned mildly serious. 'Alex seems much calmer.'

Catherine chuckled as she tore a tiny amount of bronzed skin from the enormous turkey resting on the side. 'She's getting there. It's hard for her, not drinking, but with Nikki and us behind her, she'll make it.'

'You must support her,' Beth said, narrowing her eyes at Catherine. 'Every day is a battle for her and she needs to know that you're close by. Promise me, Catherine?'

'Hey, of course, I promise.' There was real fear in Beth's eyes. 'We'll both be there for her. We're her family and she knows that.'

Catherine would have liked to say more but an eruption sounded. They both looked to see the source. Jess and Lucy had commandeered two horses in the name of Nikki and Alex and were riding them bareback in a race. Both teams had reached the doorway at the same time and were tussling to get through first. Jess and Lucy were crying with laughter and it warmed Catherine's heart to see her oldest daughter enjoying such a childish game. Pure light shone from her eyes.

'Get back, you cheat,' Nikki shouted as Alex tried to barge her way through. 'Reach over, Jess, and tickle her feet, she hates that.'

Jess did as she was bid and reached for Alex's feet and although she had no chance of reaching them from atop Nikki's back, the mere threat forced Alex to squirm around, giving Nikki the opportunity to force herself and her jockey through.

'I declare Jess and Nikki the winners,' Catherine cried from the kitchen doorway.

'And I reckon they did it in nineteen point seven seconds,' Tim said, looking very pleased with himself for mastering his gift.

Beth ushered them out of the kitchen and instructed them to sit. Catherine took charge of the seating arrangements and placed Jess between Alex and Tim, and Lucy between herself and Nikki, with Beth at the head of the table.

Beth produced a feast of festivity that was devoured amongst laughter, cracker pulling and joy. The playful banter between Catherine and Alex lasted throughout the meal and was particularly enjoyed by Beth, who was the quietest of them all but contented.

After a delicious dessert of Christmas pudding and cream they returned to the front room and settled in the places they had been previously, still wearing their cracker hats, Beth refusing any assistance with the clearing up.

It was with disappointment that Catherine realised the time and, despite her enjoyment of the day with her family, felt it was only fair to arrive at Tim's parents punctually.

Catherine packed up the presents while Beth retrieved the jackets. They bid farewell to Alex and Nikki who had already taken possession of the sofa.

'Thank you for a wonderful day, Beth. It's been lovely.'

Beth nodded and swallowed, a sad and distant look in her eyes. Catherine felt that she was already somewhere else.

Catherine reached out and hugged her sister tightly, almost too tightly.

During the drive to Tim's parents, Catherine allowed the contentment of the day to wash over her. Jess and Lucy were busily comparing bracelets in the back seats. Tim hummed some festive tunes and she stared out of the window imagining the ties they would forge over the coming years.

CHAPTER 20

Alex

'No, no, no, no, no. I don't want to get up.'

'Alex, it's almost ten. Get out of bed, you lazy lump.'

Alex threw a pillow that missed Nikki by inches, but then had a marvellous idea. 'Why don't you join me?'

Nikki laughed. 'Yeah, right, and we won't see daylight until tomorrow. Forget it, pal. We're taking that walk, remember?'

Alex groaned and rolled over. It was Monday 27th and still a bank holiday because of Christmas falling at the weekend. The previous day had been dull and rainy and they had spent the most part of it snacking on festive treats and watching Christmas films curled up on the sofa. At the end of the day Nikki had stated that, weather permitting, they would work off their indulgence with a brisk walk around the park.

'Come on, lazy bones,' Nikki said, pulling the covers from Alex's grip. 'There's something in the kitchen to prepare you for the arduous journey.'

'A taxi?'

'Use your nose and smell the love.'

Alex tentatively stuck her nose out from beneath the pillow and caught her favourite smell.

'Is there brown sauce?'

Nikki answered the affirmative with her eyes only. 'But it's going in the bin if you're not out of bed in five minutes.'

Alex made noises as she forced herself out of bed. Nikki surely knew how to use her own passions against her. Nothing started her day like a bacon sandwich with brown sauce. She dressed quickly, drawn by the inviting aroma of her favourite meat.

Secretly she had hoped for a day like yesterday, grey with rain and mist, so that their activities of the previous day could be repeated. Maybe it would rain later, she hoped, glancing out of the window. The air looked cold and fresh but no clouds cluttered the clear blue sky. *Damn.*

The sandwich was hovering above the bin as she closed the bathroom door behind her.

'Just in time.'

'Give it here.'

'You haven't forgotten about tonight, have you?'

Alex's blank look said that she had.

'Jay and Nicolas?'

'Oh yeah.' She had recalled that they were coming over some time, but she'd been wrapped in a blanket of contentment that had precluded everything and everyone else.

'Must we let the real world back in?' she whined.

Nikki came up behind her and put her arms around Alex's waist. 'I'm afraid so, sweetie, but always remember that they have to go some time and you don't. You're here, inside your home, and the day we had yesterday can happen any time you want. Including this,' Nikki said, biting suggestively on Alex's ear.

Alex dropped her bacon sandwich. 'Now?'

Nikki roared with laughter. 'You're insatiable. What time did we get to sleep last night, or rather this morning?'

Alex shrugged. 'Five, I think.'

Nikki moved away. 'After a walk in the cold, bright air I always fancy a nice hot shower, shared, of course,' she teased.

Alex finished off the bacon sandwich. 'Hang on, I'll have my trainers on in ten seconds.'

Alex turned and stood and walked straight into the waiting embrace of Nikki. She returned it hungrily, savouring the feel of the woman she loved in her arms as though it might be lost to her any minute. Occasionally she caught her own surprise at how easily they had fallen back into the best time of their relationship.

There were shared glances and looks that only they could translate. They could barely pass each other without touching, just a shoulder, arm, hand. Alex knew it was better than it had been, no longer clouded by self-doubt. She now knew that she deserved to be happy, just as Nikki deserved it too. And she was going to make sure that they both got what they deserved.

'I love you more than anything,' Nikki whispered.

'And I love you more than that.'

Their embrace was disturbed by the doorbell.

'Jeez, Jay wouldn't be this early, surely?'

Nikki answered the intercom as Alex headed to the bedroom to change for their walk. The temptation of the shower was just too much to argue with. She stopped in her tracks when she heard Catherine's voice.

Nikki pressed the button to let her in and within seconds she was knocking on the door.

Alex saw immediately that Catherine's face, devoid of make-up, was troubled and drawn.

'I've just had a call from Alan Wilkinson, Beth's doctor. He's asked if we can go to Beth straight away. He wouldn't say why.'

Alex's heart caught in her throat. She looked to Catherine for reassurance but her eyes danced with fear. She looked to Nikki.

'Hurry, go get dressed. Beth needs you.'

Alex sprang into action and was dressed in record time. She hugged Nikki and then followed her sister down the stairs, taking them two at a time.

'Didn't he say anything?'

Catherine shook her head as she pulled the car away from the kerb. 'He just said that Beth needed us to come straight away.'

The roads were almost empty, families taking advantage of the extended festive period. They talked of their activities since Christmas Day when they had last been together but both barely listened to the other, each aware that the sound of their voices was only filling the distance between themselves and Beth.

The street was quiet as Catherine parked the car. As she stepped out Alex felt a spot of rain on her hand. She looked up to find that the clouds had gathered and in their whiteness had blocked out any promise of a bright, fresh day.

'Alan, what's going on?' Catherine said, finding the doctor sitting in the front room, awaiting their arrival. The room looked unchanged from two days earlier yet the house held a quiet, eerie quality. No noise from the television or radio lifted the atmosphere. 'Is Beth ill?'

He stood and Catherine tried to see around him, to find Beth.

'Please sit down.'

'Where is she?' Alex demanded.

'If you'd just—'

'We don't want to sit down, for God's sake. Just tell us what's wrong,' Alex barked, her eyes flashing.

He nodded his solemn understanding and remained standing despite his whole demeanour shouting that he needed to sit. 'Beth called me last night. It was a surprise. I hadn't heard from her for weeks. Not since she turned me down.'

'Turned down what?'

He removed his glasses and wiped at his eyes. 'I asked her to marry me.'

Alex's gaze met with Catherine's and it was communicated between them by a look that Beth had not mentioned this to either of them.

'She told me that she needed some space and that she didn't want me to contact her any more. I tried to reason with her but eventually I did what she wanted in the hope that she would realise I truly loved her and could make her happy.'

Alex was in no doubt that this man she barely knew could make her sister happy. She made a note to try and talk Beth into rethinking her decision. It was clear that the doctor loved Beth very much.

Catherine urged him to carry on.

'Last night she called and asked me to come over for breakfast. She said she wanted to talk to me about something. I hoped that finally she had changed her mind...'

'And?' Alex felt sorry for the man standing before her. He was obviously in great pain but she wanted to know about Beth.

'I arrived at nine thirty as she'd asked me to and there was no answer. I knocked for a while and then remembered I had a key from when I used to treat your mother. I let myself in.'

He looked to them for approval of this decision. Alex nodded when all she wanted to do was shake him. Her heart was beating wildly in her chest and she could see that Catherine wanted to lay him down to cut him open and surgically extract the information from him.

'The house was so quiet. I called to her but there was no answer.' He rubbed his forehead, confused. 'I couldn't understand it. She'd invited me over so she couldn't have gone out. I mean, why would she...'

Alex moved forward but Catherine held her back. 'And what did you do?' Catherine asked. Her voice was gentle but covering a hard edge of impatience and fear.

Alan shook himself back to the present and realised who he was talking to. 'I went looking for her.'

'And did you find her?' Alex asked, fearfully. The house was eerily quiet around them.

Alan nodded slowly and raised his eyes upwards. 'I found her in the bedroom.' His eyes widened, physical pain accompanying his next words. 'She's dead.'

Alex barely heard the last two words as she tore past Alan, almost knocking him to the ground. She heard Catherine one pace behind as she mounted the stairs three at a time. She pushed open the door to their old bedroom, which now housed one single bed, Beth's old bunk.

The scene that greeted her was a vision that imprinted itself on her memory via and would stay with her for the rest of her life. A second later Catherine came to a halt behind her and made a noise of surprise mixed with pain. Alex approached the bed softly, not daring to believe the validity of what she could see with her own eyes.

Beth's hair was fanned out across the pillow framing her face like a warm mist. Her eyes were closed with a finality that Alex found hard to understand. Her face appeared soft and smooth, and Alex had the strange feeling that she could see a half smile playing on her features.

Alex stayed still as Catherine moved around her. Catherine reached out and gently touched the bare skin of Beth's arm. Alex guessed that her sister needed no further proof that Beth was gone.

'Why?' Alex murmured, before the rising tears arrived at her throat and strangled her.

Catherine stood beside her, tears streaming over her cheeks, shaking her head silently.

Alex fell into her sister's arms and cried hot, bitter tears for the sister they couldn't save.

* * *

The sun came out for Beth as she was laid to rest in the place she had requested, close to where her mother's ashes had been scattered.

Catherine felt it was because it was where she had always felt comfortable, but Alex had other ideas. She sensed that Beth wished to haunt their mother for all eternity and never leave her alone until she understood what she had done wrong. Alex hoped that there was an afterlife and that Beth would find there what she had never found in life.

The service was beautiful and attended by them all, Alan and a few well-wishing neighbours. At twenty minutes to four only Alex and Catherine remained by the graveside.

'I don't want to leave her,' Catherine said, her voice thick with emotion.

'She's no longer there. Remember what Father Stevens said, the body is just a jacket that you throw off when you no longer need it.'

'Are you ready?' Catherine asked, reaching into her handbag.

Alex nodded. Two letters had been found beside Beth's bed. The first one had been to Alan giving instructions for her burial and, they hoped, words that would comfort the man who had loved her. The second one had been addressed to them both, but neither had felt strong enough to read their sister's words and by silent agreement they had both known they would read it on this day.

Catherine opened the envelope and moved closer to Alex. They each held a top corner of the single page and read:

To you both,

Please don't blame yourselves for what has happened. There is nothing you could have done to stop it. Your actions at no time have contributed to my decision to leave this world. I have felt warmed by your love my whole life.

Catherine, you protected me with your big heart and your fierce loyalty to the bonds that held us together. You shielded me from as much evil as you could and absorbed it yourself. You made my childhood bearable.

Alex, you would have fought lions to protect me. Your fierceness and spirit were a daily inspiration to me. Even when you were no longer there I felt your love reaching out to me and always knew that we would be together again.

Since remembering the horrors that we lived through I have understood that I do not fit into this life and will never be able to adjust myself to the world around me. I do not view it as you do. My place is no longer here and I have grown comfortable with that. I am not frightened and welcome the next stage of my existence. Please do not be sad for me. I believe I will be happy with the choice that I have made.

I ask only one thing of you both. Stick together and take care of each other. It is my only wish as I leave you both that you will always take care of each other and will be separated by nothing again.
My love to you both, always.

Beth

Catherine's hand shook as they reached the end of the letter. Her sister's tears matched her own in the understanding of Beth's words. Even at the last, her thoughts had been for the both of them and not herself.

'She did it, didn't she?' Catherine asked, folding the letter. 'She brought us back together.'

Alex nodded, wiping viciously at eyes that had barely been dry during the last week. 'It was always her that got us talking again when we were kids. She hated it when we fought and always took responsibility for making the peace between us.'

'She was such a generous person. I've often wondered from where she inherited that trait.'

'Maybe we should have done more.'

Catherine reached for her hand. 'We did everything we could. We tried to get her to see someone but she refused. I think she had already made up her mind. The memories of our mother were much harder for her to bear. Not only because she had buried them for years but also because she took care of the woman until she died. Her brain gave her the memories back when it thought she could deal with them, but it would never have been the right time. The enormity of it was always too much for her to bear.'

'We have to make her proud.'

Catherine nodded and squeezed her hand tightly. 'We will.'

Alex knew that life was not going to be easy. There were still the memories of their childhood that she had to come to terms with without the assistance of alcohol.

Her insatiable need for a drink was something she would have to battle every day. She also understood that she had to let her barriers down. She had lived too long behind the safety of solitude and misunderstanding. She had to take risks and open herself to the world and all it had to offer. But somehow, Alex knew that she would make it. Her life was not being handed to her on a plate but she had been given the tools to forge it.

It would be hard to put the past behind her and learn to trust the people she loved. She had to leave behind the safety of having nothing in case her mother returned to take her life away. It was within her control now and she would get there because she would do it for Beth and she refused to let her sister down.

'Beth deserves to be remembered,' Alex said, staring down at the coffin covered with handfuls of dirt. 'I'm going to write about her loving nature. I'm going to tell our story, her story. I shall write about "The Middle Child".'

LETTER FROM ANGELA

First of all, I want to say a huge thank you for choosing to read *Dear Mother*. I hope you enjoyed the story of the three sisters despite the emotional ride. There are many types of childhood abuse and all are damaging. I chose to explore the subject of physical abuse in this book.

This story burned inside me for a number of years after reading much about being a 'middle child'. The story of the three sisters became so clear in my head that I just had to commit it to paper.

Although much of the book focusses on the stories of Catherine and Alex I wanted to emphasise Beth's role in reuniting them.

If you did enjoy it, I would be forever grateful if you'd write a review. I'd love to hear what you think, and it can also help other readers discover one of my books for the first time. Or maybe you can recommend it to your friends and family…

Thank you for joining me on this emotional journey.

I'd love to hear from you – so please get in touch on my Facebook or Goodreads page, twitter or through my website.

And if you'd like to keep up-to-date with all my latest releases, just sign up at the link below:

www.bookouture.com/angelamarsons

Thank you so much for your support, it is hugely appreciated.

Angela Marsons

www.angelamarsons-books.com

www.facebook.com/angelamarsonsauthor

www.twitter.com/@WriteAngie

ACKNOWLEDGEMENTS

I cannot complete a book without acknowledging the support, encouragement and patience of my partner, Julie. She has spent many, many nights with headphones attached to give me the space and peace to write. She has been and continues to be my rock.

I would like to thank Bookouture for giving this book the opportunity to benefit from both their tender loving care and their expertise. Knowing that this book is important to me, the team could not have been more sensitive during the process of helping it to reach a wider audience. I remain eternally grateful to Keshini Naidoo, Oliver Rhodes, Kim Nash and the entire fabulous Bookouture team.

Thank you to my mum, Gill Marsons, for telling me how much she loved this story. That meant a lot.

I remain grateful and honoured to be amongst some truly talented and inspiring authors within the Bookouture family. Every single one of them has a place in my heart.

Finally I would like to thank the fantastic readers who have taken a chance on this non-crime book and have trusted that I will still carry them on an emotional and rewarding journey.

45913266R00148

Made in the USA
Middletown, DE
21 May 2019